YOU&YOU&YOU

YOU

Per Nilsson

& YOU

TRANSLATED BY
Tara Chace

& YOU

Front Street ▮ *Asheville, North Carolina*

Also by Per Nilsson

Heart's Delight

Designed by Helen Robinson

First U.S. edition

Library of Congress Cataloging-in-Publication Data

Nilsson, Per, 1954-
[Du & du & du. English]
You & you & you / Per Nilsson ; translated by Tara Chace.—1st U.S. ed.
p. cm.
Summary: Young Anon, who marches to the beat of a different drummer
in galoshes to protect himself from radiation, touches the lives of all around him,
resulting in disillusionment, loss, love, and more than a few surprises.
Originally pub.: [Sweden]: Rabén & Sjögren Bokförlag, [1998],
under the title Du & du & du.
ISBN 1-932425-19-5 (alk. paper)
[1. Friendship—Fiction. 2. Family life—Sweden—Fiction.
3. Schools—Fiction. 4. Love—Fiction. 5. Sweden—Fiction.]
I. Title: You and you and you. II. Chace, Tara. III. Title.

PZ7.N5888You 2005
[Fic]—dc22   2004030660

This edition was produced with the support of the Swedish Institute

FRONT STREET
A Division of Boyds Mills Press, Inc.
A Highlights Company

YOU & YOU & YOU

Anon

My father is a god.
My mother is an ordinary woman,
but my father is a god.

Zarah

You say you want to win my heart. Well,
what are you going to give me in exchange? Words?
What good are your pretty words to me?

Nils

First you live. Then you die.
There's nothing to fear.

Anon

"Anon?"

She means, Has anyone seen Anon today? Is he coming sooner or will he be coming later? Or maybe he isn't coming at all?

She throws the question out to the class in general without directing it to anyone in particular.

First everything quiets down. Everyone has taken a seat, all the desks and chairs have stopped scraping against the floor, and as usual the teacher's question has caused all the chatter to die down.

But no one responds. Someone shrugs his shoulders. Someone steals a glance at the empty desk all the way in the back right-hand corner of the room. Someone breaks the silence with a heavy, theatrical sigh. Then someone says, "He's probably on his way."

Someone else nods out toward the playground. "There he is. He's coming."

Everyone turns to look out the window; everyone sees the boy, who is slowly walking by outside. A little hunched over, a little stooped, as if his backpack were a heavy burden to bear, or as if he were following some exciting tracks on the ground. Slowly, slowly, his blue rubber galoshes shuffle over the asphalt.

The students lose interest after a few seconds. Most of them sit back down at their desks again, face the front of the classroom, and wait quietly or lean over to the person next to them and start talking. Two boys get up from their seats, walk over and squat down next to a third boy, and start discussing something. They are talking about something that happened last night, obviously something funny because they are all talking over each other excitedly and their laughter is getting louder and louder: "… and then in the locker room … ha ha ha … and then he went … but she didn't know … ha ha ha …"

A girl yawns loudly and studies her nails. Another disappears into a dream world of her own and sits there with a vacant look in her eyes and her mouth hanging open.

Most of them don't care about him at all, the boy outside the window, the boy who isn't in class yet, whose name is Anon.

Anon has stopped now. He stands still and seems to be studying something on the ground with great interest. Inside the classroom there are only two people who are still watching him.

One of them is Stoffe. He looks out the window and thinks: Jeez you're a hard shake, you damn boot-wearing tardy-ass. And other thoughts like that. When Stoffe thinks about Anon his thoughts usually have swear words in them.

"Stoffe, come here a minute!" Henke yells from across the classroom. And Stoffe gets up out of his seat, goes over to him, and doesn't devote any more thoughts to Anon for now.

Now the only one left who's interested in Anon is Miss Larsson, the teacher. If you look closely you can see a little wrinkle on Miss Larsson's forehead, which usually looks so smooth and youthful. I'll have to call tonight, she thinks. This is not acceptable. It never gets easier. But soon it will be over, soon I won't need to make any more phone calls, she thinks.

Miss Larsson exhales a sigh of relief, her drawn face breaks out into a tranquil, teacherly smile, and she walks over to the window and opens it. A delightfully warm spring breeze sweeps through the classroom.

"Hello out there!"

The boy doesn't react.

"Hey, Anon!"

"Huh?!"

Confused and surprised, as if he had never seen the woman who was leaning out of the window before in his life or as if he had never been on this playground before, Anon looks around. But right away he gives Miss Larsson a big smile.

"Oh! Hi! Is that you? Did we start already? Did the bell ring?"

Miss Larsson nods seriously. "Mmm. Five minutes ago."

"Oh! I didn't hear it. Sorry. But I'm coming now. I'm on my way."

Anon laughs and looks Miss Larsson squarely in the eyes.

"I was just thinking about my father," he says.

There's a recess after two not-quite-awake-yet hours of geography class with a sleepy group-work assignment about the Nordic countries. Swedish cars yawn and Norwegian fjords yawn and Danish exports yawn and Finnish lakes yawn and hot yawn yawn yawn springs in Iceland.

But now there's a fifteen-minute recess and Miss Larsson drinks coffee and eats a cheese sandwich in the teachers' lounge and chats with her colleagues about a TV series that ended last night and about the school's new computers that are acting up again and about a student who is almost always tardy.

It's recess and the playground is full of kids. Girls and boys of different ages and different-colored jackets: red, blue, green, and black. An unusually large number of black jackets this year.

The playground is also full of sounds: shouts and laughter and wild shrieks and secret whisperings and bits of songs and talking.

And the playground is full of activity. On the soccer field almost the entire fourth grade is playing soccer. Other students are walking around and just talking, in groups of twos and threes. Some students are hopping around like a flock of sparrows all over the courtyard. Some boys are chasing some other boys, and some girls are standing in a tight ring and playing a game with a lot of giggling. Some students are jumping rope, and all the tire swings are occupied by first graders and kindergartners.

Four girls are sitting with their backs leaning against the south wall of the building letting the spring sunshine warm their cheeks. They've taken their jackets off to sit or lean on and are just wearing T-shirts. Four sixth-grade classmates, four girls who've known each other for a long time, who've been the best of friends and the worst of enemies for years, cherished friends and bitter enemies. From left to right: Magdalena, Ida, Kristina, and Frida.

Three boys who are in the same grade are standing a few yards away. One of them is a head taller than the other two. His name is Henrik, but he goes by Henke. And Kristofer and Filip go by Stoffe and Fille.

Henke and Stoffe and Fille are standing close together. Maybe Henke is showing the other two something, probably something secret, because every so often he lifts his head and looks around to make sure no one else is nearby. Occasionally it seems like

Henke's eyes stop on the four girls. Maybe it's one of the girls in particular that his eyes linger on before he turns back to his buddies again. There's whispering and boyish grins and laughter from voices that haven't started changing yet.

The bell rings. Brrring, brrring, brrring. That same persistently grating major triad. The bell rings and the youngest children stop their games and hurry back to the classrooms. The older children are calmer about it. The four girls, for example, keep talking as they get up and brush off their clothes. And Henke shoves something down into his back pocket and scans the playground.

Now Anon walks by.

"Hey, you!" shouts Stoffe, taking a few steps toward him.

Anon stops and waits.

"Hey, Anon," Stoffe says, standing a little too close to Anon.

"Mmm," Anon says, standing his ground without stepping back.

"Do you think it's going to rain today?" Stoffe asks.

"Aw, leave him alone," says Henke, trying to drag Stoffe along.

But Stoffe pulls his arm free and mumbles something and keeps standing in Anon's way. And Anon glances up at the clear blue spring sky and calmly says, "Nope."

"Then why," Stoffe asks, leaning forward, "are you wearing galoshes? Hmm?"

Anon doesn't answer.

"Why do you always wear those goddamn ugly, disgusting galoshes?"

"The bell rang," Anon says.

Yes, the bell rang and the playground is almost empty now. The four girls are still standing there. They're standing a few yards away, trying to see and hear what's going on. And two late third graders come darting around the corner at full speed. Otherwise the playground is deserted again.

But Anon can't go back to the classroom because Stoffe is in his way.

"Come on," says Henke, trying to drag Stoffe along again.

Stoffe isn't listening. Instead, he says to Anon, "Maybe you're afraid that it's going to start raining."

Anon stands there in silence.

Then Stoffe clears his throat, leans forward, and lets a big glob of spit drop down toward Anon's feet. "Uh-oh! It's definitely starting to rain. Lucky for you you're wearing your galoshes."

Yes, the glob of spit lands in the middle of one of Anon's galoshes. It lies there like a dead jellyfish, and all four boys stare at it. And no one says anything.

Why didn't he pull his foot away? Stoffe wonders. He saw what I was planning to do. He had time. Why did he just stand there?

Without a word, Henke turns around and heads back toward the classroom, and Stoffe and Fille follow him.

"Hi, Anon."

Anon is still standing there staring at his boot when the girls walk by. He looks up and says, "Hi ..."

"Ida," Ida says.

"Huh?"

"My name is Ida," says Ida.

"I know," says Anon.

"Say it, then," says Ida. "Say: Hi, Ida."

"Hi, Ida," says Anon.

"Hi there, Anon," says Ida. "It's nice to see you, but unfortunately I have to go now. You have something disgusting on one of your galoshes."

"Bye, Ida," says Anon.

"Idiot," says Ida.

And Frida and Kristina giggle contentedly, and together they head back toward the classroom for math class.

But Magdalena is still hesitating. "Anon …"

"Mmm."

"Come on. The bell rang. Otherwise you'll be late. Again."

"Mmm. I'm coming," Anon says.

But nothing happens. Magdalena looks at Anon and Anon looks at his boot and the playground is empty and quiet now.

He doesn't look upset, Magdalena thinks. He doesn't have tears in his eyes. Then she starts counting silently to herself. She's at thirty-two, and that's counting very slowly, when Anon looks up.

But he doesn't look her in the eye, his gaze stops somewhere around Magdalena's shoulder, and he says, "I'm coming now."

"Good," says Magdalena, and she turns around and goes.

As Anon follows her he tries to scrape the spit off his right boot with his left boot. It seems like it's difficult. If you didn't know what he was doing, you might think he was practicing a Silly Walk.

—

Girls' breasts are neat, Anon thinks.

Now it's lunch period and Anon is sitting in the cafeteria. He's sitting alone at his table and Ida and Frida and Kristina and Magdalena are sitting at the table in front of him. Kristina and Magdalena are sitting with their backs to Anon.

It's neat when you see a girl like this, diagonally from behind, Anon thinks. And you can see how it kind of sticks out on the side. That's how it is on Kristina, but Magdalena next to her there might just as well have been a boy.

Yes, Kristina is attractive when you see her from behind, Anon thinks. And he almost felt her breasts against his back a little while ago, when he was standing in front of her in the food line and someone pushed a little bit back in the line behind them.

"Uh-oh, Magdalena! Don't turn around, but a *certain someone* is staring at you. A *certain someone* looks like he's thinking about asking you if you like him! Uh-oh, Magdalena …"

It's Ida who notices Anon looking, and Magdalena and Kristina turn around, and Magdalena tells Ida to cut it out, and Anon stares down at his plate.

Battered cod fillets.

They're calling it battered cod fillets today, but it looks exactly like fish sticks. Anon pokes the last bit of fish into his mouth.

Now two potatoes that have been boiled to pieces and a ladleful of boiled carrots stare back at Anon from the plate. And that was even from the *nice* cafeteria lady and even after he'd told her. But she just said that Anon knew what the school nurse had said, and so she ladled out potatoes and carrots for Anon and didn't take any notice of his protests.

Anon sits there without moving for a long, long time, gazing down at his plate. Then he gets up and goes and gets two napkins. Anon scans the room as he sits back down at his place again. Anon doesn't notice Kristina.

Anon thinks that no one is watching when he scrapes all of his boiled carrots into one of the napkins and his two potatoes into the other. But Kristina sees. She's standing over by the cart where you put your trays away, watching. And she sees how Anon folds the napkins into two small bundles and then gets up off the bench and quickly stuffs one of the napkin bundles into his right back pocket and one into his left back pocket.

When Anon picks up his tray and starts walking toward the cart, Kristina hurries out of the cafeteria.

But she waits outside.

Kristina waits around the corner, in the cloakroom, and watches Anon walk by. His pockets are bulging out. That must be really sticky, Kristina thinks.

She watches Anon go into the sixth graders' bathroom.

"Kristina!" Ida calls from over on the soccer field.

"I'll be right there!" Kristina calls back.

When Anon comes out of the bathroom, his pockets aren't bulging out anymore. And Kristina hurries into the bathroom as soon as he's out of sight, and there, down in the swirling water in the toilet bowl, she sees a single piece of carrot swimming around.

Zarah

"Let's fuck."

"Again?" he asks.

"Yeah. Let's fuck again," she says.

The young man smiles contentedly, leans back in the armchair, and clasps his hands behind his head, his tan arms and weight-lifting muscles stretching his short-sleeved summer shirt.

He smiles and shakes his head. "No, not again. It's so fucking hot. I'm getting all sweaty. I don't want to have to shower again."

The young woman slides down onto her knees in front of him. She puts her hands on his thighs and begs, "Oh, pleeeaase. I want to."

The young woman looks up at the young man's smiling face.

Soon he'll want to, she thinks. Now he's just being an irritating little boy.

She leans forward, undoes two buttons on the young man's white shirt, and kisses his stomach. I've never met anyone with such smooth skin, she thinks. Never met anyone so soft and so hard. And never anyone who tastes so good.

Now he wants to. Now she can feel that he wants to.

He's still smiling his sunny smile when he slides down onto the floor in front of her.

"Don't you ever get enough?" he asks, chuckling.

That's a line from some movie, she thinks. And of course she responds, "Not of you."

—

The young woman's name is Zarah. The young man's name is Victor.

Now Zarah and Victor are fucking. In Zarah's apartment in the living room on the floor on the red rug in front of the TV, they're fucking on a sunny afternoon in May.

Afterward Zarah sits on the windowsill and smokes. She sits there in just her underwear and a camisole with her feet pulled up and her chin on her knees. The spring sunshine is warm and she's feeling good.

The blue cigarette smoke follows the brick wall up toward the roof. Down on the street a little boy stands, he stands completely still, and stares upward. It seems almost like he's staring at Zarah.

She waves. He waves back. Then he walks on.

"Who are you waving at?"

Victor is standing in the middle of the room, freshly showered and naked, with his jet-black hair combed back.

You're scrumptious, you bastard, Zarah thinks, watching him without answering. And Victor keeps standing there, smiling and posing. You're scrumptious and you know it, you self-confident bastard, Zarah thinks.

"Oh, that was just one of my secret lovers walking by down there," she says.

"Sure, sure," Victor says, nodding, and starts getting dressed.

And Zarah keeps watching him and feels a small wave of pleasure rippling through her body. Damn, I almost think I love you, you bastard, she thinks. She laughs, surprised at herself for thinking that.

—

And then Victor says that he has to get going, that he has to settle a few things, and Zarah knows what kinds of things he's going to settle and doesn't ask any questions, and Victor says that he'll be back in the evening and that he supposes they can pop out and have a beer then, and Zarah says "Sure" and kisses him on the cheek.

Ow, like rough sandpaper. Stubble already, even though he shaved this morning. But he sure smells good. Yes, he does.

"Bye" and "See you later."

Zarah stands there in the hallway, staring at the door that Victor closed behind himself. She's contemplating Appearance. Beauty. The Exterior. The Body. You always hear that it doesn't mean anything, Zarah thinks, that it isn't important, that eventually everyone gets old and wrinkly and that beauty fades. So what? Who's going to care about what they look like in fifty years? In fifty years the world may have come to an end.

Question: Who says looks don't matter?

Answer: Ugly people.

Ugly people and talented people say that looks don't matter. The ugly girls, the ones that can have sex with a Victor only in their innermost dreams. The ones that have to settle for hunch-backed, pimply, four-eyed, scrawny, pasty guys with good grades who know a lot of fancy words and have lots of theories but not a single hair on their chests.

The beautiful get the beautiful and the ugly get the ugly. That's the way it is.

And the ugly have decided looks don't matter. What's on the inside matters more than what's on the outside. And size isn't important. Ha, if only you knew, sisters!

That's what Zarah's thinking about in her hallway. And then she turns toward the hall mirror and studies the image of herself.

"You're beautiful," she tells her reflection.

Her reflection nods in agreement.

Yes, Zarah has always been one of the beautiful ones, one of the sweet ones, one of the desirable ones, one of the two or three girls in her class that the boys dreamed and fantasized about. She's played the starring role in lots of X-rated fantasies. The image of Zarah has been found in the heads of many a pubescent boy, alone in his bedroom at night.

And when she was in ninth grade she played the starring role in her school's Saint Lucia Day festivities. She stood there on the stage in the auditorium, hung over and bleary-eyed with dark circles under her eyes after a passionate, sleepless night. It was as if the verse she was supposed to read had just blown away in the wind, even though the music teacher had gotten her to rehearse it over and over again. "Be not afraid of the dark, for there lies the light …" Nope, the rest was gone, and still hasn't returned. Something about "stars." Something about a "dark pupil." And candlewax from her crown of candles was dripping on her hair and all the other girls' candles were making her dizzy and when the last performance was over she ran to the bathroom and threw up over and over again.

But she was the school's Saint Lucia. She had won the vote. Zarah was the most beautiful girl.

"Which part is it?" she asks her reflection. "What's your secret? Is it your eyes, your hair, the composition of your face, your smile, the way you move, your voice?"

The mirror doesn't answer.

"Maybe it's my pretty breasts," Zarah says, and smiles. She lifts up her camisole to display them. "See for yourself."

She sticks her other hand into her underwear, pulls them down a little bit, and shows a little of her dark pubic hair. That, Zarah thinks, is how I would look in one of those men's magazines. She parts her legs a little and slowly licks her lips: "Zarah, seventeen. Your wildest dreams can come true. If you want me, come and get me."

Zarah, seventeen, stands in front of her hall mirror and bursts out laughing at herself. Her reflection laughs with her. No, you don't have to be dumb just because you're good-looking. Airhead, bimbo, no thanks. Forget about it. Ugly people don't have to be intelligent either, for that matter.

"I'm not dumb," Zarah tells the mirror, shaking her head and continuing to laugh. "Not dumb like the dumb ones. Not ugly like the ugly ones."

She takes off her camisole and her underwear. Her laugh falls silent but she's still smiling as she inspects the image of her naked body in the mirror. Isn't that birthmark there new? she thinks, turning her side toward the mirror. How do you know which birthmarks are dangerous? How do you recognize skin cancer? Maybe I ought to go to a doctor. Maybe I should have all my birthmarks removed.

Who cares, who cares about that now?

Not Zarah, seventeen, at any rate.

She smiles at her reflection.

Freshly fucked. It shows in her eyes as a faint gleam. And she feels it in her body as a gentle, happy tiredness. Freshly fucked. What beautiful words!

Naked, freshly fucked, and almost happy, Zarah stands in front of the mirror for another little while, then disappears into the bathroom to shower.

Nils

Para conocer a la Vida tienes que conocer a la Muerte,
para conocer a la Vida tienes que morirte.
—from *La Búsqueda*

At quarter past four Nils and Hannes met outside the funeral
home. Nils gave a quick nod, Hannes opened his mouth to say
something, but Nils held the door open and gestured for him to
go in instead. Everything went according to plan.

Hannes introduced himself as a student, explained that he
was working on a project about "burial rituals in different cul-
tures," and the friendly woman behind the little desk said that
she would be happy to try to answer his questions.

"The owner isn't in at the moment …"

"I'm sure it'll be fine anyway," Hannes said, and smiled a
smile that he tried to adjust to the place and the occasion. And
he asked some questions and pretended to jot down the answers.
And he picked up some tastefully worded brochures so he could
read more about it on his own, as he told the woman.

Nils stood there quietly behind him.

"I wonder if it would be all right to just take a quick peek at
the coffins?" Hannes wondered once he'd run out of questions.

"Sure, that would be fine," and the short woman led the way
down half a flight of stairs into a darkened room. A fluorescent
light blinked on, and Nils and Hannes stood in the middle of
the room and looked around.

"Ah, yes," said Hannes.

Along the long wall there were coffins of various designs and models, from the simplest kind made of plywood (Price: $165) to an elaborately decorated, "protective" coffin with a luxurious stainless steel exterior (Price: $3,200). The tax was already included in all the prices, Hannes noted.

Along the shorter wall, across from the door, there was a display case with various types of urns. And big color pictures with examples of the different floral arrangements you could choose for the funeral ceremony were hanging on all the walls.

"Number 272: Two-tiered autumnal harvest arrangement with oats, heather, ivy, natural stones, echeveria, and greenery," Nils read. He wondered, *natural* stones?

"So the coffins have locks, too?" Hannes observed.

"Yes, on those models over there, but on these slightly simpler ones over here the lids are screwed on," the woman explained.

"Ah, yes," said Hannes.

Nils didn't say anything.

But while they were standing by the door on their way out and Hannes was saying "Thank you so much for your help" and "That was most kind," Nils exclaimed, "Oh!"

Hannes and the woman both looked at him.

"Oh, I forgot my bag in there," Nils said, heading quickly back to the coffin room to get it.

"Let me help ..." the woman began.

She was about to follow him, but then Hannes quickly said, "So is it true that you don't always have to wear black to a funeral nowadays?"

The woman glanced after Nils, hesitated a little, but then turned toward Hannes. "No, but people don't usually think about ..."

The woman had time to explain quite a bit about funeral attire, about traditional ideas and new ways of thinking, and Hannes had time to ask a few interested questions and follow-up questions, before Nils returned with his bag in his hand.

"Well, then ..."

"Thank you so much for your help," Hannes said, opening the door.

"Thank you," said the woman.

On the sidewalk outside Kjellgren's Funeral Home Inc., Nils stopped.

"Did it go well?" Hannes asked.

Nils ignored the question. He said, "What other kind of stones are there besides *natural* stones?"

Hannes shrugged.

"Plastic stones?" Nils suggested. "Artificial stones? Headstones? Or ..."

"Rolling stones," said Hannes. "Did it go well?"

"Yeah, yeah. It definitely went well."

Now it's night. Late at night.

The little yard is empty, and without difficulty Nils manages to climb in through the small cellar window that he had latched open during his few moments alone in the coffin room earlier. Then he lets Hannes in through the back door of the funeral home.

It is dark but not pitch black in the room.

"At least it's not as dark as being in a grave, heh heh. Nice …"

"Shhh …"

"What do you do with the key?" Hannes whispers after he's looked around the room for a bit.

"What?"

"What do you do with the key to the coffin? After you put the dead person in the coffin and lock the lid, then what do you do with the key? Toss it in the grave? Or keep it as a keepsake?"

"I don't know." Nils isn't listening. He walks around the room lifting up the lids on the various coffins and peering down into them. Finally he stops in front of one of the plainest, least expensive ones.

"Have you decided?"

Nils nods.

"On that one? Why not choose a luxury model instead, like that one over there?" Hannes wonders, pointing.

"It has a white lining," whispers Nils, "and a pillow and … I don't want to mess it up. This one will be better."

Hannes peers down into the coffin. It's lined with burgundy cloth. "It looks hard."

"It's supposed to be hard," Nils says, taking off his shoes and jacket. "Being dead isn't a fancy vacation."

Hannes holds up the lid while Nils climbs in.

It's a tight fit. He can't stretch his legs out properly and, even though he has narrow shoulders and is thin, it's a really tight fit widthwise too.

"Comfy?" Hannes asks, peering down at him inquisitively.

"No," says Nils.

He squirms and wriggles around to find the position that hurts the least. There, like that. But it's not going to be comfortable.

"You can shut the lid now," he tells Hannes, "but ..."

"Yes?"

"Don't leave until I make sure that I can open it from the inside."

"OK," Hannes says.

Carefully he closes the lid of the coffin and then stands in front of it and contemplates it thoughtfully. Nils's jacket and sneakers are sitting on the floor in front of the coffin.

Hannes sighs and thinks: Nils isn't like other people.

Spending the night in a coffin in a funeral home ... I mean, you can see how people might sit around and talk about something like that for an evening if they were in a group, having a good time and coming up with sort of crazy ideas. But the difference with Nils is that he doesn't just talk about it, he does it.

And he doesn't do it to make himself seem interesting or exciting. No one will ever know about this, no one besides me.

No, when Nils gets an idea ... it's like there's some kind of restraint that he's missing. He's not like other people.

That's what Hannes is thinking as he stands in front of the coffin. And now the lid is shoved aside and Nils peeks out.

"How does it feel?"

"Lonely," says Nils. "And quiet. And black."

"Were you expecting something else?"

"No. You can shut me in now and go home. I'll see you in the morning." He arranges himself in the coffin again.

"Good night," Hannes says, leaning in over Nils.

Hannes suddenly gets a weird feeling. A sense of uneasiness

comes over him that he's not at all prepared for. A bitter taste in his mouth, a feeling of fatigue in his body. He sighs again and shivers, as if to shake off the gloomy feeling.

"Good night," Nils says from down in the coffin. "Shut the lid now."

Anon

"Anon."

When Anon answers the phone, he answers by saying his name. Just his first name and nothing else.

When Anon answers the phone it's almost never someone who wants to talk to him. If he answers a hundred calls, then about ninety-two of them will be for Mother and about five will be wrong numbers. Three of the calls might be for Anon. And in that case, the three calls will all be from the same person. There's only one person who calls Anon, just one in the whole world.

Now it's evening. Anon and his mother have just finished supper when the phone rings, and Anon answers it.

"Mother! It's for you! It's my teacher."

He holds out the receiver. Mother takes it, gives a little sigh, and says, "Galoshes or potatoes?"

What a funny way to greet a schoolteacher! But of course Anon knows what Mother is referring to, and he keeps quietly clearing off the kitchen table while she talks to Miss Larsson.

"Mm-hmm," Mother says.

The teacher says something.

"Ah," Mother says.

The teacher says something. Something that doesn't take much time.

"Hmm," Mother says.

Then she flips through a calendar that's next to the phone,

squeezes the phone between her shoulder and ear, and writes while she talks. "Thursday, no, that won't work, that's when I have my exercise class. Wednesday, sure. Five-thirty? That'll be a little tight ... Well, I could certainly duck out of work a little early. Wednesday at five-thirty, then."

The teacher says something and then Mother says, "Goodbye."

She hangs up, turns toward Anon, and asks, "So how are things going at school, anyway?"

Anon looks like he's considering the question. It seems like he's trying to remember: School? Um, yes. Yes, how *am* I doing at school, anyway?

"Very boring," says Anon once he's finished considering. "I already know most of it. Of what they're working on, I mean."

"Your teacher said you often get there late. Almost always. You're almost never on time, she said. You walk around day-dreaming, she said. And then she was afraid you might be being teased."

Anon shrugs his shoulders. "I get there late sometimes," he explains. "But not always. Sometimes I get there on time. And I don't get there late because I'm daydreaming. I think. I don't dream."

"What do you think about?"

Anon hesitates before answering.

"Maybe I already know what you're thinking about?" Mother says with a serious smile.

Anon nods. "Mmm."

Then Mother walks over to him where he's standing by the sink with the dish brush brandished. She puts her soft motherly hand on his shoulder. "When you get to be a little older I'll tell you more," she says.

"Mmm," Anon says without turning around.

You. You, Anon.

Why do you call your mom "Mother"?

What of it?

"Mother and Father" aren't that common these days. Most people say "Mom and Dad." Or "Lena and Göran" or whatever their parents' names are.

It was Father. He's the one who wanted that. For me to call him "Father." And mother "Mother." I've always done it.

Yup.

"And the other thing?" Mother asks a little later once the dishes are washed and they're drinking coffee at the kitchen table. "What about your being teased?"

Anon takes a deep breath and shakes his head. "There are a few people who are childish," he says, "but I don't mind."

"You sure?"

Mother studies Anon carefully, searching for signs of sadness or fear in his voice or in his face. But she doesn't find any.

"That's what I've always thought," she says. "I've always thought that you could handle things, even though …"

"Even though I'm the way I am." Anon laughs.

"Exactly. Or maybe because you are the way you are."

They both drink from their coffee cups in silence.

Later, as Mother sits down in front of the TV and Anon is going to his room, she asks, "So do you have someone to hang out with? At school, I mean? If you want to, I mean?"

"Yeah," Anon answers quickly. "Of course."

Mother waits.

"Stoffe," Anon says. "Or …" He hesitates a little. "… or Magdalena."

Mother turns away from the nightly news to look directly at him. "Magdalena … Oh, I see."

"Yes. And Stoffe."

"You mean Kristofer who you used to play with when you were in elementary school?"

"Yeah, him."

And Mother turns back to the nightly news and Anon goes into his room and closes the door behind him.

"Anon?" There's a knock-knock on the door. "Can I come in?"

"Yeah … sure …"

Anon is sitting in his room. Mother is standing outside his door, knocking. It's gotten quite late; it's almost bedtime.

"Hey, it's locked! You locked the door."

"Oh, right, yeah," Anon calls from inside his room. "Just a sec."

Mother listens to the sounds coming from Anon's room. It sounds like a desk drawer being opened and shut. A little rustling. And then Anon's footsteps coming to the door. He unlocks it and lets her in.

"Why did you lock the door?"

"Uh …" Anon says.

"Oh, that's all right, never mind. You don't have to answer that. Of course you can lock your door if you want to."

"Mmm."

Silence. Now she's thinking that I've started puberty, Anon thinks. Now she's thinking that I've been sitting in here reading pornography, Anon thinks. And maybe that I've been playing. With myself.

"I just wanted to say good night," says Mother. "Aren't you going to go to bed too?"

"Mmm," says Anon, yawning. "I was just thinking about doing that."

"Good night, then."

"Good night."

When Anon hears toothbrushing noises from the bathroom, he carefully closes his door again and locks it as noiselessly as he can. He returns to his desk, opens the right desk drawer, and takes out what he hid in there, all the way in the back.

Sara's wallet.

Sara's wallet that Anon found in the tall grass behind the bus stop three days ago. Once again he places the black wallet on the desk in front of him, contemplates it for a minute, and then empties out its contents again. There isn't much in it:

A library card.
Two crumpled receipts:
> one from the Writer's Corner and
> one from some clothing store.
A picture of a fat, yellowish white cat.

That's it. No credit cards and no money. Not even a single coin. Well, there was one more thing in the wallet when Anon found it. There was one other picture, a picture of a guy from one of those automated photo booths. He looked like he was about eighteen or twenty, and since Anon thought the guy looked like a gangster he tore the picture up into tiny, tiny pieces and then flushed them down the toilet.

Maybe the guy in the picture was Sara's big brother. Anon has never seen Sara, but he knows exactly what she looks like and of course it would be strange for a sweet little girl like Sara to have such an ugly big brother.

Anon is sitting at his desk, staring at a library card.

It's thanks to the library card that Anon knows that the wallet belongs to Sara. And that Sara's last name is Enoksson. Thanks to the library card he also knows that Sara Enoksson lives at number 14 Östra Storgatan and her phone number is 445637. Anon could call Sara and say that he found her wallet. But he has a much better idea. He'll go to Sara's house in person and return her wallet.

But not right away. He has to prepare first. Today, for example, he went to her street, Östra Storgatan, and found out which building was number 14. Tomorrow he'll go into the apartment building's lobby and see what floor Sara lives on. Then, one day, he'll bring the wallet and go there and ring Sara's doorbell.

This is how it will be, Anon thinks:

Sara will open the door and she'll be extremely happy when she sees what I'm holding in my hand. "Thank you so much," she'll say and she'll be so cute when she laughs and her straight bangs will hang almost down over her perky little squirrel eyes, and she'll peek out curiously, slightly inquisitively, at me, and her mom will invite me in to have some juice and freshly baked rolls, the whole kitchen will be filled with the scent of baking bread, and we'll sit there directly across from each other at the kitchen table, Sara and I, and eat soft, warm rolls and talk a little reservedly about nothing in particular and Sara's eyes will smile gently and right then the phone will ring and Sara's mom will go answer it and then Sara will lean over to me and say, "You know what?" "No," I'll say. Then she'll say that she dreamed about me last night and then I'll say that I've dreamed about her every single night since I found her wallet in the tall grass. Then she'll look me in the eye, slightly searchingly, with a somewhat questioning smile. And before Sara's mom comes back from the phone, Sara and I will manage to arrange to meet the next day after school and do something together. And the next day and the next day and the next.

That's how it will be, Anon thinks.

Anon gives Sara Enoksson's library card a small, gentle kiss before he tucks it back in her wallet. This wallet has been in Sara's back pocket, it's been close to Sara, Anon thinks, and he holds it against his cheek for a moment. The wallet smells of dirt and leather.

Before Anon falls asleep he thinks more about Sara, and about how it will be when he meets her. Maybe she'll ask about my parents, Anon thinks. I suppose she will. I expect she'll want to know a little about my parents.

Then I will tell her that my father is a god.

Zarah

Children are disgusting.

And the more of them there are, the more disgusting it is. Children are always disgusting and snotty and sticky and messy, but it's worst when they eat. And when they pee and poop. Children aren't just disgusting; children are self-centered, ungrateful, naughty, spoiled, and egotistical too.

Compassion—what's that?

Helpfulness and Cooperation—what's that?

Sharing and Being Considerate—what's that?

Kids don't understand stuff like that. Kids aren't really people. Kids are small, clumsy, helpless, silly animals. They're not really people yet.

"Now what do you say, Robin?"

"Tank-oo."

"That's right. Thank you. Go wash your hands now. Zarah will be right there to help you brush your teeth."

Yeah, yeah, yeah.

Zarah gets up from her cramped little kid's chair. Ouch, damn it, her leg fell asleep; she limps after disgusting Robin, out to the bathroom, swearing under her breath.

You. You, Zarah.

Why did you choose to work in a daycare, then, Zarah?

Well, I thought it would be the easiest. I guess I thought three days a week, how bad can that be? Fuck, now I'd choose anything other than daycare. Sitting behind a cash register. Cleaning. Being a mailman. Working in some sweaty, filthy garage. Anything to get away from all these disgusting kids.

"Toopase!"

"Yes, yes, you'll get your toothpaste, Robin."

"Mo toopase!"

"You have a ton of toothpaste already, Robin. Open your mouth now and do a good job."

"Mo, mo!"

Robin squeezes his lips shut and shakes his head.

Zarah sighs heavily and closes her eyes for a second. Then she says, "Okay, then. Are you ready?"

And then she squeezes toothpaste onto Robin's toothbrush, covering the whole brush and continuing up the whole handle. She covers Robin's little fingers and his whole hand with toothpaste. Zarah empties a tube of toothpaste that was almost brand-new.

"Oh," Robin says, staring first at his hand and then at Zarah. "Oh."

First he just stands there with his mouth open. He looks at her with round, dumb eyes. Then he starts sobbing. His face and the area around his mouth start trembling, and then Robin starts to shriek at the top of his lungs, like a fire alarm, with heavy tears running down his apple cheeks, and snot starting to bubble out of his nose.

"Oh dear, oh dear, what seems to be the trouble in here? Oh dear, oh dear, a little accident, a little toothpaste accident …"

It's Mia who has come in. Just as calm and self-assured as

always. No matter what happens, Mia always has something comforting to say, like a reliable mother. Not just a mother, really. Out of all the sensible, gushing women who work at the daycare center, Mia is the only one who has actually cared about Zarah, the only one who has shown any interest, the only one who has taken the time.

Now Mia takes a firm hold of Robin's right hand and starts to rinse it off and comfort him, and to Zarah she says, "Couldn't you be in charge of naptime today? With me. Maybe you could play guitar like you did last time? And maybe read something. Would you like to? Go on in there now and help them with their mattresses and I'll take care of this."

Zarah nods and leaves a sniffling, snotty Robin at the wash-basin.

Ha, take that, you disgusting kid, she thinks.

"I feel it in my fingers, I feel it in my toes …"

Zarah sings "Love Is All Around" and plays the guitar, and eighteen children lie on mattresses on the floor with yellow blankets over them and listen. Most of them are holding something in their hands; most of them are lying there snuggling and cuddling with a security blanket or a teddy bear or a doll or a stuffed animal or something. All of them are lying quietly and still; only Jenny and Hanna are sniffling and snuffling a little.

"…You know I love you, I always will …"

Mia sits in the corner. She watches Zarah closely, her eyes settling on the back of Zarah's neck, but Zarah doesn't notice. She's singing and accompanying herself like she learned at music school a long time ago: thumb-index-middle-ring-index …

"… And if you really love me, come on and let it show …"

The song fades out:

"... come on and let it show ..."

And Zarah whispers:

"... come on and let it show ..."

Zarah lets the final D-chord reverberate as she looks around the room. Elin and Viktoria and Mikael and Albin and Bermina and Faton are already asleep. Robin is lying there with his eyes open and snuggling with a snotty security blanket. His cheeks are glowing red and Zarah has a brief attack of Guilty Conscience. It feels kind of like a mosquito bite and it passes just as quickly.

But now Zarah thinks: No, not just disgusting. Not when they're sleeping, not when they're lying still on a mattress and snuggling with their old teddy bears. No, then the children look so soft and good, almost like fruit, like a bowl full of sun-warmed peaches. Imagine just sinking your teeth into those rosy cheeks, mmm ...

"Story," snuffles Hanna. "Read us a story."

Zarah doesn't answer. Zarah doesn't move; she sits completely still with her guitar in her lap, as if she didn't hear Hanna's whimpered request.

But just as Mia's about to get up and pick a book from the bookshelf, Zarah whispers, "Once upon a time there was a girl ..."

With the hint of a smile on her lips, Mia sinks back down in the corner again and listens to Zarah, her eyes still resting on the back of Zarah's neck.

"Once upon a time there was a girl whose name was Sara," Zarah begins.

"Just like you," Rebecka whispers with a sleepy giggle.

"Mmm, just like me. Hush now and I'll tell you the story."

And Zarah says:

"Once upon a time there was a girl whose name was Sara, and Sara always got her way. If she said, 'I'm not going to bed,' then her mom said that, of course, she could stay up all night. And if Sara said, 'I want candy for dinner today,' then her father would hop on his bike and go to the store and buy a pound of bulk candy. Everything Sara wanted, she got. And everything Sara wanted to do, her mom and dad let her do. They never said no. Sara always got what she wanted. Still she was never satisfied. Still something was always missing."

"What, what?" Rebecka whispers.

"She was missing her mirror sister."

"Her what? Who?"

"Sara had a twin sister. They were exactly the same, it was almost impossible to tell them apart, and Sara and her sister had so much fun together when they were little. They always played together. They did everything together. And they had secret places where they did secret things and—"

"Hey, Zarah ...?" Rebecka whines.

"Yes?"

"What was her name? The sister. What was her name?"

"Her name was also Sara," says Zarah. "They were both named Sara. Sara One and Sara Two."

"Oh."

"Yes. But anyway: Sara and her sister were always together, they made noise together and played together, they laughed together and cried together. Until one day ..."

"Yes? What?"

"One day Sara's sister was gone. Disappeared."

"What? Why?"

"Sara didn't know. She didn't understand. She looked everywhere and she thought maybe her sister had done something dumb, something forbidden, and that Mom and Dad sent her away …"

Zarah stops for a minute and waits for Rebecka to ask "What, why?" but Rebecka's eyes are closed now. She's breathing calmly and slowly, and in a quiet little voice she says, "Mmm …"

"… and Sara asked her parents," Zarah whispers, "but they would never talk about her twin sister that disappeared. But that was the day Sara discovered she could get everything she wanted, she got everything she asked for from her parents, still Sara was never truly happy again, still there was always something she was missing …"

Zarah falls silent. All of the children are asleep. Not a single child tells her to keep going. No, it's Mia from the corner diagonally behind Zarah who whispers, "Then what happened?"

Zarah shakes her head without answering.

"OK," Mia whispers, getting up.

They sneak out of the room together.

After coffee Zarah stands out by the garbage cans. She's sneaking a cigarette when Mia comes out.

"How did things turn out for Sara?" Mia asks.

"What?"

"How did things turn out for Sara who was missing her mirror sister? Did she find her?"

"Nah. She's still looking," Zarah answers, putting her cigarette out against a post.

Zarah doesn't really know why she asks if Mia wants to come over to her place some evening. She hadn't thought about it before and she hadn't planned on asking. And when Mia answers right away, "Yeah, thanks, sure, I'd love to," then Zarah gets a weird feeling that Mia had been waiting for her invitation.

"But not tonight, we have an away game tonight."

"Maybe tomorrow?" Zarah suggests while at the same time trying to remember if she had anything planned with Victor tomorrow night.

"That'd be great," Mia says.

"I live on—"

"I know where you live," Mia says. "I checked in the office."

Mia has short hair. Mia plays soccer. Mia walks firmly and confidently wherever she goes. Mia can laugh and comfort people.

As Zarah sits outside on the playground watching Mia play a game of tag with the big kids over by the swings, she thinks: Mia isn't like me. Mia is like a big sister, like a big sister should be. More sister than mother.

Or like a friend, maybe, a pal. A friend you can rely on.

That's the kind of friend I need, thinks Zarah.

Nils

Para ser hombre
Tienes que acordarte de la muerte
Cada día de la vida
tienes que acordarte de la muerte.
—from *La Búsqueda*

"So …?"

"So … what?"

"You know what I mean," Hannes says, taking a bite of his Danish. "How was it?"

Nils contemplates his friend in silence. "You have something yellow by the corner of your mouth there," he says finally.

It's a normal afternoon, and as usual Nils and Hannes are sitting at a window table at Hansen's Café. Nils pulls a crinkled pack of cigarettes out of his jacket pocket, shakes a cigarette out for himself, and then offers Hannes one.

"Five days," Hannes says, shaking his head. "Everything in my head feels so clear and healthy now. Smoking really makes everything foggy. I figured that out when I quit. You should give it a try."

"Mmm," Nils says, lighting his cigarette.

"Do you remember that Sandburg poem about how the fog comes on little cat feet? Or was it Robert Frost? Anyway, it's a great image, don't you think? The fog coming and going without any fuss or noise, stealthily, like a cat. Nice, huh?"

"Mmm," Nils says, gazing out the window.

"So, tell me," Hannes urges again. "How did it go?"

"I survived," Nils says with a wry smile.

You. You, Nils.

Yeah, so how did it really go, Nils?

What did you learn? What do you know now that you didn't know before you spent the night in a coffin?

I don't know. Maybe nothing. Maybe something.

Maybe a feeling, maybe a little bit of knowledge that can't be put into words. Yet. And anyway, I didn't stay there the whole night.

"Humans are the only animal that knows it's going to die," Nils says, looking directly into Hannes's clear blue eyes.

"And …?"

"And that's the basis of all religion," says Nils. "Humans know that they are going to die. So they think about life. And about what happens after life is over. That's why there are churches. That's why there are ministers. That's why there are gods."

"How do you know that?"

"What?"

"Maybe cats also know they're going to die. Maybe cats have a religion too. Maybe there's a Cat Jesus and a Cat God."

"Cats wouldn't spend so much time licking their butts if they were religious," Nils says, grinning.

A moment of silence. Some thoughts. A mouthful of lukewarm coffee, a puff on a cigarette.

"Seriously, though," says Nils. "That's how it is. Humans are the only animal that is conscious of the fact that it is going to die."

"Not me," says Hannes.

"You're not?"

"Nah," he says, shaking his head resolutely. "I'm not conscious of the fact that I'm going to die. Quite the opposite. I know that I'm *not* going to die. I'm going to live forever."

"Amen," says Nils.

"Seriously, though," says Hannes, "you still haven't told me what it was like in the coffin. Did you have an intense near-death experience?"

Nils gives Hannes a slightly sheepish look and then says, "I fell asleep." It almost sounds like he's apologizing.

"Huh …?"

"Yeah, I fell asleep. It was super cramped and hard and uncomfortable, but I fell asleep. And when I woke up it was completely pitch black and I didn't know where I was and then I kind of freaked out because I started thinking the lid was screwed shut, but then I was able to open the coffin and …"

"Yes?"

"I sat up and I think I screamed out loud. But I couldn't see anything, the light totally blinded me, everything was completely white. I couldn't see; it really was like I was blind. But I heard sounds. A howl, a thud, someone running. And after I'd sat there in the coffin blinking for a minute and my eyes adjusted to the light, then I saw …"

Nils stops talking and takes a sip of coffee. There's an annoying little twinkle in his eye as he watches Hannes, who's waiting for him to continue.

"What did you see?!" Hannes finally pleads.

"Well, when I was finally able to see, I discovered an old woman lying completely still on the floor there in the coffin room. She was lying right in front of my coffin, and that old lady that you interviewed the other day was standing in the other room, she was standing at the desk with the phone in her hand and staring at me with eyes as wide as saucers and opening and closing her mouth like a fish. I awkwardly pulled myself up out of the coffin and I was stiff and I could hardly stand, so I was staggering around among the coffins for a bit. The old funeral home lady just stared and stared and stood there as if she'd been turned to stone, and the old woman who had fainted was lying on the floor—I guess she was in there to pick out a coffin for her dearly departed husband or something when I arose from the dead. Tough break for her. Hope she didn't suffer any long-term injuries."

"And then?"

"Then I left. I just left through the back door. Didn't think I could really add anything to that. Not after my grand entrance."

A big smile spreads across Hannes's face as he looks at Nils. "Really?"

Nils puts out his cigarette. Still serious, he looks Hannes in the eyes, but then he finally can't hold it in any longer and at exactly the same instant the two young men both burst out laughing, laughter so loud that for a second everything in the café freezes and all the other customers stop talking and turn to look at their table.

No, that wasn't the truth.

The truth was much less dramatic. The truth was that Nils

didn't spend the night in the coffin. It was too cramped, too dark, and too hot. And as long as we're telling the truth, he felt dumb. Foolish. He started giggling to himself and climbed out of the coffin after only half an hour and left the funeral home and biked home.

So what have I learned? he thought as he lay at home in his soft, warm bed.

Nothing, he thought. But that was only step one. Steps two and three were still to come.

"I need you to help me one more time," Nils tells Hannes once they're done laughing.

"Yeah?"

"Yeah."

Nils doesn't say anything else; he doesn't want to say anything else for now. He'll explain it when the time comes.

Small talk. Chatting.

About the world. About life.

About things that have happened.

About two new movies that came out.

More coffee. Two more cigarettes.

That old, familiar café feeling. Always the same, always safe. Familiar sounds, familiar scents, and familiar faces at the tables.

And the conversation winds down toward a feeling of departure, a feeling of "Bye, see you tomorrow," but then something happens on the street outside the window. Just as Nils is about to get up he sees something out there, something that makes his face light up with an unusually radiant delight.

"What is it?" Hannes wonders, leaning forward. "Is Jesus standing out there?"

"Maybe," says Nils without turning to look at Hannes. "Do you see that guy over there?"

Hannes surveys the street. "Which guy? You mean him—the one in the galoshes?"

Nils nods eagerly, and Hannes finds himself staring at a boy of about twelve who's standing there, right outside the café, looking around in confusion.

What's so special about him? Hannes wonders. "What's so special about him?" he asks.

Nils doesn't answer; his eyes light up and he quietly shakes his head. His eyes are riveted on the twelve-year-old boy in the blue galoshes outside the window.

Only after the boy walks away does Nils turn toward Hannes.

"Did you see that?" he asks as he leans back with his hands clasped behind his head.

"What?"

"That little boy—he walked right into that lamppost! Thwack! He was walking along daydreaming and then *thwack*, right into that lamppost. And then he just stood there, feeling stupid, and looked around to see if anyone had seen him. Ha!"

Nils is filled with a childlike glee, as if he had just opened the Christmas present he wanted most of all. "That could have been me," he says.

Hannes watches Nils as he lights another cigarette.

"I used to be just like that," Nils continues. "When I was eleven or twelve. I was the kind of person who was always walking into lampposts. I always had a bruise on my forehead. And Göran would laugh at me and my mom would get all annoyed and irritated."

The wistful smile remains while he takes a deep puff on the cigarette and loses himself in his memories of when he was twelve. Hannes waits.

"I used to play Invisible Jesus," Nils says after a while.

"What?"

"Invisible Jesus," Nils repeats. "That was my best daydream. It was like I was God's secret agent. God would come to me with his biggest problems. And I would fix them. Always. And sometimes …"

"Yes?"

"Sometimes I would be the fastest runner in the world. For all distances. That was another one of my favorite dreams. I had this secret magic phrase and when I said it to myself I could run faster than anyone else. I won all the gold medals. Every single one."

Nils puts out the cigarette and looks Hannes straight in the eye. For a brief instant he considers revealing his secret runner's prayer:

O Lord
give me my running feet
my wingèd feet
once more

But no, then it would lose its power, Nils thinks to himself with a little laugh.

"And all my daydreams ended the same way," he said instead.

"Thwack!" Hannes says, laughing.

"Thwack!" Nils says, nodding. "Lamppost. Thwack! Bruise."

Nils tilts his head to one side and looks at Hannes. What did you dream, Hannes? Were you Invisible Jesus too? Were you also the fastest runner in the world for all distances?

A gentle, liquid warmth permeates Nils's body; he can even feel it in his fingertips. I am just one human being out of many, he thinks. We are all the same and we are all different. The world is both safe and wonderful.

"Earth to Saint Nils!" Hannes laughs. "Boy, do you look saintly."

Nils nods. The little boy outside the window reminded him of something. Something he'd almost forgotten. He gets up.

"I have to go home and cram. Test on Friday."

"Mmm," Hannes says, getting up too. They say goodbye to each other in front of the coffee shop.

"See ya."

"Mmm."

Nils has gotten only a couple of yards when Hannes calls after him, "Hey!"

"Yeah?"

"Watch out for lampposts!"

Nils waves without turning around and walks on.

Those days are gone, he thinks. I was a child then. Dreams had a different sort of power back then.

Anon

"Anon?"

"Here! I'm here!"

"Oh, there you are! I didn't see you. Please come on in!"

Nurse Ekdal holds the door open and Anon walks into her office. He sits down on the chair directly across from her desk and looks around.

It looks the same as ever in here, Anon thinks. The scale there and the height chart there and the eye-test chart there and small Band-Aids and bandages and the medicine cabinet and files. And No Smoking posters on the walls. The normal smell too—all the normal smells.

"It's been a little while, Anon …"

"Mmm."

It had actually been a little while. All the same, Anon must have been number one at the top of the list for most visits to the school nurse. School champion.

"Do you know why I wanted to see you?"

Anon shrugs his shoulders and purses his lips. "The galoshes?" he guesses.

Nurse Ekdal shakes her head. "Not this time. But you know what I think about that."

Yeah, yeah, Anon thinks. How can I possibly make you understand? "Then I guess it's the potatoes?" he tries.

Nurse Ekdal shakes her head again. "Mrs. Gustafsson in the cafeteria says things are going much better now. They are, aren't they?"

Um, yeah, thinks Anon. But how can I possibly make you understand?

Nurse Ekdal studies Anon in silence for a moment. "No, this time it's something completely different," she says then. "I thought you might already have some idea what this was about."

Anon shakes his head energetically. "No idea," he says.

It's true. If it's not the galoshes and not the potatoes, then he can't understand why Nurse Ekdal wants to talk to him. Because it doesn't seem like she wants to give him a shot and it doesn't seem like this has to do with finding out how much he weighs or how tall he is.

"There's been a bit of a problem in the bathrooms," Nurse Ekdal says.

Then she doesn't say anything else, just stares Anon right in the eyes, so intently that it's like she's trying to see inside his skull.

She's trying to read my mind, Anon thinks, and he can't help but laugh. He pictures Nurse Ekdal dancing naked with the principal in the middle of the playground and all the students watching and clapping along with the music. He stares back at Nurse Ekdal, curious. Nope. Nope, it doesn't work. She can't read his mind.

"You're laughing?"

"Just thought of something funny," Anon mumbles.

"What I'd like to speak to you about is no laughing matter," Nurse Ekdal says. "Quite the opposite."

Anon tries to make his face look serious.

"There's been a problem in the bathrooms," Nurse Ekdal says again. "There's been quite a bit of discussion about it in recent weeks. But you don't have any idea what I'm talking about?"

"No," says Anon succinctly.

Nope, he has no idea. And he's starting to get tired of this guessing game. Bathroom problems seem more like something for the janitor than for the school nurse, he thinks.

"Then I suppose I ought to explain," says Nurse Ekdal with a little sigh, as if she were tired too. "It's been happening in your bathroom, and in the fifth graders' bathroom, and in the bathrooms by the cafeteria. Someone has been peeing."

Anon can't help but laugh. Did Nurse Ekdal call him in here to tell him that someone was peeing in the bathrooms? Wasn't that what bathrooms were for? Among other things.

Nurse Ekdal silences him with a stern, serious look.

"Someone has been peeing outside the toilets," she continues. "It's definitely on purpose. On the floor, on the walls. And on the inside of the door. And in other places."

Now Nurse Ekdal stares at Anon intently again.

"You haven't ever noticed this?"

"Nope. Although …"

"Yes?"

"Although I do wear my galoshes. So it doesn't matter that much to me. If there's pee on the floor, I mean," Anon says, lighting up as if he were thinking: Ha! You see?! It's not so dumb to wear galoshes after all!

"Don't you think it's disgusting?" asks Nurse Ekdal, wrinkling up her nose.

"Well, yes, I suppose it is." He feels bored again. Is that all? What does it have to do with him if someone is peeing outside the toilets?

"I find it *very* disgusting," Nurse Ekdal says, and her *very* is heavy, like a sandbag. "The boy who's—"

"Boy?" Anon interrupts and a glimmer of interest shows in his eyes.

"Yes, it has to be a boy, and—"

"Why does it have to be a boy?"

"Because …" Nurse Ekdal is irritated now. She hesitates before continuing "… because a girl can't pee … so high. I did say that someone had peed on the walls. And in other places."

"Hmm …"

Now Anon is interested. He ponders. How high can girls pee anyway? Can girls pee only straight down? What if a girl bends over forwards? Or backwards? Or if she …

"I know!" Anon exclaims. "Now I know!"

Nurse Ekdal eyes him suspiciously.

"It's not necessarily a boy," Anon says. "What if it's a girl who's standing on her hands!"

Not much else is said in the school nurse's office.

When Anon emerges, Stoffe is waiting for him. "Well?"

"What?" Anon wonders.

"What did she want? Why did the school nurse want to talk to you?"

"I'm not sure," Anon says. "She told me that someone has been peeing in the bathrooms. Outside the toilets. A boy, probably."

Stoffe nods. "Did you confess?" he asks, and starts walking away without even waiting for a response.

That afternoon Anon hears it five times. Someone whispers it as he walks by, someone yells it out loud so it can be heard halfway across the playground, and when the class comes back in after the last recess someone has written it in big childlike letters on the black chalkboard:

PISS ANON.

Everyone sits there in silence; not a sound is heard as Miss Larsson marches quickly up to the board and erases the writing.

"Well?"

She lets her eyes wander around the room. Silence. Everyone knows that she means: Now, who wrote that? No one answers, although most of them know who did it.

Finally Anon raises his hand.

"Yes?"

"I'm not the one who's peeing in the bathrooms," he says. "I mean, I'm not the one who's peeing outside the toilets."

He's completely calm as he says it. As if this whole thing had nothing to do with him. As if it actually didn't bother him that it said PISS ANON on the blackboard a minute ago.

Miss Larsson looks at Anon seriously. She isn't concerned that a little murmur goes through the class, she isn't concerned that a little "Tsss" and a little teasing "Nya nya" and other small comments can be heard, she just looks at Anon and knows: He's telling the truth.

And a feeling that resembles sadness is born in Miss Larsson; a heavy, bleak sadness starts to grow in her as she looks at Anon.

Miss Larsson stands there in silence for a long time. All the murmuring and mumbling and whispering and gossiping in the classroom grows into quite a hum before she snaps out of it and looks around, and immediately her sadness turns to anger.

"Silence!" she roars.

Her voice unusually harsh. Her cheeks an unusual, angry red.

The classroom unusually quiet, the students astonished.

"Is there anyone in here who knows that it was Anon who peed ... who peed outside the toilets?" Miss Larsson asks, her voice unusually biting and firm.

Silence.

"Well?!"

A little murmur that sounds like "Nooooo ..."

"In that case I do not want to hear any more about this," Miss Larsson continues, nodding toward the chalkboard. "Is that understood?"

A little murmur that sounds like "Yeaaaah ..." And then silence again.

Anon is surprised. He thinks: She doesn't have to defend me so vigorously. Just think if she's wrong. Just think if I am the one who's been peeing.

Kristina sits in front of Anon, one row over. She thinks: I should say it. I should say that I know Anon isn't the Pissman.

Because Kristina has been watching Anon for a couple of days. She saw him smuggle his potatoes and vegetables out of the cafeteria, she saw him go into the bathroom to flush the contents of his pockets, and she had Anon under surveillance yesterday when, for example, someone peed in the fifth graders' bathroom. She could be an alibi for him.

In the past, Kristina thinks, in a black-and-white movie, I would have stood up right now and said something. And been the hero, the cute, curly-haired heroine. That's not how it is now. Maybe I'm a little chicken. And why should I care about Anon? And besides, maybe it *is* him anyway, I can't really know for sure.

So Kristina doesn't say anything, and finally Miss Larsson

says, "Let's continue. Take out your math books."

Her voice is almost normal again.

When math class is over and school is done for the day, Anon sits alone in the cloakroom. He's always the last one to leave school; he puts his jacket on calmly and peacefully, checks to make sure he has everything in his backpack, and usually sits there for a little bit while everyone else rushes off as if they'd just been released from jail every day at ten to three.

Right when he stands up to go home, Ida comes back into the cloakroom.

"I just want to say one thing," she says.

Anon waits.

"I just want to say that I think you're disgusting," Ida says, turning her nose up at him.

Then she turns her back on Anon and goes back out to Frida, Kristina, and Magdalena, who are waiting on the playground.

But on the way home, Anon isn't thinking about what happened at school. Not a single thought about pee or bathrooms or classmates.

No, his head is filled with Sara.

Sara who he has never seen.

Sara who lost her wallet.

Sara who Anon will meet when he returns her wallet, Sara who he will get to know, Sara who will get close to him. She will get closer to me than anyone ever has before, Anon thinks. I will be able to talk about everything with Sara. I'll tell her about my father.

And in his head, Anon sees how he and Sara sit facing each other at her kitchen table, and he hears himself tell Sara:

My father is a god. My mother is a normal woman, but my father is a god.

He's not one of the biggest, most powerful gods, no, quite the opposite. But a god at any rate. And even the smallest, most minor gods have more power and strength than all of the kings and presidents, yes, more power and strength than all of the people on earth.

Imagine someone strong. My father is stronger.

Imagine someone powerful. My father is more powerful.

And still he's only a basement god. Way at the top, on the thirtieth floor, is the Über-God. Then there are the head-of-department gods and the mid-level gods and the sub-gods with their secretaries on the floors below, and way down in the basement are the basement gods.

The three basement gods share responsibility for Transportation & Distribution & Repairs.

"I'm the deputy assistant manager here," my father usually says, and laughs his thunderous god laugh.

Anon smiles to himself as he walks along the sidewalk. That's what I'll tell Sara, he thinks. And her jaw will drop and she'll say "Oh," and then I'll say:

Yeah, my father is a god. But it isn't as unusual as you might think. At the last meeting there were three hundred and fourteen. Three hundred and fourteen children whose father is a god or whose mother is a goddess. And then there are a lot of kids who are too little to attend the meeting, and quite a few who've already turned eighteen and been transferred. And then the gods and goddesses also have a lot of god-children with each other, right and left, higgledy-piggledy.

I would bet there are four or five thousand of us. Five thousand children of gods on earth. Given that there are only twenty-seven gods, there are a lot of us. And one thing is easy to see:

They mate like rabbits, the gods and goddesses. They are very lustful. Mating for life? Being faithful? "What's that?" a god would say. "Why?" he would say. Or she.

But I'm not complaining. Sure, I don't see Father that often, and I have a ton of half-brothers and sisters that I've never even seen, and my mother has cried many lonely tears. But there are also advantages to having a father who's a god.

Being immortal, for example. I think.

Anon wrinkles his forehead and stops walking.

Maybe I shouldn't say that part about mating like rabbits to Sara, he thinks. Maybe that will alarm her. Maybe she'll think I have certain intentions. No, I won't go into all that, Anon decides. I'll just tell her how many of us there are.

And as Anon starts walking again he keeps thinking about his conversation with Sara.

"You really can't tell from looking at you," Sara will say, laughing. "That your father is a god, I mean."

"No," I'll say then, "I'm just like an ordinary person. I have the same number of fingers and the same number of toes as an ordinary person. And a nose in front and a rear end in back."

"Hee hee," Sara laughs. "But can you tell by looking at your father?" she asks then. "Does it show when you look at him that he's a god?"

"Only if you know," I answer. "Then it's quite obvious. Good heavens, some of the gods look so godly. But they walk around on earth just like ordinary people. Just like your mother. They shop at the local grocery store and pick up their children at—"

Thwack!!!

A lamppost. And Anon walks right into it, and there's a ringing in his skull, and his Dream Conversation With Sara comes crashing down to earth, and Anon clutches his forehead, ow, ow, ow, and he looks around. Did anyone see him? No, apparently not. People are walking on the sidewalk around him as if nothing had happened. Good. Walking right into a lamppost makes you feel like such an idiot. And it happens a little too often.

Anon shakes his head as if to shake away the pain. Where am I anyway? he thinks. Ah, outside Hansen's Café. Well, then, I'm almost home. I'll go home to Mother now, Anon decides. And I'll pay attention and keep my eyes open and not daydream.

Bye, Sara, Anon thinks. Bye, see you later. See you tonight.

Zarah

Did I say "Make yourself at home" when she got here? Zarah wonders.

No, I didn't. "Make yourself at home" is an old-fashioned house-wifey thing to say. But she seems like she's making herself at home anyway, Zarah thinks, glancing out toward the living room where Mia is walking around, pulling books off the book-shelf, looking at her CD collection, and studying the mess on Zarah's desk with interest. Almost a little too much at home.

Yes, Mia arrived at seven o'clock sharp. A gray bag from the liquor store in her left hand and a bag from the grocery store in her right hand.

"I was supposed to be inviting you over and you brought the whole party with you," Zarah had said, laughing, as she took the bags and looked in them.

Two bottles of white wine, frozen shrimp, mayonnaise, tomatoes, and a loaf of white bread that smelled as if it had just come out of the oven.

"I make plenty of money," Mia said, smiling. "You don't, even though we work at the same place."

And Mia stepped into the apartment and right away she wanted to "take the tour" and look around, and Zarah was forced to quickly step in front of the closed bedroom door. "No, not in there. That's just the bedroom. It's a total mess."

"OK," Mia said, shrugging. "And this must be your kitchen. It's so cozy …"

Just to be on the safe side, Zarah makes sure to lock the bedroom door now while Mia's in the bathroom.

Now the shrimp are all eaten and the good bread. Zarah is standing in the kitchen rinsing the plates, and Simson, who smells alluring aromas, is rubbing against her leg and purring in anticipation.

"Should I put some coffee on?" Zarah calls out to Mia.

"We might as well drink the wine up first," Mia calls back.

So Zarah finishes the dishes and goes out to Mia in the living room, hops up on the sofa, pulls her legs up under her, and lets Mia fill the wineglasses.

"It's really good," Mia says. "This wine, I mean."

"Dangerously good," Zarah says with a little giggle.

And Mia raises her glass and clinks glasses with Zarah, without a word, with just a smile, and Zarah takes a sip while Mia drinks a big gulp, and before she sets her glass down on the coffee table she looks directly into Zarah's eyes.

Mia's smile is contagious. Her laugh too. Mia is easy to spend time with, she's good at both talking and listening, and the evening has sped by.

Still, there's something bugging Zarah.

You. You, Zarah.

What? What do you mean? There's something bugging you? What?

There's one thing I'm wondering, one thing someone once said.

What? Pray tell …

Ugh, it's so stupid …

Say it anyway.

All right, OK. At least half of the girls on Sweden's national women's soccer team are lesbians. That was something that someone told me once, and it sounded like it was true. It sounded like the person who said it knew it was true. And now that thought is bugging me. What if Mia …

Would that matter?

Yes. Now and then I've thought: I would like to know someone gay. A guy. Be friends with a guy, just friends of course, without an ounce of the tension, the suspicion, the lust that gets in the way and ruins things. Every now and then it would just be so nice and relaxing not to have to deal with that whole game. Now maybe everything will be exactly the opposite with Mia. She's nice and cheerful and fun to be with. But what if she has certain intentions? What if she's here to seduce me? Then everything would come crashing down to earth. Then nothing would be worth anything anymore.

Zarah raises her wineglass again and contemplates Mia over the edge of the glass. Zarah feels like an idiot and is ashamed of her thoughts.

Almost the first thing Zarah did when Mia got there was show her a picture of Victor. "This is my boyfriend." Like a kind of warning label. Or a vaccination. And Mia had just nodded and said "Mm-hmm" and seemed moderately interested.

Zarah's ashamed. Go away now, all you suspicions, she thinks. Girls can have short hair and be friendly and play soccer. I'm glad Mia's here. I like her. Not a single other thought about that other stuff for the rest of the evening!

She fills Mia's wineglass with the last of the wine. "Damn, if only we had another bottle."

"We have to work tomorrow," Mia says, laughing. "Don't forget that."

They each drink from their glasses, and Zarah feels pleasantly, cheerfully tipsy, and she leans back on the sofa and meets Mia's searching smile without any more hesitation.

"You should tell me about Sara," Mia says.

"Sara?"

"Sara who's looking for her mirror sister. Sara who got everything she wanted from her parents. Sara that you told the story about at naptime. Do you remember?"

"Mmm." Zarah nods.

"Are you her? Was the story about you? Is Sara Zarah?"

Zarah shrugs her shoulders. "Not the part about the parents. I never got anything from my parents. I never had any parents. At any rate, not …"

When Zarah falls silent, Mia raises her eyebrows in a wordless question, but Zarah shakes her head.

"No, I don't want to talk about that. Not now. But about the other thing, yeah, Sara is me. There was a time when I dreamed all the time, every night I dreamed, every night was like a fairy tale, an adventure …"

She speaks slowly, with long pauses; she searches for words and thoughts. This might be the first time she's told this to anyone.

"I must have been eleven or twelve years old … and I remember a couple of those dreams so clearly, so unusually vividly, almost as if they were real, and one in particular, it was a dream I had lots of times, a recurrent dream …"

Zarah sinks into her memories, and Mia waits without interrupting her.

"Yeah, I dreamed that I had a twin sister. A girl who was my mirror image. I dreamed about everything we did together, and when I woke up I missed her. I missed her so much it hurt. I missed her so much I got goose bumps. I didn't want to wake up from my dream. And I stood in front of the mirror every day, and what I saw in the mirror wasn't a reflection of myself—what I saw was my sister who'd disappeared."

Zarah falls silent, hesitates, thinking.

"I eventually forgot my mirror sister later on."

Zarah gets up, finds a pack of cigarettes on the desk, gets a lighter from the kitchen, opens the window, sits on the window-sill, and lights her cigarette. Mia swivels halfway around in the swivel chair to sit facing her.

"Well, then in junior high there was so much other stuff. Boys. And, well ... a lot of other stuff. And trouble. A lot of trouble. I forgot my sister. But then one day in ninth grade, in the spring, we had a substitute one day, or maybe it was a guest speaker or something; at any rate there was this guy who talked so seriously and said something like 'Each person is unique, in the whole world there is no copy of you, in the entire history of the world there has never been a copy of you, and there won't be a person who is just like you in the future either. It's truly remarkable. Everyone is different. Everyone is unique. And yet we are all alike.'"

Mia laughs because Zarah has been talking in a serious, almost religious voice. As if she were giving a sermon.

"Well, that's what he sounded like," Zarah says, laughing. "And I happened to be in school on just that day, and when I heard that guy talk, I remembered my twin sister and I thought,

'Ha, you're wrong, dude.' I've never forgotten her again since then. And since that day I've missed her. And longed for her. Every day."

Zarah stamps her cigarette out against the metal window frame, tosses the butt out into the dark spring night outside, takes a deep breath, and closes the window.

Mia watches her while she squeezes past the coffee table and sinks down onto the sofa again. She's closed herself off again now, but Mia knows that Zarah opened up to her, that Zarah told her something from deep in her heart. She gave me a present, thinks Mia. That's what it feels like.

After they've sat silently for a bit, each of them deep in her own thoughts, Mia whispers, softly, as if afraid of interrupting, "Do you think you'll find her?"

Zarah doesn't answer. Doesn't want to talk anymore now. Thinks: Why did I tell Mia all that? It's not because of the wine anyway, I haven't had *that* much to drink, I can take a lot more without starting to ramble.

So Zarah just shrugs her shoulders and sits there silently.

The silence thickens between the two young women, and when it's broken—*riiiiinng*—by an angry signal from the doorbell, they're both startled, give each other a look as if they'd just been awakened from a deep sleep, as if they'd each awakened from a dream, and laugh.

"That'll be Victor," Zarah says.

She cocks her head to the side, almost as if she were apologizing for her boyfriend's arrival. And she doesn't get up right away to open the outer door; she waits until Mia has said something about its being "probably about time to get going now," and another sharp ring slices through the apartment before Zarah goes to the door and lets Victor in.

"Hi. What the fuck, were you asleep or what?"

Mia hears Victor's voice from the hall as she gets up. And then he comes into the room, struggling with two heavy paper bags that he sets down in front of the bedroom door. He tries to turn the doorknob.

"What the fuck, why'd you lock the door?"

"Victor, this is Mia," Zarah calls from out in the hall and then pushes her way past him into the living room. "Mia works at the daycare center, at the daycare center where I ... work. And this is Victor."

She stands there between Victor and Mia, feeling like nothing is right.

"Hi." Mia gives a little nod.

"Hi," Victor says and turns toward Zarah. "Why'd you lock this door?"

Fucking Idiot Victor, Zarah thinks, sensing the icy chill between him and Mia. Could you be just the slightest bit civilized, you goddamn fucking immigrant. You're usually so goddamn charming. Shit, Victor, if I had to choose between you two right now, I wouldn't choose you.

She takes a key out of her pants pocket and unlocks the bedroom door, and Victor lugs his bags in.

Mia can't help but peer in. It's impossible to tell what's in the bags because there's some black plastic on the top. And she's only able to cast a quick glance into the bedroom before Victor shuts the door behind him. Cardboard boxes. Brown cardboard boxes along one wall is what Mia is able to see.

"Thanks for ... a nice evening."

Mia is standing in the hallway now, with her jacket on. Zarah feels like she ought to apologize for Victor in some way, find some little explanation or something, but ... uh ... She says something about the shrimp and the good wine instead.

Then she stands there in silence directly opposite Mia, until Mia takes a step forward and puts her soft daycare hand on one of Zarah's shoulders. For a brief second, Zarah thinks Mia is going to lean in and hug her or give her a kiss on the cheek, but Mia just stands there and says, "You're not going to oversleep tomorrow, right?"

"No, no, don't worry," Zarah says.

There's a bit of a question left in Mia's eyes, Zarah sees it, but Mia never asks the question, she just lets her hand leave Zarah's shoulder and says, "Bye. And thanks."

"Mmm," Zarah says, closing the door behind her.

Zarah stands there facing the closed outside door for a while.

She giggles. How dumb can I be? she thinks. How could I believe that whole thing about the women's national soccer team? That must have been a long time ago anyway. These days I'm sure there are plenty of girls who play soccer. As many girls as guys.

Zarah giggles again and goes back into the apartment, to Victor. Anyway, then half of the guys on the men's national soccer team should be gay too, she thinks. How stupid can I be?

Nils

El viejo sabio de China dijo:
Los duros y los fuertes
son los compañeros de la muerte,
los suaves y los débiles
son los compañeros de la vida.
Digo yo: ¡Sí!
—from *La Búsqueda*

Kristina is dancing.

She's dancing alone in the living room. Music fills the apartment, misty Irish music, synthesizers, and a woman's voice with a lot of echo. Loud.

Nils sees Kristina dancing.

She thinks that she's home alone; she didn't hear Nils come in. Now he lingers in the hallway, hides behind the doorframe, and peers in at her.

Kristina closes her eyes and dances. The music fills her body, she can't ignore it, has to move, has to follow the music. She is music. She is dance. She is melody and rhythm and sound.

Something has happened. Only a year ago she was a gangly fawn, Nils thinks, following his little sister with his eyes, astonished. Now it's not a scrawny twelve-year-old girl who's dancing there. Not just that. There's a little softness in her body, a little roundness, a little hint of a young woman.

Almost a young woman.

Only twelve years old and still a little girl, of course, but all the same ... And it's not just puberty, there's something else too, Nils thinks. Something about the way she carries herself, the way she moves, a kind of deliberate, womanly pride.

Kristina has always danced. Now Nils remembers a little baby in diapers who would waddle around and sway in time to his rock music until she landed on her butt with a plunk. A long time ago.

This is the second time in one day that Nils is filled with a warm, childlike sense of happiness, warm and soothing like the oatmeal Mom might fix on a cloudy Monday morning. Twice in the same day. Strange, Nils thinks.

First it was that boy who crashed into the lamppost outside of Hansen's, the boy who reminded me of the dream world of my childhood. And now I'm standing here watching my little sister starting to grow up and I almost have tears in my eyes.

What's going on? Nils wonders. Am I starting to get old and maudlin? Or is it Sentimentality Day today? Is it Think-About-Childhood-and-Have-a-Warm-Fuzzy-Feeling Day?

Now the music stops and Nils quickly sneaks back to the front door, opens it, and calls out as if he'd just come in from outside, "Hello! Is anyone home?"

Almost immediately Kristina answers, "Yeah, I'm home. Hi!"

"Hi, Stina!" Nils shouts, slipping off his shoes without untying the laces.

"Kri!" he hears from the living room.

"What?"

And now Kristina is standing there in the doorway, she's

leaning against the doorframe, watching her big brother, and she says again, "Kri!"

"What?"

"Is this so hard for you to get? My name is Kri-stina. Kristina. Can't you remember that? You have only one sister."

"Hi, Kriiiistina," Nils says, smiling broadly as he looks at her. "Why are your cheeks so red?"

"None of your beeswax," Kristina says, and she disappears into her room.

Before she shuts the door, she sticks her head out and yells, "Nilsy! Hello there, Nilsy! Spillsy-Nilsy! Are you home?"

She manages to lock the door exactly one second before Nils gets to it. He stands there fiddling with the doorknob for a minute and shouts, "Just you wait!" and hears Kristina giggling in there; then he goes out and sits down in the kitchen.

As Nils gets milk and margarine and sandwich fixings out of the fridge, he thinks: That's weird. My little sister is starting to become a woman. My little brother stopped being a child years ago; he's a little computer engineer in disguise, playing the role of Perfect Student. But I'm becoming more and more childlike. And I wouldn't want it any other way.

Although I ought to be a man now. A young man. Becoming a man ... Brrr. A man, what is that? Nils smiles to himself, sitting at the kitchen table with a sandwich in his hand and a big glass of milk in front of him.

Question: What is a Man?

Answer: A hairy being
who is always right,
who always wants to compete,

who wants to win,
who wants to fight,
who knows best,
who knows most,
who wants to decide,
who wants to be in charge,
who's finished growing,
who's finished learning anything new,
who isn't curious anymore, and
who has an answer to every question.

Question: Who wants to be a Man, then?

Answer: Not me, anyway.

Nils smiles to himself. To grow up, yes. To be a grownup, no.

"Hi, are you home … Hey, don't fill up on sandwiches now, I'm just about to start dinner. Why don't you put a pot of water on for the pasta? And set the table."

Mom, Mom, Mom. I'll always be a little boy to you. I'll never be a man to you.

"Sure," Nils says, getting up.

Of course, it would be better not to live at home, he thinks. Not to be someone who still lives with his mother when he's twenty, that isn't normal. Even if you don't want to turn into a boring old grownup, you still have to leave the safety of the nest sometime. Test your wings. Set out into the world. See new things, learn new things.

That's what he'd thought, anyway. But nothing became of all his big plans, of all the wild and crazy ideas he had about what would happen when he finished high school almost a year ago. Yes, sure there was: Study math in college. ("Are you thinking of becoming a teacher, then?" "No way, I'm just going to school for the fun of it.") Still living at home. Still meeting Hannes for coffee. Contemplating Life & Death.

It's been a year in the waiting room.

Something has to happen now. It's about time to get things started.

"Well, you sure seem lost in thought," Mom says, putting a hand on his shoulder.

"Just contemplating life," Nils says with a sigh, twisting away.

"And?" Mom says, cocking her head.

"And death." Nils smirks.

Dinner. Knives and forks clattering against plates.

And there sits Göran and there sits Mom and there sits Oskar and there sits Kristina and here sits Nils, all at their usual places, everything is as usual, everything is normal.

"Can you pass the pasta, Stina?" Nils asks, but he corrects himself right away: "Kristina, I mean. Kri-kri-kri-kri-kristina, would you be so kind as to pass the pasta?"

"Nope," Kristina says, pushing the pasta bowl further away from him.

Nils sighs and looks around helplessly. "I'm moving out," he says.

"Well, what are you waiting for?" Kristina says.

This is love, Nils thinks. What I'm feeling for my irritating little sister now. What she's feeling for me. This is love. Some type of love. Something that resembles love. I may never get any closer, Nils thinks.

—

Yes, there sits Göran.

Papa Göran. A little older now. Even slower, even more sluggish, even more lost inside himself and his own world.

"Hey, Göran ..."

"Huh? Hmm," Göran says, looking around.

"Did you ever walk straight into a lamppost when you were a kid?" Nils wonders, studying his dad carefully and curiously.

Göran licks his lips, smacks his lips a little, and then dries them with his napkin before responding, "Sure. Every day."

Then he devotes his attention to his helping of pasta again.

Yes, there sits Mom.

Same old Mom. Always the same.

"You did that sometimes, didn't you?" she says, smiling at Nils. "Crashed into lampposts, I mean. When you were a kid."

Nils nods.

"I've never known a kid who daydreamed as much as you," Mom says, shaking her head. "And who could get into such messes ... Do you remember the time you were supposed to buy a present for Aunt Maggan?"

Nils nods and smiles at the memory.

"What?" Kristina says, looking up. "Do tell!"

Nils and Mom look at each other.

"Oh, it really wasn't anything," Nils says, shrugging his shoulders.

"Come on, tell me," Kristina pleads.

"There was this one time," Nils begins, "when I was supposed to buy a birthday present for Aunt Maggan, so I took the bus into town and I found a book for her, but then when I went to go home again I wound up on the wrong bus because I … well, because I was walking around daydreaming and I wound up at the harbor instead and then I forgot the book on the bus and the bus drove off but at the harbor I met eleven Japanese tourists who had arrived on the ferry—or were they Chinese?—and I showed them the way to the train station and to thank me for my help they gave me a package and then I met an old woman who needed help carrying some heavy furniture so I helped her and then an old man gave me a ride home and the old woman gave me a book, too, and strangely enough it was the same book I'd bought for Aunt Maggan and then anyhow in the evening we were at Aunt Maggan's party and then I gave her the present I'd gotten from the Japanese tourists. Or were they Chinese?"

By now Göran is chuckling so hard that two curlicues of pasta are working their way out of his mouth. "Yeah, oh my God …"

"What? What? What's so funny?" Kristina wonders.

"Well," Nils says, "there was a tie in the package. But the tie had this picture on it …"

"What? What? What's so funny?"

"It was a tie with a picture that wasn't meant for children to see. A picture of two Japanese people. Two naked Japanese people. A man and a woman. Who were f—"

"Who were hugging," Mom fills in.

"Oh!" Kristina says, and starts chuckling too. "What did Aunt Maggan say then?"

"She was pleased as punch," Nils remembers.

And there sits Oskar.

Little Brother Oskar, fifteen. He's been sitting there quietly the whole time they've been eating, but after the laughter subsides he says, "We got our French tests back today."

"And?" Mom wonders.

"Fifty-nine out of sixty. A+."

"Très bien," Mom says, and gets up to serve dessert.

Dessert: Ice cream with chocolate sauce. Bowls and eager spoons.

This is a nuclear family, Nils thinks.

This is the foundation upon which society is built. Or at least that's how it used to be. That's what this is. A mom and a dad and three healthy children. One who's studying math and thinking about death, one who will be finishing ninth grade in a few weeks with straight A's in all of his classes except possibly woodshop, and a daughter who can dance.

No divorce, no half brothers or sisters, no pretend stepparents, no shared custody, and no child support. No drug problems, no criminality. No physical or sexual abuse in the family.

A Swedish nuclear family. Pasta and ice cream.

Pleasant respectability and stifled dreams.

The foundation upon which society is built.

That's how it used to be, Nils thinks. It's not that way anymore.

Of course Göran forgot that the parent-teacher meeting with Kristina's teacher is tonight, so of course he decided there was something else he had to do and of course this makes Mom angry and she mutters something like "Typical," but then Nils says why doesn't he go along with Mom and Kristina to the parent-teacher conference and at first Kristina says "No, no, no" but very quickly she says "OK then," and then they head out to the school together.

And once Nils is there in Kristina's classroom she seems kind of proud and extremely chatty, and she wants to show him some of the stuff she has in her desk and some of the stuff she's done that's up on the walls and she wants to explain things and talk about things. And Mom and Miss Larsson sit politely and wait and let her do so. And Nils looks and listens and remembers.

Then there's the parent-teacher conference and Mom and Kristina get to hear more or less the same stuff they've heard at all the parent-teacher conferences they've had for six years. That Kristina is a good student with good penmanship and a good attendance record and she's mature for her age and doesn't have any problems and that the girls in her class all get along so well.

But when Miss Larsson asks Kristina various things, she doesn't say much. Mostly "Mmm" and "Yeah" and "Nah" and "Kind of." Now she's not so chatty anymore.

"And I'm sure it will go well in junior high," Miss Larsson says. "You're not worried about it, are you? Changing schools and all that? And getting new classmates? But a lot of your friends will still be in class with you."

"Nah ... mmm," Kristina says, unsure of which question to answer.

"No," Miss Larsson says and then it's quiet while she flips through her papers and notes. "Well, I don't have much else to add. Maybe you have some questions or things you're wondering about?"

Silence in the classroom.

I've been here every day, Kristina thinks. Five days a week.

For three years. But tonight it's like a foreign world, so empty and quiet. She looks around at the room. All of the chairs are up on top of the desks, the floor has been mopped, and the chalkboard is clean and empty except for a few small boxes all the way up on the right: Math homework, Friday, page 124. Geography test, Monday, May 26.

"Kristina is particularly good at math. But of course that runs in the family," Miss Larsson says, flashing Nils a charming smile.

Is she flirting with me? he thinks, smiling back.

Then he says, "Oh, she's not really that good. I've been doing her homework for her all the way through elementary school. She paid me to do it. Ouch! Why are you pinching me?"

"Hee hee," Miss Larsson laughs, standing up as Kristina starts chasing her big brother around the classroom.

Mom says goodbye to Miss Larsson while Kristina keeps chasing after Nils. He escapes from the classroom with plenty of noise and laughter, but in the cloakroom he stops dead in his tracks and suddenly falls silent. Because there's a boy sitting there with his mother waiting, and Nils recognizes the boy instantly.

It's the one who crashed into the lamppost. The one with the galoshes.

"Hi," the boy says, but it's not Nils he's saying hi to. No, he's saying hi to Kristina, who's peeking around from behind her big brother's back.

"Hi," she says back.

Then Mom comes and says hi to the boy's mother, and Miss Larsson says, "Oh, hi, you're here already, great," and shows the boy and his mother into the classroom while saying goodbye to Kristina and Nils and their mother.

"Who was that?" Nils asks once they're out on the playground and the door has closed behind them.

"His name is Anon," Kristina says. A brief pause, then she continues, "He's crazy."

"What?"

"He's a little … peculiar."

Mom doesn't say anything.

"In what way?" Nils wonders.

"He always wears galoshes, for example," Kristina says. "The whole year he walks around in those blue galoshes. And then … well, there's a lot of other stuff."

But she doesn't say anything else. She doesn't say anything about boiled potatoes and boiled carrots in his pockets. And she doesn't say anything about the bathrooms.

"Are you nice to him in class?" Mom asks.

Kristina shrugs her shoulders.

"Are you nice to him?" Nils asks.

Then Kristina gets mad. She stops outside the gym and says in a defensive tone, "What's that supposed to mean? *Nice?* I'm not nice or mean. I don't have anything to do with him. Enough already."

Why so much talk about Anon? It was *her* parent-teacher conference. Why not talk about her, and about everything the teacher said? She doesn't want to talk about Anon. She doesn't want to talk about Anon at all.

Anon is disgusting. He's the kind of guy who eats his boogers. He's the kind of guy who sits and studies his boogers carefully before he crams them in his mouth. And he doesn't even care if people are watching him.

"It's really great that your teacher had so many positive things to say," Mom says. "That she thinks everything is going well."

"Mmm," Kristina says, kicking a rock.

Anon

"Anon, yes …"

Miss Larsson leafs through her papers before she begins.

"Yes, this will be the last time we have one of these meetings. To talk about school. And about Anon."

"Yes, I hope so."

From the moment they walked into the classroom, everything was off-kilter for Miss Larsson. Anon's mother isn't like the other mothers. She doesn't smile encouragingly like the other mothers. She doesn't answer politely and graciously. Anon's mother makes Miss Larsson uneasy—it's always been that way, ever since fourth grade. Anon's mother has never been grateful, Miss Larsson thinks.

It's as if Anon's mother doesn't understand how special Anon is. Or maybe she doesn't want to understand, Miss Larsson thinks, and she tries again. "Yes, now there are only a few weeks left. Here. At this school. Then he starts junior high. After summer vacation."

Anon's mother scowls slightly. Either she finds it a little cramped and uncomfortable sitting there at Anon's school desk or she thinks Miss Larsson is just making small talk. And while Miss Larsson struggles to get the parent-teacher conference going, Anon's mother scans the classroom with her eyes. All of the other chairs are on top of the desks, there are drawings and big group-work reports about THE BODY and THE NORDIC COUNTRIES and THE MIDDLE AGES up on the walls.

The Week's Vocabulary is on the bulletin board, and there's a reminder about the math homework and a geography test on the chalkboard. Her eyes come to a stop on Miss Larsson, who's sitting directly across from her with a manila folder open on her knees.

"Sorry," she says.

Miss Larsson stops. "What? I don't understand …"

"Sorry," Anon's mother says. "I wasn't listening. You said something about junior high."

And Miss Larsson starts again, saying that she thinks that the class has learned to accept Anon now, that he can be himself, but obviously in junior high Anon will have new classmates and he'll be with students from other sixth-grade classes and also older students who don't know him, but surely it will go well, although obviously it would be easier if it weren't for the galoshes, with those you can tell right away when you look at Anon that he's … well, he stands out, so to speak, but we've talked so much about this …

"Yes," Anon's mother says.

"Things are going well in the cafeteria now," Miss Larsson continues. "It seems as if Anon has realized that he has to eat his potatoes and vegetables too, so there's no problem anymore, and at school, well, in the actual classes, well, he's certainly very knowledgeable and is good at everything, actually, he often knows more than I do, he often asks questions I can't answer, but now he knows how to look the answers up himself on the computer and he does that often, then of course sometimes it happens that he gets tired and that he isn't that interested in what we're covering and in a way I can understand that, and one thing that he's actually bad at is cooperation. He prefers to work on his own, and for the most part I let him. Also because it's more or less impossible to force Anon to do anything."

"Umm," says Anon's mother.

She's heard all this before.

Then silence. Talk about his being bad at cooperation, thinks Miss Larsson. It's nice, ohh so nice, that this is the last time. Soon spring term will be over and then I never have to subject myself to Anon's mother again. Or to Anon. Thank goodness.

Miss Larsson feels guilty almost instantly. I shouldn't think that way, she thinks. All the children in the class, including Anon, have to benefit from my ... good will? consideration? care? love? Well, I suppose love is too much to ask. But anyway. And it's the mother who's the biggest problem. Miss Larsson turns to face Anon.

"What would you say, Anon?"

No response.

"What are you sitting there thinking about?"

Anon is thinking about Kristina's breasts. And he's thinking that she was cute and had such rosy cheeks when he saw her in the cloakroom a few minutes ago. And that must have been her big brother. What a big big brother Kristina has, Anon thinks. A grown-up big brother.

"Nothing in particular," he says.

Miss Larsson looks at him. No, love is asking too much. But actually ... a kind of affection, really. Despite everything.

"There's been a bit of a problem here at school in recent months," she says then, turning back toward Anon's mother. And then she explains about the Pissman.

"You haven't heard anything else about that, have you?" she asks Anon once she's finished explaining. "I mean, no one has said anything else to you?"

Anon pretends to think about it.

"No," he says when he's done pretending.

That's not true.

Some people still shout "Piss Anon" at him, but he's never managed to figure out who's doing it. Something else happened too: When Anon came back to the locker room after P.E. on Monday, one of his galoshes was wet. On the inside. Someone had peed in one of Anon's galoshes. He rinsed it out in the shower and trotted home with his right boot soaking wet. "Yuck, that is sooo disgusting," Henke had said.

But Anon hasn't thought about it since, he hasn't been worried. Mostly he's been thinking about Sara.

Now Anon notices that Mother seems uneasy and concerned. She is eyeing Anon with an inquisitive look.

"You didn't tell me about this," she says.

Anon shrugs his shoulders.

Since I'm not the one who's been peeing in the bathrooms, I guess there's no need for us to talk about it, Anon thinks. But says nothing.

When his mother realizes that she's not going to get any response from Anon, she turns back to face Miss Larsson again.

"Was there anything else?"

Miss Larsson takes a deep breath. First she thinks about saying something, some phrase, one of the many phrases she's said at the twenty-three other parent-teacher conferences with the twenty-three other parents and students, but then she thinks: Why? Why should I put on an act if she's not going to put on an act?

And suddenly Miss Larsson feels completely calm, like a burden has been lifted, and she breaks into a smile, gets up from her chair, and just says, "Well. There wasn't anything else." But she smiles at Anon warmly and genuinely and says, "I'll see you tomorrow, Anon."

"Yup," he says.

"You'll be on time, right?"

"Of course," Anon says.

And "Thanks" and "Goodbye."

"Come on! What are you doing?"

Mother has made it halfway across the playground. She's all the way over by the swings when she discovers that Anon has stopped and is still standing outside his classroom. The light is still on in there; Miss Larsson is clearly still there. What is she doing? What does Anon see?

This is what Anon sees: Miss Larsson is sitting there behind her teacher's desk in the empty room. She's resting her chin on her hands and smiling.

It's her smile that made Anon stop, made him linger outside the window there. A smile he's never seen before, a smile that comes from the inside, that lights up her face, a smile so full of sorrow and warmth and serene pleasure that Anon stands there as if he's been turned to stone, as if he's grown roots into the ground or been frozen by a magic spell.

This is what Miss Larsson's doing: She's thinking. Thinking and remembering.

Miss Larsson is remembering the first time she met this class, and her first meeting with Anon. In this very classroom, almost three years ago. Sure, she'd gone over to their third-grade class-room and introduced herself to them, and she knew what all the students' names were, but this was her first day with her new 4b class.

And she had told them about everything that would be new and exciting now that they were in fourth grade, and everyone had gotten to talk about something that had happened to them over the summer, and everyone had gotten a math book and a geography book and a couple of spiral notebooks, and everyone had gotten copies of their new schedule too, and Miss Larsson had offered everyone fresh-baked cinnamon buns and juice,and had a little contest, and it had been pleasant and agreeable, and when the first day of school was almost over she asked, "Does anyone have any questions? Is there anything you've been won-dering about?"

That was when Anon raised his hand. She'd heard about Anon, of course. She'd seen him on the playground. She'd been warned, too. Still, she was completely unprepared when Anon said, "Yes. There's a word I've been wondering about ..."

"Let's hear it," Miss Larsson said, smiling her friendliest smile.

"I read it over at the Shell station. It was part of some head-line in a newspaper," Anon said.

"Let's hear it."

"What does 'orgasm' mean?"

Then Miss Larsson stopped smiling. Was he making fun of her, pulling her leg, trying to make her blush?

"Stoffe says it means living things that are found pretty much everywhere," Anon continued when he didn't get any response from his new teacher. "But I looked it up in a dictionary and it said it means something like 'culmination of feelings of desire.' But I still don't really understand what it means."

Miss Larsson hesitated.

"It's a grown-up word," she finally said. "It's a word you don't have any use for when you're ten years old. Or nine."

Actually, Miss Larsson thought, I don't know if one ever has a use for that word.

"It has something to do with sex, right?" Anon suggested.

The students' mouths were all hanging open, eagerly awaiting her response.

He's making fun of me, Miss Larsson thought, suddenly filled with a discouraged sense of weariness. Fourth graders these days know very well what that word means; fourth graders have seen pictures and movies and magazines. He's testing me. He's pulling my leg. And there had been such a good, nice, comfortable tone all day. And she had been up half the night baking so she could offer her new class fresh-baked cinnamon buns and everything had felt like it was going well. Until now. And it was his fault.

But there was no going back now. She sighed and tried to smile again.

"Yes, it has something to do with sex. The word Stoffe was thinking of is probably 'organism.' But I can't explain that other word any better than your dictionary. It's a grown-up word, like I said."

"That's what I thought," Anon said.

And then, in all earnestness, as if he meant it from the bottom of his heart, he said, "Thanks for your help."

Now Miss Larsson remembers that. Now she smiles and thinks: I was wrong back then, Anon didn't have any ulterior motive, he wasn't trying to put one over on me or show off to the class. No, but I thought so then because I didn't know Anon and it's been a thorn in my side all these years.

Anon is an exceptional person, Miss Larsson thinks, still smiling. I don't understand him. He's never cared about the class, about the other students. Just stumbled along on his own path. Although in the last few days it feels like I've gotten a little closer to him. A tiny little bit, but still. Enough to feel ... sympathy ... or something.

Miss Larsson smiles, remembering.

She remembers another thing too. Anon wasn't alone in the beginning. He and Stoffe were a pair. Real pals, good buddies, they did everything together, always wanted to sit together. And Anon used to laugh back then.

Weird that I forgot about that, Miss Larsson thinks. I've always imagined Anon alone. As the outsider. The one who trots along on his own fifty meters behind the rest of the class when we're out somewhere. The one we wait for. The one who drops a mitten. The one who gets lost, the one who comes late. Or not at all.

But the friendship between Anon and Stoffe ended a couple of months after fourth grade started. Stoffe wanted to be with the tough guys, be one of the popular kids. And I couldn't do anything about that.

Miss Larsson stops smiling and gets up from her seat behind the teacher's desk. How will things go for Anon now? When he starts junior high after summer vacation. Hope it goes well, Miss Larsson thinks. Hope he doesn't have to suffer too much. And maybe it will be easier to be Anon the Unusual in junior high, maybe it's easier to be yourself there. Yeah.

—

Now Miss Larsson turns out the light in the classroom, and that's when she discovers that Anon is standing outside and peering in at her.

She goes over to the window and Anon waves happily. Across the playground she sees Anon's mother, she hears Anon's mother calling him, and Miss Larsson feels a mild sense of triumph that Anon is lingering outside the window instead of rushing over to his mother.

"The little death," she whispers, convinced that Anon can't hear her from outside. "The little death, that's what it's called. That word you read in a headline at the Shell station that time, that word you asked me about. A long time ago. Little Anon. Anon, my friend."

Then Miss Larsson purses her lips and blows a kiss through the pane of glass to Anon. He catches it, laughs with his whole face, waves again, and then runs off to join his mother.

Is it all right for a teacher to blow a student a kiss? Miss Larsson wonders as she checks to make sure the door to the classroom is really locked. Yes, it's all right for a teacher to do that.

Anon and Mother come home.

They drink coffee and chat a bit, but not a single word about school. Then it's time for bed.

Before Anon falls asleep, he thinks about Sara.

Anon has done this every night since he found her wallet in the tall grass behind the bus stop.

This is what Anon thinks tonight: The door is ajar when I get to Sara's house and I sense right away that something is wrong, so I carefully sneak into the apartment and there in the kitchen sit Sara and her mother, each tied to a chair with their arms behind their backs, without clothes, with clothes, without clothes, with clothes, with their clothes torn to shreds, and voices and wicked laughter can be heard from the living room, and I free Sara and her mother and whisper to them that they should run away and call the police and I peer into the living room and two robbers are ransacking the apartment, but then one of them spots me and screams and then they both rush toward me and one of them has a pistol and the other one has a big knife but I run out onto the balcony and when the robbers follow me I climb over the railing and am able to swing down to the balcony below and Sara is standing there in that apartment because she and her mother moved there and she comes out to me on the balcony and hugs me tight, but suddenly she yells, "Look out!" and then I turn around and see that one of the robbers is trying to climb down to this balcony, but I give him a shove so he loses his balance and with a terrified shriek he falls down to the street below and Sara hugs me tight and sobs against my shoulder. And then the police arrive.

That's what Anon thinks before he falls asleep.

Zarah

Zarah didn't know.

How could she have known? How can anyone ever know?

A random thought, an impulse, a little joke can start a deluge. A whisper can trigger an avalanche.

How can anyone know the consequences?

Zarah is happy.

She wants to dance her way down the sidewalk like someone in a musical, she wants to hop and skip like a perky little girl with braids—hippity-hoppity-hippity-hoppity …

A happy little rabbit on her way to the pub.

Yes, Zarah is happy. She's arranged to meet Victor at the neighborhood pub, and she's been longing for him today, a longing like an expectant ache in her body, and it's been such a good day today, a good daycare day, lots of laughter with Mia, a kind of friendship that feels like friendship used to feel and the children aren't always so disgusting either, not all the children.

Not little Rebecka today when she whispered that she wanted to show Zarah something and took Zarah out into the hall and told Zarah to cover her eyes and then Zarah was allowed to look and Rebecka was standing there beaming like a little sun and holding out a crumpled package and she said it was for Zarah because she was so nice and then gave Zarah a hug and a kiss too.

A hug as soft as a pat of sun-warmed butter. A kiss as wet as warm summer rain.

And in the package there was: 1) a felt-tip pen drawing of a girl with long hair holding something that might resemble a guitar in her hand, 2) a necklace made of plastic pearls, 3) a small pink heart-shaped eraser, 4) a sticker that said "Union Bank Kid's Account."

No wonder Zarah's happy.

And it's a lovely early-summer evening. People have ventured out of their dark, dusty lairs. Some are on their way to the movies, some are on their way home from soccer practice or a game, some are just out to feel the springtime warmth on their cheeks or to watch all the other people who are out, and some are on the way to the pub, like Zarah.

It almost feels like the Riviera.

This is how it should be, Zarah thinks. Summer is her season. The city hibernates the rest of the year. The city is gray and cold and dreary with gloomy, empty streets and marketplaces. The rest of the year the city shuts down when the businesses close up for the day.

It should be crowded, Zarah thinks. People should be jostled around in crowds and meet each other at restaurants and pubs and cafés where they can sit outside. Zarah loves being in the city in the summertime.

And tonight is the first summer evening and Zarah got a little present at work today and now she's on her way to have a beer or two with Victor.

Zarah's in a bubbly, happy, hurray-it's-summer mood.

That's why things turn out the way they do.

That's why she does what she does.

How was she supposed to know?

Zarah spots Victor as soon as she enters the pub.

The murmuring and the music and the scent of beer and the heavy cloud of tobacco smoke strike her, and as soon as her eyes have adjusted to the dim lighting she sees Victor over at the bar.

He's happy too. He's chatting and laughing. Three girls are standing around him, three girls with hair just as shiny and black as Victor's, three young girls with dark eyes and last names that are hard to pronounce, and all of them have their eyes and all of their attention focused on Victor as if they were afraid of missing a single word he said, and they laugh and smile, flashing their bright white teeth. One of the girls has very long, straight hair, longer than Zarah's, and a very short white dress, shorter than Zarah's, and Victor's hand is resting very obviously on her hip.

Now you're having a good time, Zarah thinks.

But she doesn't get angry. Not annoyed. Not jealous. She smiles as she watches Victor and the three girls.

That's my man there, girls, she thinks, smiling. Laugh at his jokes, ladies, send him moist, yearning looks with your big, dumb, black eyes, he's still my man.

Smiling, not angry, not annoyed, but a little irritated.

Victor's hand on that skinny girl's hip, well, almost on her butt. And he knows I'm coming to meet him here, Zarah thinks. He's standing there fiddling around with her rear end even though he knows I'm coming.

You're a little too cocky, you handsome devil, Zarah thinks.

She looks around. The pub is crowded—all the tables are filled to capacity and there are lots of people at the bar. Zarah scans the room.

That guy over there, she decides. He'll be good. He's alone and looks sort of lost and harmless. He'll be perfect.

Zarah has an idea. She has a little plan. She's going to get a little revenge, and a childlike feeling of anticipation starts bubbling in her stomach.

Zarah takes a couple of steps toward the bar, her eyes are fixed on a guy in his twenties who's standing alone holding a beer and looking around, but she keeps track of Victor out of the corner of her eye.

Yes, now Victor's noticed her. Now he lets go of the girl and raises his hand to wave at Zarah. He's just about to holler something to her when she darts past him. As if she hadn't seen Victor at all, Zarah proceeds with quick, determined steps right over to the single guy at the bar. She stops right in front of him and bends over.

"Look like you're happy to see me," she whispers in his ear.

There are a lot of noises in the air. Music, talking, laughter, and cheerful hollering. Zarah's lips move against the guy's ear as she whispers to him, her hair brushes against his cheek. She wants him to be able to hear.

The guy stares at her for a brief second looking bewildered, then leans forward and whispers, "I'm happy to see you." His lips move against Zarah's ear.

"Well, show it then," Zarah whispers.

And the guy good-naturedly obeys and lays his right hand on Zarah's cheek. He smoothes her long hair behind her ear and takes a cautious hold of Zarah's earlobe and holds it tenderly between his thumb and his index finger.

But Zarah isn't there. All of her attention is directed at Victor, who's standing a few yards to her right. She sneaks a peek without turning her face from the guy who's holding on to her ear with a soft, firm grip. Yes, Victor is standing there staring at her; he hasn't budged. And Zarah smiles and thinks: Ha, take that. I'll teach you not to take me completely for granted. And not to stand there and pat other girls' butts when you're waiting for me.

Now Zarah sees the guy who's standing in front of her.

He has such an idiotic smile on his face that for a brief instant Zarah feels a little sorry for him, and he's raised his other hand too so that he's holding Zarah's head between his hands.

This is almost getting to be too much, Zarah thinks. It's almost too good. And that'll do.

"Sorry," Zarah says. "I had to borrow you to teach the guy that I love a lesson. And I think that'll do."

The guy smiles and shakes his head. He didn't hear what she said. "What?"

Then Zarah pushes herself up onto her tiptoes and gives the guy a kiss. She kisses him on the corner of his mouth, very quickly and very lightly, but she manages to notice that he tastes like beer.

"Bye. Thanks for the help," Zarah whispers in his ear.

Carefully she extracts herself from his hold, looks around, pretends to notice Victor, and goes over to him.

"Hi. I hadn't noticed you were here already," Zarah lies.

A feeling of triumph bubbles in Zarah's stomach as she's met with three insincere, fake, girl smiles. She pushes her way up to

Victor, presses up hard against him with her whole body.

"Are you happy to see me?" she whispers.

"Come on, we're going somewhere else," Victor says, taking hold of Zarah's upper arm. "Come on …"

He nods a quick goodbye to the three girls, and Zarah shrugs her shoulders and follows him out of the pub.

"Who was that back there?" When they reach the sidewalk, Victor stops all of a sudden and stands in front of Zarah.

"Who?" As if she didn't know what he was talking about.

"That guy in there. Who was that?" Victor asks again, his face impatient and irritated.

"An old friend," Zarah says, shrugging. "Someone I knew from before. Before I met you."

"Were you together with him?" Victor asks, nodding toward the bar.

"And those three girls that you were standing there flirting with, who were they?" Zarah asks instead of answering.

Victor's eyes narrow and there's a tension in his face that Zarah doesn't recognize. But then he scowls quickly. "Oh, fuck, that was just Nico's sister and a couple of her friends. It's nothing. I don't have anything to do with those girls. We were just standing there chatting a little. What the fuck, I was standing there waiting for you."

Silence.

"Why don't we go in and have a beer?" Zarah asks, taking a step toward Victor.

But he shakes his head. "We'll go to your place instead."

"But …"

"Yeah, we'll go to your place," Victor decides.

Zarah wasn't prepared for it.

That's why she fell. Not because it was a powerful blow; it was just a normal cuff to the ear, a brief, quick smack to her left cheek.

The surprise made her fall. Or, more accurately, collapse. She collapsed on the kitchen floor as if the mechanism that held her body upright had suddenly stopped working.

This happened: Zarah and Victor walked home side by side in silence through the city. Home to Zarah's apartment. She unlocked the door, they went in, Victor followed Zarah into the kitchen, he stood in front of her and cuffed her on the ear, and she collapsed onto the kitchen floor. All of it silently. Not a single word, just the smack of a palm against a cheek.

Now Zarah is lying there on the kitchen floor, and Victor immediately drops to his knees next to her. He grabs hold of her shoulders and pulls her up. Zarah sits there like a rag doll while Victor tries to hold her upright in front of him.

No tears in Zarah's eyes. No fear, no pain, no rage. Nothing at all, just emptiness.

"Listen, Zarah. Listen now ..."

Victor seems distraught as he tilts his head to the side and looks at Zarah.

Then he says, slowly and very clearly as if he were a teacher who was explaining something important to his students, "Listen now, Zarah. No girl disses her man."

He studies Zarah closely to see if his words are penetrating into her consciousness.

"No girl disses her man in front of other people. Do you get what I'm saying? You don't dis me. Ever. Do you get it?"

Zarah's face is blank.

But suddenly Zarah feels like she can see herself and Victor from the outside, from above, and her thoughts begin to flow clearly like a babbling mountain brook and she thinks: You're trying to train me, you bastard. Like your father and his father and his father before him trained their women, you're trying to train me. Like all men everywhere at all times. You're part of a pattern that you can't even see, an age-old stupidity, you think you can train the person you love the way you train a dog.

And a wave of heat rises in Zarah, and the life starts to glow in her eyes again, and tenderness and desire grow in her when she sees the seriously distraught expression on Victor's face.

"Do you get it?" he asks again.

A little boy who's playing at being a man, Zarah thinks. A scared little boy who's hiding behind a mask of manliness.

Almost imperceptibly she bows her head in a nod.

Yes, I get it, Zarah thinks. I get a lot more than you think. And just wait, just wait and you'll see who trains who in the end. A new era has begun.

Victor bends forward and lets his lips strafe Zarah's in a fleeting kiss.

"I'm sorry," he says, looking her squarely in the eye. "I just wanted you to get it."

Stupid boy, Zarah thinks, and pleasure and warmth and desire flood through her and wash everything else away, and she presses herself hard against Victor and whispers in his ear, "Make love to me."

Nils

¿Buscas a alguien
que te cambie la vida?
¿Un gurú, un profesor, un ángel?
Quizás busques una sagrada escritura,
o un sitio sagrado para visitar.
No te engañes.
Está todo dentro de tí mismo.
—from *La Búsqueda*

"I met an angel!"

"What?" Hannes leans in over the table. "What? What did you say?"

He and Nils are sitting across from each other in the darkest corner in the pub. A big bottle of beer, half drunk, in front of Nils, an empty bottle of German beer in front of Hannes.

"I met an angel," Nils repeats, lighting a crumpled cigarette.

"You don't say. An angel?" Hannes says, nodding to himself.

"Yeah. Just a minute ago. Right before you got here. I was standing there at the bar. Then an angel came in and kissed me." Nils smiles an idiotic smile.

"You don't say."

"Yeah. And I held her like this. Between my thumb and index finger," Nils continues, staring at his right hand as if he could hardly believe his own words.

"Obviously it must have been a really small angel," Hannes says with a snide smile.

"I was holding her ear," Nils says, sighing. "I was holding on to her earlobe."

Suddenly he gets quiet. He cannot comprehend what just happened: He was holding an angel between his thumb and his index finger. He was kissed by an angel. He felt angel hair against his cheek as an angel whispered in his ear: "Look like you're happy to see me." An angel smiled and disappeared, smiled a sad smile and disappeared.

"Hello?!" Hannes laughs.

"Yes?"

"Would you care to explain? Or are you just going to sit there grinning?"

And Nils explains. When he's done explaining, he studies his hand again. These fingers held an angel, he thinks.

Hannes sits there silently and listens. A slight smile twinkles in his eyes as he watches his friend. "And what are you going to do now?" he asks after a minute.

"Find my angel," Nils answers. Without a second's hesitation he responds. As if the answer were obvious. As if the question were unnecessary.

Hannes smiles and nods and gets up without a word.

"What is it, where are you going?" Nils wonders, waking from his reverie.

"Are those the girls over there?" Hannes asks, pointing.

Nils turns sideways, tilts his chair, cranes his neck, and tries to see through all the people in the pub ... Yes, sure, all three of them are still standing there, three radiant young beauties over there at the bar. The girls who were standing there with the guy who followed her out of the bar. Her. She. My angel, Nils thinks.

"Yeah, that's them, but— Wait! What are you going to do?"

Hannes pushes his way through to the bar without responding.

After ten long minutes he returns, with a new bottle of beer in his hand and a very contented smile on his lips. "What's her name?" Hannes asks as he sits down.

Nils doesn't answer, just looks wonderingly at Hannes.

"Where does she live?"

"I don't know," Nils answers, shrugging his shoulders. "How should I know?"

"*I* know," Hannes says, flashing a big, pearly smile. "I know her name, where she lives, and ..."

"Yes?"

"... and what her boyfriend's name is."

And Hannes explains. The three girls were suspicious, of course, but when they finally understood that Nils might be a knight in shining armor who could liberate their charming friend Victor—that's the boyfriend's name—from his bitter, haughty Swedish girlfriend, they couldn't wait to be helpful.

"I found out everything they knew," Hannes explains.

"And?"

"Sara. Her name is Sara. She has an apartment on Östra Storgatan, right across from the post office. She and Victor have been together since Easter, or the whole year, I got slightly mixed messages on that point. And one of the girls claimed that Victor still lives at home, but the other two thought he had moved in with Sara. And at least two of the three girls would gladly take over possession of Victor if he became available, that was very clear."

Nils listens attentively, with his head resting on his right hand. Now he takes a deep breath. He looks pensive. Not exactly worried, not disappointed, but ... well, pensive. Contemplative. Something like that.

"I promised that you would fix it," Hannes continues, smiling cheerfully. "That you would easily fix things. So that Victor would be on the market again and, you know, available." Smug. Very self-satisfied. "So?"

"So, what?" Nils wonders, raising his eyebrows.

"So, what do you say?"

"Huh?"

"You say, 'Thank you very much, my dear Hannes. You're really and truly a good friend. You really show—'"

"Yeah, yeah, yeah," Nils interrupts with a wry smile. "Thank you, thank you, thank you. You're really and truly an asshole."

A half hour later, Nils and Hannes part ways outside the pub.

Goodbye, goodbye, I'll see you later. And as soon as Hannes has disappeared around the corner, Nils turns around. He isn't going home. He's going to Östra Storgatan.

It isn't far. Soon he's there.

And he positions himself with his back against the post office and watches the building across the street. That must be the front door to her building there. Number fourteen. Or possibly number sixteen. There are only lights on in two of the windows facing the street, one on the third floor and one on the fifth.

The fifth floor, Nils thinks. There's a girl sitting in that apartment, a young woman, an angel whose name is Sara. She can't sleep. She's sitting there thinking: Everything's gone wrong.

Nils is thinking that Sara's thinking: Everything's gone wrong. I just wanted to make Victor jealous. And then I met Him. And He held my earlobe so tenderly between his thumb and his index finger. I don't even know His name. Will I ever see Him again?

"Yes!" Nils wants to shout. "Yes, here I am! My name is Nils. Here I am!"

He wants to shout it out into the night.

And he wants the woman whose name is Sara to open her window on the fifth floor, look out, discover him, and yell, "Hey. Is that you …?"

He wants her to be wearing her nightgown. And he wants her to invite him up for a bit, and she'll toss the key to the front door down to him, and he'll enter the building and go up to her place, into her apartment, and she'll say "Hi, I'm Sara" and he'll say "Hi, I'm Nils" and then she'll pull the nightgown over her head and carefully take all his clothes off and then they'll make love. And they'll both know they are meant for each other. In this world they are meant for each other.

None of this happens. Of course.

Nils stands there staring at the façade of a building for about fifteen minutes. Nothing happens, other than that someone turns out the light on the third floor. The nighttime cold makes Nils shiver. He wakes up from his dream world and goes home.

Just five minutes after Nils has left his surveillance position outside the post office, a guy named Victor comes out of the front door of the building on the other side of the street. He looks around, shoves his hands deep into his jacket pockets, and starts to whistle as he strolls off into the night.

He seems satisfied. That's the impression he gives.

Anon

Kristina has a plan.

She told Ida and Magdalena and Frida what they should do, but she didn't answer their "Why?"s or their "What?"s. She only said that it will be funny. She said that it had to do with Anon. When she said that, Magdalena got a little worried.

"It's not bullying," Kristina said hurriedly. "It'll just be funny."

"All right then," Magdalena said.

It's not bullying, it's just revealing the truth, thought Kristina. She didn't tell the others that it had to do with the potatoes in Anon's pockets.

So today the girls rushed to finish eating their lunch, something the cafeteria called "pizza fish." Now all four of them are standing outside the cafeteria, full of anticipation and giggling, and Kristina tries to get them to be quiet while she keeps track of Anon, who's still sitting in the cafeteria.

Ah, yes, just as usual. Kristina sees Anon look around, she sees him putting into two napkins the potatoes that have been boiled to the point of disintegrating, she sees him smuggling the napkin wads into his pockets. Just as usual, just as he does every day.

Kristina feels a pleasant tingle in her stomach.

"Now. Right now," she whispers.

Now Anon is standing by the cart where you put your trays away, now he's done, now he's on his way out of the cafeteria.

"Now!" Kristina hisses.

And Frida dashes into the bathroom by the cafeteria and locks the door from the inside while Ida and Magdalena disappear out the door. Kristina hides behind the coat hangers; she stands there and tries to look as if she's getting her jacket when Anon comes out of the building.

He looks around again and goes over to the bathroom. When he sees that it's occupied, he shrugs his shoulders and calmly proceeds out onto the playground.

Now he's heading for our bathroom, Kristina thinks, sneaking after Anon. The tingling in her stomach almost makes her laugh out loud to herself.

She sees Anon go into the sixth graders' cloakroom. Everything is going according to plan. Anon comes out again before the door has even had time to swing shut behind him. The bathroom is occupied. By Magdalena.

Now he's heading for the fifth graders' bathroom, Kristina thinks. It's almost time now …

She doesn't get any further in her thoughts, and Anon has only gotten halfway across the playground on his way toward the fifth graders' cloakroom when a scream brings everything in the school to a standstill.

A howl. A shriek. "IIIIIIIIII!!!"

Everything goes silent. Everyone stands still for a few seconds.

Then Ida comes out of the fifth graders' cloakroom, she stands right outside the door and screams again, "IIIIIIIIII!!!"

Right out loud. At the top of her lungs.

Her hands are wet. They're dripping as she holds her arms out in front of her like a sleepwalker. "IIIIIIIIII!!!"

People come running from all directions. A crowd gathers around Ida and keeps growing and growing. Of course Kristina runs over there and pushes her way to the center of the crowd.

"What is it? What happened? Where's Ida?"

Rumors and murmuring and a thousand questions and a few small yelps and shrieks, and finally Miss Larsson and Mr. Lagerkvist, the fifth-grade teachers who were serving as lunch monitors, arrive, and Mr. Lagerkvist makes his way through the crowd to Ida.

"Come, come, everybody back up a little bit! There, that's right, good. What in the world happened? Quiet, don't everybody talk at once. And stop pushing! Back up a little. There, good."

And he gets everyone who's crowding around Ida to back up several paces, and now everyone can see Ida, who's leaning against the wall with her eyes closed, and Mr. Lagerkvist asks her what happened, and everyone can hear her answer.

"It was so … yechhh … disgusting … repulsive … yechhh …"

Her voice is frailer than usual. She's witnessed something awful; that much is clear to everyone. Perhaps, some think, Ida is enjoying being the center of attention now, with half the school crowding around her, being the focal point. Maybe she's hamming it up, trying to keep the excitement alive as long as possible. That's what some think.

Silence as Ida explains:

"I went into the bathroom, and the door handle was wet when I shut the door, but I didn't think about it and … yechhhh …"

Now everyone starts to understand. Ohhhh. Yuck.

"… and then I noticed the lid of the toilet was wet, completely wet, yellow, and the whole bathroom stank, and then I realized ... yechhhh ... and on the door too, it had dripped, and I realized that ..."

She holds her right hand out limply in front of her and looks at it as if she doesn't want to touch it, as if she wants to chop it off, as if she had contracted some horrible infection.

"... and I just screamed right out loud ... yechhh! That's so disgusting, and I washed and washed my hands and screamed and ran out and ... well ..."

Mr. Lagerkvist nods. It's completely quiet. It's so quiet that everyone can hear it when Stoffe turns to Henke and whispers, "Piss Anon has struck again. Now we'll catch that jerk. Where is he?"

"No. It wasn't Anon."

Everyone hears Magdalena too.

As if she were thinking out loud, as if she can't help it, Magdalena speaks. In a steady voice she continues, "It wasn't Anon. We know that it wasn't Anon. We saw him. Right?"

Everyone follows her eyes as she looks toward Kristina. Everyone is waiting, everyone is silent. The grin on Stoffe's face has tightened.

Kristina gulps, nods almost imperceptibly, and in a flat voice finally says, "No, it wasn't Anon. We saw him."

A sense of bewilderment spreads through the students. How can Kristina be so sure that it wasn't Anon? Restlessness spreads through the crowd. Well, if Anon isn't the Pissman, then it could really be—anyone ...

Everyone looks around. It could be him. Or him. I could be ... Anyone. Some people step sideways, some back up a little. What if I'm standing next to the Pissman, some think.

A cloud of anxiety spreads.

Mr. Lagerkvist also seems concerned, but he says, "Well, I'm sure we'll get to the bottom of this. For now I'll ask the janitors to clean the fifth-grade bathroom. Well, then. There's ten minutes left in the lunch period. Let's make sure that ..."

His voice fades away, and he looks around as if he is expecting all the students to stream out across the playground and start jumping rope and playing soccer and swinging on the tire swings.

But nothing happens; most of the students keep standing there. Most of them start talking to the people next to them, and only slowly does the dense group that gathered around Ida and Mr. Lagerkvist disperse.

Magdalena happens to notice Miss Larsson, who's standing a little off on her own, lost in thought. She doesn't seem to be aware of what's happening around her. She's contemplating something, and an earnest smile flutters across Miss Larsson's face.

What is she thinking about?

On the way to the classroom, Kristina runs into Anon.

He has no idea what's happened, she thinks. He just walks around in his own little world. He doesn't care; it doesn't bother him in the least that everyone thought he was the Pissman. And now he doesn't even know what's happened. And if he did know he wouldn't care.

I was supposed to be the one playing a trick on you, Kristina thinks. You tricked me instead, although you don't even know it.

She looks at his pockets. Flat. No potatoes, just a damp spot by his pocket.

—

When the last class is about to start, Henke is standing at the front of the room by the chalkboard along with Miss Larsson.

"Henrik wanted to say something before we get started with our Swedish lesson," Miss Larsson says, taking a step to the side.

"Talk for a long time!" Stoffe shouts, and a few people laugh.

Henke looks around the room, grins at Stoffe, waits for everyone to be quiet, and then says, "Yeah, I just wanted to say, in case anyone doesn't know, that on Thursday right before the last day of school there's going to be a big party for our class at my house, and it'll be the last time we do anything together as a class so everyone has to come, and our band is going to play and there'll be games, and those of us who are taking drama will put on a little play, and there'll be candy and chips and soda and everyone has to pay me three dollars by Tuesday and—"

"And there'll be dancing too!" Ida hollers. She seems to be over her horrific bathroom experience now.

"Obviously there will be dancing," Henke says. "I just forgot to say that. Fille will be the disc jockey."

"But Fille has no taste in music!" Kristina yells.

"Yeah!" some of the other girls agree.

"Oh, I can play some nice slow make-out music," Fille says, laughing as he turns toward Kristina, "so that you can press yourself up against ..."

"*Shut up!*" Henke shouts. "Quit blabbering or we'll miss our whole, extremely useful Swedish class." He winks at Miss Larsson.

"Are you finished?" she asks calmly.

"I just wanted to find out if there's anyone who won't be able to come," Henke says, scanning the classroom.

No one raises a hand. Everyone can come.

"So you guys are going to be there?"

"*Yeah*!" everyone yells.

Almost everyone.

After school Anon goes straight to Östra Storgatan.

Today he goes right up to the front door. Number fourteen. He checks, yup, the door's unlocked, it's heavy and unlocked, and he pushes it open and steps into the little mailroom at the bottom of the stairs.

It smells different in here, it doesn't smell the same as the stairwell at home in his building. Older. An older scent in here, like the scent of old people, old forgotten things and rotten apples.

Z. ENOKSSON

Anon finds the name right away when he starts examining the list of residents. There's a Z. ENOKSSON on the fifth floor.

Z? Does Sara's mom have a name that starts with a Z? Anon wonders. What could her name be? Zoey? Zena? Anon almost starts chuckling to himself, but then he thinks: I'm such an idiot. Maybe it's Sara's dad. Why should Sara be fatherless?

Zarduk. Sara's dad's name is Zarduk Enoksson and he's not home that much, Anon decides.

You. You, Anon.

Why are you sitting on the stairs, Anon? Aren't you going to go up and return Sara's wallet now?

No, today's not the day to do it. Today I'm just checking to make sure the Enoksson family really lives here. And I see that they do. Up there on the fifth floor live Zarduk Enoksson and

his wife and their cute twelve-year-old daughter Sara and her
nasty big brother who looks like a gangster.

Yup.

Yes, well now, I guess I'll just sit here on the stairs for a bit.

Are you waiting for Sara? Do you think Sara is coming?

Maybe she will.

Will you say hi if she comes? Will you start talking to her?

Maybe I will.

And Anon sits there in the darkness in the stairwell and thinks about what it will be like once he's gotten to know Sara. Sara will think it's exciting that Anon's father is a god.

"Can you walk on water, then?" she'll ask. "Can you raise the dead?"

"I don't know," Anon will answer. "I've never tried. But Father can, of course. He can if he wants to."

Then Sara will ask how often he sees his dad and then Anon's eyes will look a little sad and he'll answer that it's not that often.

"At the Meetings, of course," he'll say. "And sometimes Father is waiting in the parking lot when school gets out. Then we go to a café and have a piece of cake. Father loves cake."

Then Sara will suggest that they sit in the dark, cramped cloakroom for a while, and Anon will think that's a good idea. And in the dark, cramped cloakroom they'll sit so close to each other that Anon will be able to feel Sara's breath on his cheek. That's how it will be.

Anon sits on the stairs only for a little while longer, then he gets up. No, today's not the day he'll meet Sara. Today he's just checking. Better go now before Sara comes, he thinks, and he opens the door.

The bright sunshine blinds Anon, but once his eyes have adjusted to the daylight he realizes that someone is leaning against the brick wall by the door. It's someone Anon recognizes, but he can't think who it is.

He makes it halfway home before he remembers. Of course. That was Kristina's older brother. Her big older brother, the one who went along to the parent-teacher conference. Why was he standing there outside the door to Sara's building?

Zarah

Zarah in front of the mirror.

Early morning, and Zarah is sitting on a kitchen stool in front of the hall mirror staring at her own reflection. She's wearing a white T-shirt that's way too big, nothing else. Five minutes ago she called Mia and said she couldn't come in today, said "Fever," said "Headache," said "Didn't sleep a wink last night," said "I'm sure I'll be in tomorrow." And Mia said that Zarah should Get Well Soon and then Mia talked about a Good Idea and a Pleasant Surprise that she wanted to talk to Zarah about, and "Maybe I can swing by tonight if you're not feeling too bad," Mia said, "and tell you about it," she said, and then she also said something about Zarah having to decide in the next two days.

"Sure, sure, sure," Zarah said, getting curious and excited. "Stop by after work, yeah. I'm sure I'm not contagious."

This is good. Mia is coming over tonight with a Pleasant Surprise. And I'm staying home today and taking it easy and am kind of a little under the weather, Zarah thinks. But she doesn't smile at her reflection. She's serious when she looks deep into the reflection of her eyes and whispers, "Mirror, mirror, on the wall, who's the dumbest of them all?"

Her mouth in the mirror is serious when it answers, "Zarah Enoksson."

Now Zarah leans forward on the kitchen stool. She points her shoulder toward the mirror, pulls up the roomy arm of the

T-shirt, and displays her upper arm.

"Look at this," she whispers. "Look at what he did."

There's a bruise on Zarah's arm, like fingerprints in blue ink, a blue stamp that reminds her of yesterday, that reminds her of hard words and a hard grip.

Something had happened to Victor since that miserable night last week when Zarah had teased him at the pub. Suspicion has started gnawing away at Victor. He wants to talk to Zarah about it again and again.

"Picture this," he said last night. "Just imagine if someone says the girl I'm going out with is a slut. What do I do then?"

Zarah just glared at him and shrugged her shoulders. Five nights of the same nagging now, she was sick of it.

"If someone says you're a slut, what do I do then?" Victor persisted.

Zarah glared at him without responding.

"I hit him, obviously," Victor said. "I tell him, 'You're a motherfucker and your little sister is a whore who'd spread her legs for a dirty old man for ten bucks and a beer.' And then I hit him. You see?"

Zarah glared at him, scowling slightly.

"I hit him because he's calling you a slut," Victor said, taking a firm hold of Zarah's arm. "But what if he's right?"

Drop it, Zarah thought. Enough already!

"But what if he's right? Who's the joke on then?" Victor asked, squeezing down harder on Zarah's arm.

It would've been so easy for Zarah to say, "I have never, ever, even looked at another guy since I met you. I haven't even wanted to." It would have been true too. Not even a fleeting shadow of a thought of anyone else since she and Victor had started going out. But she can't say that, doesn't want to, not now; no one has ever been able to force her to say anything, not even Victor can do that.

So Zarah said nothing, and Victor kept squeezing her arm, harder and harder, and finally Zarah yelled, "Cut it out! Enough already! Are you out of your fucking mind?!"

And Victor let her go, and the evening eventually ended in reconciliation. Reconciliation and sex.

Now Zarah's sitting in front of the mirror. Now her reflection whispers, "Dumb …"

Her reflection is serious, looks at Zarah with serious, worried eyes.

"Dumb, dumb, dumb …" it whispers.

Yes, Zarah's reflection looks worried as it contemplates Zarah.

"Take a look around, sister. You know what usually happens to girls like you."

Zarah nods. "Never again," she promises, and stands up.

Never sunglasses. Never a stupid excuse about how she'd walked into a door or tripped on the stairs.

"Never again," Zarah promises.

Victor is still asleep in the bedroom.

With one of his hands tucked up under his chin and his body only half under the covers, Victor is sleeping so soundly in Zarah's bed. And she stands there in the doorway and watches him.

Thinking and Feeling, Zarah thinks. Thinking and Feeling, what are they? The title of some movie? It's a good movie title anyway, because that's exactly what it's about. Life. Thinking and Feeling. And if Feeling whispers yes, then it doesn't matter how loud Thinking tries to scream no. Feeling is a hundred thousand million times stronger.

Zarah smiles. Zarah is filled with joy again.

The sight of Victor in the bed makes her forget all of her somber morning thoughts. And the scent of Victor. The whole bedroom is filled with the scent of Victor and the scent of love. The heavy scent of love.

Zarah creeps up onto the bed and kneels next to Victor, she leans down and kisses his shoulder, the back of his neck, and lets her lips rest against his spine. He tastes like salt. He tastes like a man, Zarah thinks, resting her cheek against Victor's back.

And when Victor rolls over and opens his eyes, he's greeted by Zarah's smile.

"Help," she whispers. "There's a pirate in my bed!"

Then she pulls the T-shirt over her head and Victor kisses the bruise on her arm and whispers, "I'm sorry ..."

Feeling, feeling, feeling. Goodbye, thinking. Ciao, adios, sayonara, Zarah thinks, smiling at her thoughts.

And she pulls the covers off Victor and lies down on top of him, all of her body against all of his, close, so close that there's not even room for a single little millimeter of thinking between their naked bodies.

"Sleepy today?" Zarah whispers, rubbing her nose against Victor's.

"Mmm." Victor nods.

"Trouble rising? Trouble getting up? Is the gentleman having trouble getting up?"

Victor shakes his head. "I never have any trouble ..."

"So I shouldn't help him up, then?" Zarah asks, kissing Victor's neck.

Victor responds with a little grunt, and Zarah can tell that the grunt means yes, so she does. She can. She knows how to do it.

She knows how to get him up.

Afterward, Victor and Zarah eat breakfast together, a very short, quick breakfast because Victor has to get going, he has someone to meet, something to arrange. As is so often the case.

It's almost as if he were a regular old punch-the-timecard slave, Zarah thinks as she closes the door behind Victor. He goes off to work and comes home from work, and there's Beautiful Zarah waiting for him with some dinner and some loving. Like a married couple. Like someone with a job and his wife. Frequently Victor works overtime. Frequently he works late into the evening and in the middle of the night. His Zarah thinks that's a little sad. Yes, like a regular old punch-the-time-card slave and his little wife.

It's just that Victor doesn't have a job. Never in his life has he even been close to anything that could be called a Respectable Job. He has learned to survive in this new country that his parents brought him to. He has learned how one can live quite well here. But a job? No, never. A paycheck in the mailbox on the twenty-seventh of the month, a regular old wage slave? No, never.

Zarah goes back to the bedroom. The scent of love fills the room even more thickly now. The scent of desire. The scent of bodily fluids. The scent of sweaty love gymnastics. And Zarah opens the window wide and thinks: I'm going to miss that smell.

But it'll be nice to get rid of all this crap, she thinks, letting her eyes roam over all the boxes and bags that are piled up along one wall. The other night when Zarah was grumpy she told Victor that she didn't want his stuff in her apartment anymore. She reminded him that he had promised. And Victor said that he would have it all sold soon, "but there was this guy that was trying to put one over on us," Victor had said, but now he was working on some other guy and soon everything would be sold and then there would be money, money, money.

It's all about money. It's not just about getting by, no, it's about doing well. Almost as well as the people who are doing really well: the high and mighty, the well-to-do. Not settling for a small-time life, a life of poverty, the life of a wage slave.

The phone rings just as Zarah has started wondering what "doing well" means. She hurries over to the phone.

"Hello ... Oh hi, it's you, I was thinking about calling you today ... No, nothing much ... Mmm ... A little under the weather ... Nah, not that bad ... Nah, I wasn't feeling that good this morning ... Sure, yeah, that would be great ... I'll be home all day. Thought I'd tidy up a bit ... Sure, good, good ... Well, actually, a friend from work was going to stop by then ... Yeah, yeah, that'll be fine ... Good ... I'll see you ... Kisses ..."

After she hangs up Zarah sits there next to the phone. She runs her index finger over the gray telephone handle as if she wishes she could stroke the cheek of the person whose voice she just heard.

"I'm glad you're out there," she whispers to the phone. "You'll always be out there, I know that. And now I'm going to pop down to Hansen's and buy a cookie for you, and some rolls, and then we'll drink coffee when you get here, and you ..."

She keeps stroking the telephone handle as if the phone were a purring, gray cat.

"... and you, I love you. Did you know that?"

A real cat comes and rubs against Zarah's leg as she stands in the hallway, a fat, yellowish white cat.

"Do you want to go out, Simson? I'm just going down to the café. Do you want to go outside for a bit?"

"Mmmyes," Simson meows.

And Simson pads along behind Zarah down the stairs. She lets him out into the backyard before she herself exits through the front door onto the street.

Outside the door, leaning against the wall of the building, stands a guy. A young man. He follows Zarah over to Hansen's Café without her noticing him.

Nils

Para conocer al Amor tienes que conocer a la Muerte,
para conocer al Amor tienes que morirte.
—from *La Búsqueda*

Today he heard her voice.

Again. For the first time since that night in the pub. That makes three times that he heard her voice today.

First at Hansen's Café. He followed her in there, passed just a few feet behind her back as she stood at the counter, sat down in the café, and heard her voice say, "Hi. Two of those cookies. And two dinner rolls. Actually, make that three. No, those ones with the poppy seeds on top."

Then she went home again, but he kept sitting there with a cup of coffee and a roll before he returned to his post outside the front door to her building.

He stood there for the rest of the day. The sun was shining. A few hours flowed by. Many thoughts flowed by. He made up his mind: If she comes out again, I'll talk to her. Make contact. Explain.

No, maybe not explain. Pretend to run into her by chance. Chat, but not explain.

But she didn't come out. It wasn't until afternoon when hunger had already started rumbling in his stomach and he had almost decided to give up on his surveillance activities for the day that something happened.

First a woman came striding up at an energetic pace, a young woman with short hair, her face beaming in cheerful anticipation. Without any hesitation she pulled the door open and disappeared inside. Nils followed her in through the front door, stood there in the lobby, and pretended to study the list of residents at the foot of the stairs as he listened to the woman's brisk footsteps making their way up the stairs. Second floor, third floor, fourth floor … No, now she stopped abruptly, probably because she heard the same thing as Nils; a male voice could be heard from up above, probably from the fifth floor, and the woman on the stairs stood still, silently. And she and Nils heard a male voice say, "Bye, sweetheart. Take good care of yourself. And call. Call if you need anything."

Then Sara's voice could be heard. Her voice, but not what she was saying. Just mumbling that ended with "… see you. *Kisses*."

A door closed. The elevator cables rattled. The man got in the elevator up there and rode down. Nils stayed where he was. The young woman with the short hair stood still somewhere near the fourth floor.

And the elevator came down, and the elevator doors opened, and a man who was about forty-five or so got out, and Nils pretended he was studying the list of residents again while he peeked at the man. Gray suit. Civil servant, office worker. Banker. High school teacher. Right as the man opened the door he turned and looked at Nils, and for a brief moment their eyes met. The man smiled, a knowing little smile, as if he and Nils shared a secret.

"She spells Sara with a Z," the man said, nodding toward the list of residents. "A Z at the beginning and an H at the end.

Z-A-R-A-H. A little coy, huh?"

His nice, knowing eyes looked directly into Nils's eyes. Happy laughter wrinkles on the man's face.

But Nils didn't smile back conspiratorially. He also didn't say, "I don't know what you're talking about." He just looked away and mumbled something inaudible, and the man opened the door and disappeared without saying anything else.

When the door clicked shut again behind the man, Nils thought: Oh, I see.

Sara is actually Zarah. I see.

A dream that begins with a Z instead.

Now Nils hears the young woman start walking up the stairs again. He hears her stop, he hears a door up there opening, and he hears her yell so that it echoes through the entire stairwell: "Milan! Parma! Florence! Bologna! Departing next Friday from the airport. Six-thirty in the morning. We come back on Tuesday night. What do you say?"

Silence. After a long silence in the stairwell, Zarah's voice could be heard: "What? What are you talking about?"

The answer was a gleeful holler: "We're going on a trip!"

And then talking and laughing and questions and answers and the voices faded away as the door to Zarah's apartment closed.

Yes, he's heard her voice three times today.

The first time when she bought the cookies and rolls. The second time when she said "*Kisses*" as she said goodbye to the high school teacher in the gray suit. The third time was a surprised "What?" when her friend told her about a trip to northern Italy.

Now it's evening, now it's late evening, the pale twilight is slipping into night, and Nils is standing outside the cemetery. The main gate was closed and locked so he went around to the back. Now he casts a few quick looks around. Now he quickly climbs over the low fence.

The gravel crunches under the soles of his shoes. When Nils stops to figure out where he is in terms of the various walkways, silence closes in around him.

It must be over here to the left. And then over there by that little pond to the right. Of course. Nils quickly finds the grave he's looking for and then squats down in front of the headstone.

EMIL MÖRCK
October 7, 1914 - October 7, 1974

Somewhere deep within
we will always be together

A long time ago, when Nils was a daydreaming child, he would sit by this grave.

I was someone else then, Nils thinks. I was living a different life. I was fully engaged in living then. Living and daydreaming and smashing into reality, over and over again. And a backwards life started here, Nils remembers, smiling. Then he gets serious and thinks: Now I don't want to be a child anymore, now I want to be a man, now I want to get to know death. So that I can live. And so that I can love.

Next to the grave there's a small strip of grass. Nils lies down there; he lies down on his back. When he reaches out his right arm he is just able to reach the edge of the headstone. He lets his fingertips trace the outline of the rough, cold stone and thinks: How are you doing, Emil? How are you doing down there? What's left of you?

It's quiet. Unusually quiet.

Even though the cemetery is in the middle of downtown there's almost no noise at all, just a few car engines now and then like a distant hum. Somehow the city's noise has been shut out of the cemetery. Somehow all sound seems to stop outside the wrought-iron fence that runs around the burial ground.

Nils listens to the sound of his own breathing. He tries to make his breathing calm and even. He feels his heartbeat. He thinks: Now oxygen from the air is kissing my blood. Kiss, kiss. Now the blood is pulsing throughout my body, now I am alive. Those who are no longer breathing live down in the earth. Someday I will live there too.

What's there to be afraid of? Nils thinks.

Now we're alive. Then we're dead. What's there to fear?

Nothing at all, Nils thinks. Not a thing.

A mild, warm, almost gleeful happiness fills Nils's body. It starts down in his toes; then the sweet, bubbling happiness rises up to the top of his head, like when you pour champagne or sparkling wine into a champagne flute. He thinks: Here I lie in a cemetery on a May night. I am twenty years old and I am almost laughing with joy at this thought:

First we live. Then we die. There's nothing to fear.

A beaming smile shines in the dark cemetery night.

Completely still, flat on his back, Nils lies there. The earth beneath him. He feels the profound coldness of the earth against his back. The entire mass of the earth under him. He can feel how it pulls.

Yes, I will come to you, he whispers. But not now, not yet. The earth pulls, the earth calls, the cold, black earth down there. Yes, I'm coming. But not yet. First I'm going to live. If I may. If I may be so blessed. Give me time to live my life, please.

I've just learned: There's nothing to be afraid of. Life is a beautiful and exciting adventure. I'll talk to her tomorrow. What have I been waiting for? What have I been afraid of?

His head is spinning. The cold ground beneath him. The warmth in his stomach. His breathing is calm and steady.

That little timid, cowardly child must die, Nils thinks. Then I can live. Grow. Maybe grow up.

Darkness. Ice cold.

With a shiver Nils sits up. Where am I? Why? What happened? Everywhere he looks his eyes encounter the black of night.

Slowly his consciousness returns. He remembers. And he remembers the thoughts he was thinking.

I must have fallen asleep, he realizes as his eyes adjust to the darkness. I feel so safe that I fell asleep in the cemetery! There's nothing to fear.

Brrr, he shivers. But from the cold, not from the fear of death.

I've lain on the cold, cold earth, Nils thinks, standing up with difficulty. His joints are stiff like an old man's.

Brrr, now I'll get pneumonia and then I'll die, he thinks, and he almost laughs. What time is it? It's almost impossible to make out what his watch says in the darkness. A little past one, what? He was asleep for barely half an hour.

Brrr, he jumps up and down a little, jogs a little in place next to Emil Mörck's grave to warm up.

Now I'll go home to my soft, warm bed, Nils thinks. I don't have anything left to do here now. I learned something tonight.

Clang!

Right when Nils takes his first step onto the walkway he stops. He hears a noise. The silence has been broken. He hears a laugh and right after that another clang, and he understands that he's not alone in the cemetery.

Nils pricks up his ears and hears voices not that far away. Eager voices and happy laughter.

He hesitates. Just go home. Just walk away. But he's starting to feel irritated and a little curious. Who dares disturb the peace, who dares disturb the dead? And who dares disturb him?

With determined steps, and without worrying whether the gravel crunches under the soles of his shoes, Nils starts walking toward the voices.

Now he sees a light too, a fluttering light among the bushes.

And he hears the voices and the laughter even more clearly. Now he's close and he squats behind a bush and carefully peers through. On a patch of grass in front of a few tall rhododendron bushes there are four young people—four teenagers, fourteen, fifteen, sixteen or so, three guys and a girl. A small bonfire in the middle of the grass lights up their faces; there are a few cans of beer on the ground between them. One of the guys is sitting with his arm around the girl. Someone must have just said something funny because one of the guys is laughing so hard he ends up on his back, rolling around in the grass.

"Heads up!" the third guy shouts.

He takes the empty can of beer he just finished and throws it straight toward Nils. Clang! Bull's eye, right into a trash can on the other side of the bushes.

"Three points!" hollers the guy who threw it.

"Shit, watch this!" says the guy sitting with the girl.

He throws his can. It misses the trash can by more than a yard and plunks down onto the gravel in front of Nils's feet. Nils looks down at the beer can on the ground and thinks: Back to reality.

Time to get real. Bye-bye, profound, spiritual contemplation of life and death. Back to reality, gritty old social realism. Young people's problems and problem young people.

What do I do about it?

a. Go home. Think: What does it have to do with me? Let the kids party and have a little fun. They're not bothering me.

b. Call the police.

c. Walk over there, have a polite, grown-up conversation with those young adults, and explain how inappropriate it is to party in a cemetery.

d. Retaliate.

Well, Nils thinks, they *did* disturb me. They are disturbing me. And they're disturbing Emil Mörck. And calling the police is cowardly. Time now for a little Personal Responsibility & Moral Courage. But I don't want to risk getting caught up in a big fuss or make a big scene or take any nasty blows to the head.

So that leaves option d.

This is a case for the Punisher.

Nils takes a look around. Right next to him there are a few big garbage cans, and behind the garbage cans there's a compost bin where the groundskeeper throws the leaves and wilted flowers. In between the garbage cans there's a spigot, with a hose neatly coiled on the ground front of it. A mischievous smile lights up Nils's face.

The Punisher is here, boys and girls, here to teach you some respect.

Nils carefully creeps over to the spigot. He lifts the hose, makes two crimps in it, and squeezes it tightly in his right hand as he turns on the water. He hears the water rushing through the hose. Good pressure, he thinks, nodding in satisfaction. Hope it's good enough.

He slowly moves back over to the edge of the bushes, holding all the loops of hose together in his lap so that no one will hear it dragging over the gravel. I could probably drag a vacuum cleaner around over here without being noticed, Nils thinks as he hears another volley of laughter from over by the bonfire.

He peeks through the bushes. It's now or never.

Hope the pressure is good enough that I don't end up standing here with a pathetic little trickle of water, Nils thinks, and he takes a deep breath.

Now. The Punisher is here, boys and girls.

The water pressure is good. Really strong and good. It's definitely up to the task.

The first jet hits one of the boys on the back of the head. He lurches forward and almost loses his balance. "What the hell …"

Nils quickly aims the water at the fire. A few seconds later it's out, sizzling with a *pssshhtt*. And little bits of charred, soaking wet wood are flying up off the ground. Nils presses his thumb against the end of the hose to spread the water out more.

Once the fire's out it gets dark. Unexpectedly dark. But not quiet.

"What the hell! What the fuck! Cut it out! God damn it!"

And over all the swearing a high-pitched, very loud girl's voice screams, "Iiiiiihhh!"

A scream of panic. And chaos. Footsteps running. Someone falls. Nils sprays and sprays.

"Jeez, Jenny, knock it off! Chill out! It's just someone playing a trick on us. Henke, is that you? Cut it out, Henke. Enough already!"

No, my friend, Nils thinks. This isn't Henke. This is the Punisher. He smiles with satisfaction and tries to aim the water toward the voices.

"Shit, come on, you guys, let's get the bastard ..."

"Wait! Hang on!"

"We're leaving!"

Running footsteps fading away. Shouting and yelling.

Right when Nils shuts off the water he hears a gruff voice from over by the big iron gate: "Hello? What's going on here?"

He peeks over the bushes. Flashing blue lights. Yelling. Swearing. Stern police voices, angry teenage voices, and footsteps running on a gravel walkway. And a girl voice sobbing.

Time to go home now, Nils thinks, quickly heading in the other direction.

Anon

Anon's at home.

Evening. Anon is lying on his bed. He just lay down. Mother and a friend of hers are sitting in the living room, a new friend that Anon has never seen before, someone Mother met at the gym. Anna-Lena? Anna-Karin? Ann-Marie? Anon has already forgotten her name, but anyway it's something with Ann or Anna in it. She has big horse teeth and nice cow eyes and a face full of cheerful freckles, and she laughed almost the whole time when she was talking to Anon a minute ago. As soon as Anon said something she would laugh, as if he were an unusually amusing child.

Anon liked her right away. Her laughter was sincere and genuine and she smelled good.

And now Mother and Anna-Something are sitting in the living room. There are several bottles and some small bowls of peanuts and snacks on the coffee table between them, and the women are each holding a glass in their hand. There's some kind of milky white alcohol in the glasses. Now they look at each other and smile and raise their glasses.

"Skoal! So nice of you to come."

"Skoal! So nice to be here."

Anon lies in his bed in his room.

The women's murmuring voices form the backdrop for the movie in his head. The movie is called *Anon and Sara*. Anon has watched this movie every night since he found Sara's wallet in the tall grass behind the bus stop.

Sometimes the movie is about what Anon and Sara do in the dark closet. Sometimes Anon saves Sara from evil robbers. Very often, Anon tells Sara about his father. Tonight he does that, in the movie in his head. This is what Anon says:

My father is a Good god. And I'm going to be a demigod.

You get to pick, so I picked Good.

We got to pick at the last meeting. The ones who wanted to be Good got to stand in one corner of the room, the ones who wanted to be Evil in the other. The ones who wanted to be Cool & Popular went to the third corner, and the ones who wanted to be Useful in the fourth. So we broke into groups and then we stood there and waited.

Those of us who chose to be Good mostly stood there feeling a little miffed and staring at the ground. The Evil ones and the Cool ones were kissing up and laughing and irritating the rest of us and getting all worked up. And the Useful ones lined up in a nice, neat line.

After a long time it got quiet. The Game God, who was leading the exercise, stood in the middle of the floor. He slowly examined us. He didn't say anything, just smiled as if he'd just thought of some kind of dirty joke.

"Interesting," he finally mumbled.

Then that was it.

There weren't that many of us who'd chosen to be Good.

That's what Anon tells Sara. In the movie in his head. And Sara watches him the whole time, attentive and interested, and when he's done she says, "Let's go in the closet for a bit."

—

Anon doesn't get to watch what happens in the closet this time because the movie gets interrupted. A word forces its way in and interrupts the movie, a word forces its way in from the living room—into the bedroom and into his head—a single word, a word with three letters, and the movie ends right away, and Anon slips out of bed, sneaks over to the bedroom door, and listens with his ear against the chink of the door.

Mother is speaking. Anon can hear that she's had more than one glass of the sweet, strong, milky-white liquor, there's something in the tone of her voice, the pitch, an unusual kind of eagerness to her voice.

"Yeah, it's true," Mother says. "He looked like a god, like a Greek god."

The word was "god."

And Anon hears Mother tell her friend Anna-Something:

"… and I noticed him right away, he came walking along the beach, oddly enough he was alone, they usually come in pairs, two by two, but he wasn't all full of himself, not cocky like some people, you know, he was just walking along completely calmly right through all the people lying around sunbathing, it was almost as if he were lost in thought. And I nudged Jenny, who was lying there next to me, and she giggled and said, 'Well, there's one I wouldn't mind sharing a shower with,' and right when she said that he turned around and looked at us. No, no, it was just me he was looking at, he never saw Jenny, and he smiled a slightly sad smile and …"

It was quiet for a little bit.

"I hadn't gone there to … pick up guys," Mother continues

with a little giggle. "I just wanted to relax for a week. Sunbathe, swim, eat good food, and chill out. Some people really put a lot of effort into meeting someone when they're on vacation, if you know what I mean, but … no, that's not why Jenny and I went to Crete. But …"

A short pause.

"… but then anyway that same night we were sitting in a little taverna and the same guy came over and asked if he could join us, and he seemed so nice and he was kind of courteous in an old-fashioned way and, you know, he looked so Greek … but he turned out to be from Gothenburg. Can you believe that? He was Swedish!"

A little nervous laugh, a little silence.

"Maybe that's why," Mother says, laughing again, "maybe that's why it turned out like it did. Because when he spoke Swedish he had this amazing Gothenburg dialect, and I just melted. I've always been *really* partial to that dialect."

Glasses clinking and peanuts and chips rustling.

"For as long as I live," Mother says then, "I will never forget those days. No matter what has happened, no matter what will happen in the future, I will never regret … those days. It was … intoxicating, like really being alive. Yeah, like really being alive. The way you wish life could be all the time. And then, well, then we said goodbye. He was going to stay for another week, and I left him my address but I wasn't expecting … well, I didn't expect it to go anywhere. It was what it was. And strangely, I was satisfied. I was so happy to have experienced those days that it didn't matter if there weren't going to be any more."

"But?" Anna-Something interjects when Mother stops.

"Well, exactly. One day he just showed up. It was October, the rain was pouring down; my doorbell rang and there he stood, wet like a licked kitten. Ha, I can see him now! And I let him in and … well, then he stayed."

Silence.

Anon stands inside the door to his bedroom and tries to make his breathing as quiet as possible. Noiselessly and stiff as a board he stands there, and he can sense his mother's thoughts and the way she's searching for memories through the silence. Now she continues her tale:

"He was a carpenter. He'd lost his job after they finished some big building outside Gothenburg, so he came here and moved in with me. We were happy together. I think. And Anon was born."

"Anon is an unusual name," Anna-Something says.

"Anon is an unusual boy," Mother says. "And he got his name because I read a poem one time that was written by someone named Anon, or so I thought, and I liked that poem so much, but then Anon's father told me that 'anon' is short for 'anonymous,' meaning that no one knows who wrote the poem. But we named Anon 'Anon' anyway. I had made up my mind."

"Well, he's not anonymous, is he?" Anna-Something says.

"No, he's not," Mother says.

Anon can hear her smiling.

"He seems like a wonderful kid," Anna-Something says.

Mother doesn't say anything. She's probably nodding, Anon thinks. She's probably smiling proudly and nodding.

"But it just didn't work out. We were so different. He was nice, he cared about Anon so much, but we were so different."

Now Mother continues her tale:

"More and more it started feeling like this apartment was a prison for him, a cage that I'd locked him in so we could play house. I mean ... he never said that, it just felt like that to me. He was nice. He's really the nicest person I've ever met. He never raised his voice to me, he never hit me, didn't drink too much, nothing like that. We were just different. You know ... He'd played in a rock band, he was interested in the theater ... and politics. And stuff like that. And when the romance wore off all we had in common was Anon. And he couldn't find a job here either, but then something turned up in Gothenburg and he moved back there and ... Neither of us cried."

"So does Anon see his dad?" Anna-Something asks.

"Yeah, of course. One month every summer. Some weekends now and then. And then Anon always goes to Gothenburg before Christmas and goes to the big office Christmas party there at the company where his dad works now, he's the custodian for a big company. And Anon usually goes along to the theater too."

"And you?"

"We talk on the phone now and then. Send postcards to each other when we're on vacation. Try to remember each other's birthdays. We're not enemies. But not really friends either. I guess you could say it was a good divorce. But ..."

"Yeah?"

"Of course Anon needs his father. He misses him so much, I notice it all the time. And you hear so much these days about how important it is for a boy to have a father. Not that Anon's going to turn into some kind of gangster, but still."

"Mmm ..."

—

The talking stops.

Mother is lost in her thoughts, and her friend from the gym, Anna-Something, lets Mother stay lost in her thoughts for a bit before moving on to another topic.

And Anon tiptoes carefully back to his bed.

It takes him a while to fall asleep. He lies there thinking about what he heard his mother say. It wasn't all new to him. Mother had told him some of that before, but it was still different to hear her talk about it with someone else. To hear her talking about Father.

It's good that it was Anna-Something who was listening, the one with the horse teeth and the cow eyes. She seemed smart, I'm sure she could understand, Anon thinks.

Right before Anon falls asleep he has a thought that makes him smile:

You almost said it, Mother.

You almost said that Father is a god.

Zarah

"But … but … is it all right … can I just … really? What about work? And what will it cost? And … and do I need to make up my mind right now?"

Before Mia has even entered the apartment she is explaining, tripping over her own words as she explains, and Zarah listens with her mouth wide open, trying to understand, and Mia laughs at her and answers all her questions:

"Yes. Yes. Yes. No problem. Only two hundred dollars. Yes."

"Now? Right away?"

"Mmm." Mia nods, smiling.

Zarah thinks about it for five seconds. Then she says, "OK."

"So you're coming, right?"

"Absolutely."

"Good. Awesome," Mia says, looking like she genuinely means it.

And with that Zarah has decided that she will go with Mia to Italy next week, a tour of northern Italy with the soccer team, there are a few extra spaces and Zarah gets to go.

"I've never been to Italy," Zarah says.

"I have," Mia says, laughing. "I've been to Rome. And Venice. Italy is great. And the food is good, really good. And the wine!"

She pulls the door shut behind her and hangs up her jacket.

Then she studies Zarah.

"How are you feeling? You don't look like you're gravely ill."

"I'm not gravely ill," Zarah says.

They go into the kitchen together.

"But I don't have to kick the soccer ball around, do I?" Zarah laughs.

"No," Mia says, also laughing. "It's enough if you just cheer us on."

"Great. So I have to fight against a bunch of Italian fans in the stands while you guys kick the ball around?"

"I really don't think the stands are going to be that full," Mia says. "And no, you don't need to start a fight with the Italian fans, start hitting them or anything. Girls don't hit. It's guys that hit. Besides, we're only going to play two games, two training games, one in Parma and one in Florence. The rest of the time is vacation and we're free to do what we want."

Zarah puts some coffee on to brew, wipes off the kitchen table, and removes the two coffee cups and the empty breadbasket that were on the table.

"Did you have a visitor?" Mia asks.

As soon as she asked the question, she thinks: Why am I asking her that? I mean, I know the answer. I almost crashed into that man in the stairwell who was coming out of this apartment. And that wasn't her boyfriend. Why am I asking, why am I playing detective?

"Just my dad," Zarah says, with a slight shrug of her shoulders and a faint smile. "Just my little old dad. He stops by sometimes and lets me fill him up with coffee and rolls."

"I thought …" Mia starts, but she doesn't finish her thought.

Mia was going to say: I thought you didn't have a dad, I thought you were an orphan, I thought you said that one time. But maybe I misunderstood …

That had been part of how Mia pictured Zarah: Orphaned. Foster home. Problem child. Problem teen.

Mia thinks: I let myself be fooled so easily. Or maybe I fool myself. Leap to conclusions …

"Yes? You thought what?" Zarah wonders.

"Oh, nothing," Mia says.

Mia's speculations fade away as she and Zarah have coffee and discuss Italy, and both of them are energized and giggly and start talking over each other and planning, and Zarah has a thousand excited questions and Mia tries to answer them as best she can.

"Yes, you have to bring your passport. No, no raincoat. No, no shots. No, I can't speak Italian. Yes, the hotel will have towels. I don't know. No. Yup. Yes. I don't know. Don't know."

How can I be annoyed? Mia thinks. She's just a kid. She's just a cute little girl. A very cute girl.

Mia sits at Zarah's kitchen table for almost two hours, then she has to go home, but yes Zarah will come to work tomorrow and yes Zarah will remember to pay for her share of the trip tomorrow and yes of course it's fantastic that in a week we'll be sitting in Bologna in a little trattoria and—

"What's a trattoria?"

Mia explains and describes the kinds of food they'll eat and, yes, Zarah agrees that it sounds good.

"Arrivederci!" Mia says when she leaves.

Just five minutes later the doorbell rings, and Zarah can tell from the ring who it is.

"Hi, Victor," she says as she opens the door. "Guess where I'm going?"

Victor doesn't answer, Victor isn't listening, Victor isn't alone, there's a short guy in a black leather jacket standing behind him in the dark stairwell, and between them are two large brown boxes.

"Are you going to let us in or what?" Victor says, picking up one of the boxes.

The guy in the leather jacket picks up the other box and Zarah leads the way, letting them into the bedroom. She hears Victor issuing commands in there to his buddy, and finally the boxes are put away and Victor comes out to Zarah in the kitchen.

"This is Krille," Victor says, nodding at the guy who's standing behind him.

Zarah says hello to Krille with a little scowl.

"Computers," Victor says, nodding toward the bedroom. "Lot of money."

Zarah shrugs her shoulders and starts clearing the table again. She stands in front of Victor with the coffee cups in her hands and says, "I'm going to Italy."

"Is that so?"

"Yep. And guess who I'm going with?" Zarah says with a taunting smile.

Victor makes no attempt to guess; he just raises his hands and shoulders in a gesture that means "How would I know?"

"A soccer team," Zarah says with a slight giggle, setting the cups down in the sink.

She turns to face Victor, leans back against the sink, and sticks out her tongue. Then she repeats, "I'm going to Italy with a soccer team. On Friday. With a whole soccer team."

Little Krille looks skeptically at Victor and smiles awkwardly. He can't tell if what he's hearing is a joke; he doesn't know if laughing would be right or wrong.

Victor isn't laughing. He's not even smiling, just staring at Zarah, and his face is completely blank, totally empty, absolutely no expression at all. Maybe his face contains the same question that his buddy Krille didn't dare to ask: Is this a joke or is it for real?

"But I'm not going to play soccer myself," Zarah says, laughing right in Victor's vacant face. "I'm going to cheer them on. We're going on Friday."

"Great," Victor says. He says it as if he thinks that Zarah is making the whole thing up, as if To-Italy-With-A-Soccer-Team is an unusually bad, uncreative joke.

Then Victor says that he and Krille have to go but that he'll be back later, and Zarah says "Sure," and it sounds as if she doesn't care whether he comes back or not.

Before Victor leaves the kitchen his eyes settle on the sink.

"Who was here?"

"One of the soccer players," Zarah says, wrinkling her nose at him like a confrontational little rabbit. "And my dad was here too."

After Victor disappears, Zarah sinks down into one of the chairs at the kitchen table.

Why am I doing this? she thinks. I'm irritated at Victor, he's getting on my nerves, I'm teasing him. Why am I doing that? Zarah wonders. What happened?

Zarah nods to herself. She knows quite well what happened. It's become a battle. Our love has turned into a competition. It's not about Victor's suspiciousness or jealousy, it's a power struggle. That's what Zarah thinks as she sits at the kitchen table.

I'm going about it all wrong, she also thinks. If I'm trying to teach him something, if I'm trying to train him, I'm going about it wrong. I know that, but still I can't help teasing him. And I can't help getting irritated.

Zarah puts her elbows on the table and rests her head in her hands.

You. You, Zarah.

Maybe you should be a little more careful, Zarah. Mellow out a bit. You may be playing with fire, Zarah.

I know.

Some girls get into trouble. Some girls like you get into really serious trouble.

I know. But not me. Never. Never another bruise. Never a shiner. Never. Besides, Victor isn't like that. Not deep down inside.

Aren't you even scared, Zarah? Aren't you ever afraid?

No. Never.

What about the love, Zarah? Is it still there?

Yes. But something's happened to the love. Sometimes the flame burns as strongly as ever, sometimes it's ... gone. Sometimes there's just nothing there.

So, what's it going to be, Zarah? What's going to happen?
Test the love. That's what I think.

It doesn't take long; their love is tested later that night.

Victor gets there really late. Zarah's on her way to bed. She's holding her toothbrush in her hand when she opens the door for him. She chats with Victor, small talk, tries to reach him, but he just doesn't answer, mostly walks around muttering and grumbling a little, and finally he stands close, really close, to Zarah, forces her almost up against the wall.

"What are you doing?" he asks. His eyes are piercing, his gaze is sharp like a razor blade.

This time Zarah's ready, she's on the lookout, prepared, but still not afraid, and she just says it like it is. "Sorry, but ... I couldn't help it. Teasing you a little. Because I got so pissed off when you walked in with all your goddamn boxes today. Soon you won't even be able to get into the bedroom ..."

Victor's eyes are still narrowed, but some of the edge is gone, he's a little calmer. "Money. That's money. Money for us, for you too. Food. Beer. Clothes. Maybe a car. And we can take a trip somewhere. But what was all that stuff about Italy?"

Victor has already backed down some, the kitchen fan has sucked the threatening feeling out of the room. Now we'll have a conversation, Zarah thinks, relieved, a friendly conversation. Now we'll talk about our little problems like two normal young people.

"Mia came over and told me, Mia from the daycare center, that I could go to Italy with her soccer team, there was an extra space, and it was cheap and ... Yeah, I want to go. I'm going. Next week, I'll be gone for five days."

Victor is staring at her.

"It's a girls' team," Zarah says with a little laugh.

"Why don't you want to go with *me*?" Victor asks, in the voice of a whiny little kid.

"I'd love to go somewhere with you," Zarah says, laying her hand on his chest. "Would really love to. But I thought you didn't have any money right now, right? You just have a hundred and fifty brown cardboard boxes full of stereo equipment and cameras and VCRs and computers and printers and monitors and TVs. Right? And all of that stuff is crammed into my bedroom, and it's been there for several months, and every single night it multiplies like little rabbits, and someday the cops are going to knock on my door and ..."

Victor has a smirk on his face. "Car stereos," he says. "You forgot the car stereos."

Later, in bed, Victor is in his calmest, gentlest mood.

"I promise," he whispers in the darkness of the bedroom, "you'll be rid of all this stuff soon. When you get back from Italy all the boxes will be gone. Every single one. And I'll have a ton of money. And you ... I'm working on something else too. That could *really* lead to a lot of money. A ton of money. A shitload of money."

"Mmm," Zarah whispers.

She's almost asleep. Snuggled up next to Victor, she's almost asleep with her lips against his shoulder.

Nils

Pero si hallas a tu ángel,
síguela.
No la dejes que desaparezca,
no la dejes que se vaya volando.
—from *La Búsqueda*

"Hannes? Hi ..."

Mom is surprised when she opens the door and finds Hannes standing out there.

"Um, Nils isn't home," she says. "I thought you knew that. I thought he was with you, or that you would know where he was ...?"

Hannes shakes his head. "No. No idea. I thought he was at home."

"He disappeared yesterday," Mom says, "early yesterday morning. He just left a note—it said that he would be back on Tuesday or Wednesday."

"Hmm," Hannes says.

"I mean, I'm not worried," Mom says. "Just curious."

"Me too," Hannes says.

He smiles at Mom. Mom smiles back.

"No coffee today?" Mom asks, smiling.

"No thanks," Hannes says. "Another time."

"Hi, Hannes!"

Hannes runs into Kristina on the stairs, little sister Kristina. She's happy to see him too.

"Hi, Kristina, it's been ages ..."

"Mmm. Nils isn't home. He's disappeared."

"So I heard. Where are you coming from?"

"Dancing," Kristina says, swinging the cloth tote bag she's holding in her hand.

"Dancing on a Saturday afternoon?" Hannes asks skeptically.

"Jazz. Not disco nightclub dancing, silly," Kristina says, laughing.

"Oh, I see," Hannes says.

"But on Thursday we're going dancing, my class from school. We're having a class party. Our last class party."

"Oh, I see," Hannes says. He flashes Kristina a knowing smile. "Are there any cute boys in your class?"

"Ugh, they're all so immature," Kristina responds.

She stares down at the floor and spins her tote bag around a few more times.

"Um, well ... I think ... uhh ... I think he's not ... ummm ... home. Hang on, hang on a minute and I'll check. Just hold on for one moment ..."

Papa Göran stands there with the receiver in his hand. It seems like he's not sure what to do with it. He looks around and right then Kristina walks into the living room.

"Kristina?! Do you know, is Nils home, or ...? There's someone on the phone for him. Here, on the phone."

He points at the receiver with his other hand. As if he needed to explain to Kristina what a telephone is.

"Nope, he's not home," Kristina says without stopping.

Göran holds the receiver back up to his ear. "Nope, he's not home."

Göran listens, and just as Kristina's about to disappear into her room he calls out to her, "When will he be home?"

"On Tuesday or Wednesday," Kristina says, shutting her door behind her.

"On Tuesday or Wednesday," Göran tells the receiver.

Nope, Nils isn't home. Nils is gone, no one knows where he is. But he left a little note on the kitchen table before he disappeared early yesterday morning: *Hi, I'm going on a little trip. Back on Tuesday or Wednesday. Love, Nils.*

Nils is gone, so no one's in his room. Right?

Nope, someone is in Nils's room. Someone is in there with the door closed. Someone is standing in the middle of the room, looking around. Someone has gone into Nils's room to look for something.

It's his little brother, Oskar, age fifteen.

It's nice that Nils is gone, Oskar thinks. It's nice for a number of reasons. For one thing, because then you can look around in his room in peace and quiet. Nils usually gets really pissed off if he finds out that Oskar has been in his room and borrowed some magazines or CDs. So pissed off that he scares Oskar. But now, Nils is gone and Oskar stands calmly in the middle of his room looking around.

This is what he sees. This is Nils's room:

To the left behind the door, two wide shelving units from IKEA. The first is loaded with books, books of all sorts, all jumbled together. A tall stack of *Destroyer* books is crammed next to the *Collected Works of Gunnar Ekelöf*, one of Sweden's greatest poets; Dostoevsky's *Crime and Punishment* is pressed up against an Ed McBain thriller; *The Birds of Europe: Color Edition* is sandwiched between *20,000 Leagues Under the Sea* and the *Iliad*. Three shelves of books of all sorts, all jumbled together.

There are brown cardboard boxes on the two bottom shelves. Some have been labeled with a thick felt-tip marker—AGENT X9, SPIDER-MAN, MUSIC, POLITICS—but two of the boxes are unlabeled. Oskar will come back to those in a minute.

The second set of shelves is full of magazine storage boxes and binders. All of the storage boxes are marked, bearing small labels. It says "Important Matters" on one. And there's also "Unimportant Matters" and "Maps" and "Useful" and "Papers" and "Catalogs" and many more. Oskar pulls out a folder that is marked "Beautiful Things." It contains postcards, postcards of various artistic images. Oskar chuckles to himself and puts the folder back.

It says "Secrets" on one folder. Oskar doesn't pull that one out; he doesn't check that one. He already knows that it contains only a slip of paper that says: CURIOSITY KILLED THE CAT, HA, HA, HA! (IF YOU DON'T STOP SNOOPING AROUND IN MY STUFF I'LL THROW YOUR COMPUTER OUT THE WINDOW!) I'M SERIOUS!

Oskar wonders if Mom has read that note.

In the next wall there's a window, and under the window is a white laminate desk with drawers on both sides. There are schoolbooks on the left side of the desk, thick math books called *Analysis I* and *Analysis II* and *Topics in Algebra* and *Elementary Numerical Methods*; there are study guides and spiral notebooks and an advanced graphing pocket calculator.

Order and Organization prevail on the left side of the desk. On the right side, disorder and chaos reign; there's a jumbled-up mishmash consisting of letters, pens, four old toy cars, watercolor paints, a stuffed monkey, spiral binders, a small shell collection, a few rolls of film, and a studio photo of the three Persson siblings taken when Kristina was just a baby. And other stuff, a lot of other stuff.

Left and right. Order on the left and emotion on the right. Just like in the brain.

For some reason Oskar sighs and shakes his head as he contemplates the desk for a moment. He doesn't open the drawers, he knows what's in them. He knows what was in them two weeks ago, anyway.

On the right-hand wall there are three wardrobes. Oskar doesn't plan to open those either, although he did make a find in one of the wardrobes one time. All the way up on the top shelf, under all the thick winter sweaters, he had found some rolled-up pornographic magazines. But that was a long time ago, maybe three years ago.

Along the wall directly opposite the door is Nils's bed. It's unusually neatly made; Mom's probably been here. Above the bed there's a reading light and a little homemade bookshelf from woodshop class at school. Oskar goes over to the shelf. There are about ten books there. All of them are more or less worn-out paperbacks that have been read to death. Oskar cocks his head to the side and reads the spines:

Island by Aldous Huxley
Something Wicked This Way Comes by Ray Bradbury

In Watermelon Sugar by Richard Brautigan
Earth House Hold by Gary Snyder
Leaves of Grass by Walt Whitman
Romancero Gitano by Federico García Lorca
On the Road, Dharma Bums, and *The Scripture of the Golden Eternity* by Jack Kerouac
Sometimes a Great Nation by Ken Kesey
Walden by Henry David Thoreau
Residencia en la Tierra by Pablo Neruda

Just books in English and Spanish, none in Swedish. Typical snobbery. Typical Nils. Oskar shrugs his shoulders. He doesn't recognize any of the titles or authors' names.

An old habit makes Oskar stick his hand under the pillow and … Aha! Caught him! There's a book here too! He pulls it out. Ugh, another one in Spanish, Oskar notes with disappointment. *La Búsqueda* by Lorenzo Montero (Picador, 1971). Oskar sits down on Nils's bed and starts reading what it says on the back cover. He can take his time today; today he doesn't have to worry that Nils will suddenly turn up and start screaming and yelling.

This is what Oskar reads on the back cover of the book:

Una biblia para la generación beat.
—Cristóbal Carbón, *El Universal*

Después de leer *La Búsqueda* me encontré contemplando al mundo con los ojos de una niña: el mismo asombro, la misma calidez y la misma curiosidad. Este libro me cambió la perspectiva por completo.
—Isabel Metralla de Astilla, *La Opinión*

Gracioso e ingenioso.

—Nestor Furbank, *El Nuevo Día*

Lorenzo Montero nació en Salinas, California, el 13 de febrero de 1934. Allá pasó todo su vida en una casa con su madre y hermana menor. El 20 de mayo de 1963 salió de la casa y nunca regresó. El día anterior había mandado el manuscrito de *La Búsqueda* a una editorial. Desde entonces, nadie lo ha visto.

La fotografía abajo muestra al autor junto a Jack Kerouac y Neal Cassady afuera de la casa de Montero en marzo de 1958.

The picture below the text is a blurry amateur photo in which you can just make out a curly-haired young man with narrow shoulders squeezed between two slightly older men in white shirts. The three men are leaning against the side of a big Chevy, and all three are smiling and flashing their white teeth. Kerouac and Cassady look fairly similar and both have lecherous glints in their eyes and an arm flung around Montero.

Oskar flips through the book a little. Someone has written in it, circled certain thoughts, underlined things, written brief comments and exclamation marks and question marks in the margin. Oskar nods to himself. Yup, his big brother Nils is the one who wrote in the book; Oskar recognizes his handwriting.

Oskar reads a short section that's been circled:

Tienes que vivir tus sueños, por lo menos uno de tus sueños. Escoge tu deseo más profundo, y hazlo realidad. Si no, siempre vivirás como un niñito atrapado en la autocompasión. Sé hombre, afronta el mundo, deja de llorar. Haz que un sueño se haga realidad.

A little farther down on the same page, Nils wrote two big, fat exclamation points next to these sentiments:

Pero si hallas a tu ángel, síguela. No la dejes que desaparezca, no la dejes que se vaya volando.

Oskar shrugs and shoves the book back under Nils's pillow. Then Oskar goes over to one of the big bookshelves, pulls out one of the unlabeled cardboard boxes, and flips through the comic books inside, searching for some erotic ones.

When he leaves Nils's room ten minutes later, he has a couple of comic books stuffed under his shirt.

"What were you doing in there? What were you doing in Nils's room?"

Kristina pops up just as Oskar is about to duck into his own room. She uses her nosey, accusatory little sister voice.

"I just went in there to … to get something … a book … that Nils borrowed from me," Oskar lies.

"Then why didn't you get it?" Kristina asks, suspicious.

She knows Oskar's lying.

"Couldn't find it," Oskar says.

He quickly vanishes into his room and shuts the door.

"You know you're not allowed to go in Nils's room!" Kristina screams after him.

"Bla bla bla!" Oskar screams from inside his room.

Kristina sticks her tongue out at his door.

Anon

"Is Anon ready?"

"Is that you, Kristofer? It's been ages. I hardly recognized you." Mother smiles fondly at Stoffe, who's standing in the doorway.

"Mmm," he mumbles. "I'm here to get Anon. Is he ready?"

Anon appears in the hall behind Mother. He thought he'd recognized that voice. Now he's peering out around Mother's shoulder.

"Hey," Stoffe says when he catches sight of Anon. "Ready to go?"

"Huh?" Anon says, taking a step forward to stand next to Mother.

"Don't tell me you forgot ..." Stoffe shakes his head and then turns to Mother. "There's a class party tonight," he explains. "At Henke's place. Um, I mean Henrik's. The last party we're going to have with our old class. Everyone's coming. I thought Anon and I could walk over there together."

Mother looks at Anon. "Were you planning on going to the class party? You didn't mention it."

Anon doesn't answer.

"You already paid and everything," Stoffe says. "Of course you're going. Everyone's going."

Anon shrugs. "OK," he says, pulling on his galoshes.

"Aren't you going to change?" Mother wonders. "If you're going to a party ..."

Anon looks down at his clothes. A T-shirt and jeans. Why should he change? He shakes his head.

"Have a good time, then!" Mother says. "When will you be home?"

"The party's over at midnight," Stoffe answers. "And I can walk home with Anon."

Did I really pay? Anon wonders as he follows Stoffe down the stairs.

Henke and his parents live in a big, pink house with white trim and a black roof. Anon thinks the house looks like a giant birthday cake. Henke's parents aren't home tonight; they promised to stay out until midnight so the class could have its goodbye party in peace.

A wall of noise hits Stoffe and Anon when they open the front door.

"Feedback. From the speakers," Stoffe mutters. "Come on …"

Anon follows him into the large living room. The whole class is in there sitting on sofas, armchairs, and wooden chairs lined up along the wall on one side of the room. Henke is standing on the other side of the room, in front of a big display case with glass doors that's full of porcelain and fancy china, adjusting a guitar amplifier. Fille is standing next to him, his electric bass hanging from a wide strap over his shoulder. A seventh grader that Anon doesn't know is sitting behind the drums.

Stoffe walks straight over to Henke and whispers something in his ear, but Henke doesn't seem that interested. He keeps adjusting controls on the amplifier. Then he picks up the guitar and puts the strap on. Then he tries a few notes, adjusts the volume, tries again, pushes on a pedal that makes the notes sound shrill and bleed together, and finally seems satisfied and walks over to the microphone stand in the middle of the room.

"A one, a two, a one, two …"

While all this is going on, Anon takes a seat on the floor by one of the sofas. Everyone is eagerly waiting for the music to begin. No one really cared that Anon arrived, no one noticed him. Only Magdalena. She's sitting on one of the sofas, squished between several other students, and she nodded when she caught sight of Anon and he could see her mouth the word "Hi."

Now it's time. Stoffe walks over to the microphone. He taps on it a few times. "Ahem, ahem," Stoffe says. "Ladies and gentlemen. Ahem. Let the party begin. We'll start the music now, you're about to hear the school's best punk-rock bank, the school's only punk-rock band, the school's only band … Yes, ladies and gentlemen, allow me to introduce: the Dead Camels!"

Everyone applauds. Henke nods briefly and then goes over and whispers something in Stoffe's ear.

"Ahem," Stoffe says into the microphone, and everyone falls silent. "Ahem. And their first song is called 'The Robber and the Cop' and it was written by Simon."

Stoffe turns and points at the guy behind the drums. Some people start applauding again, but after two seconds the applause is drowned out by a sonorous guitar chord, and then Henke jumps over to the microphone and shouts, "The robber and the cop …"

And with that the Dead Camels' concert is under way.

Anon's having a good time.

The music carries him away—the thunderous volume, the heavy bass and the thump of the bass drum that he feels in the pit of his stomach like a pleasant tickle, the drummer's quick fill-ins on the snare drum and the kettledrums, and the piercing clang of the guitar.

The music fills Anon up. There's no room for anything else.

When the music ends, when the first song is over, Anon feels like he's waking up from a dream. A good dream. And when everyone else is done applauding, he keeps clapping, all on his own.

Henke looks at him, a little suspicious at first, then he bursts into a satisfied grin and nods at Anon. "Our next song is called 'Run for Your Life.'"

After the Dead Camels have played three songs, Henke says into the microphone, "Well, this will be our last song. And we'll have tonight's guest performance by Kristina and Ida, who are going to sing and dance."

Applause as Kristina and Ida walk over and stand on either side of Henke. They are both wearing black dresses.

"Are you ready?"

The girls nod.

"And the song is called 'Want to See You.' One, two, three, four …"

There's only one microphone. When it's time for Kristina and Ida to sing along with the refrain they have to squeeze in close to Henke. Cheek to cheek, all three of them sing, "Want to see you. I want to see you I want to see you …"

And then Kristina and Ida dance.

Flawlessly. Perfectly coordinated, perfectly synchronized.

Anon is fixated on Kristina. He's almost embarrassed when she spreads her legs apart so that her underwear shows and when she caresses her own butt. But mostly he watches her breasts. They sway so nicely in time to the music. That looks good, Anon thinks, that's how it should be.

"Encore, encore!" everyone screams when the band finishes, but it doesn't lead to anything because "We don't know any other songs," Henke says, and besides, the drummer, Simon, has to go to another party. While the band puts away their instruments and amplifiers and cords, everyone gets up and starts talking and walking around, and out in the kitchen there's chips and soda and Cheetos, and "In a couple of minutes we'll start the games," Stoffe yells, and "You guys, don't spill on the rug!" Henke shouts.

One of the doors to the porch is open, and Anon seizes the opportunity to duck out into the yard. It's quiet and still out there. It's a nice, warm evening, and the sweet, sickening smell of lighter fluid and charcoal smoke wafts over from one of the neighbors' yards. A few swallows dart across the sky, and a blackbird starts singing. Anon belches from the soda and feels happy, the music still echoing in his head.

"Hey, everyone! Games! Come on, we're going to start the games now!" someone shouts from up by the house, and Anon goes back up to join everyone else.

Stoffe is the game leader. He divides the class into two teams. He explains all the rules and keeps track of the points and serves as the referee, and there are relay races and quizzes and an obstacle course. Everyone gets all sweaty and has a good time and hoots and hollers, and finally Stoffe says, "OK! Listen up! There's only one game left, and right now the two teams are exactly tied—team A, Ida's team, and team B, Henke's team. So listen up! This is going to be the big finale. Listen! The team that's able to make the longest line of clothing, I mean, from the clothes that you're wearing, and that you have to take off to do this, the team that makes the longest line wins, and you'll start here next to the porch and go to that flowerbed over there and then back again and so on until the clothes run out. Does everyone understand? On your mark! Get set! Strip!"

With a howl Henke pulls off his shirt and runs out into the yard, and both his team and the opposing team follow him. And the clothes start coming off. First it's mostly socks and T-shirts and the boys' pants, but then Ida pulls off her dress, stands there in just her bra and underwear, and says, "I mean, it's no worse than at the beach, come on …," and a couple of the other girls follow her example, and soon the whole lawn is covered with a confused muddle of more or less undressed twelve-year-olds.

Ida and Henke each stand at the head of their troops. Ida is the most ardent of all. In just her underwear she is running around and urging her team on. She's running back and forth and shouting, but by now everyone has pretty much taken off everything they can, and Henke's team is still leading by a few inches. Ida peers around; she scrutinizes everyone …

That's when she discovers Anon.

Anon is on her team. He's standing off to the side and watching. He's taken off his shirt but nothing else. Ida rushes over to him.

"Anon, come on! We can totally win! Take your pants and galoshes off. And your socks. You must have a couple of yards of clothing on. Hurry up! We can totally win!"

Ida is so eager that she's jumping up and down. Anon doesn't know what to look at. Ida is standing just a couple of feet in front of him, jumping up and down and yelling, and all she has on is a black bra and a pair of black lace panties. Anon doesn't think it's anything like the beach. He looks to the side, tries to make it look as if he's noticed something interesting over there behind Ida.

"Your galoshes, Anon! Galoshes and pants! Come on!"

Now several other team members rush over. A small group clusters around Anon, and soon everyone is shouting in chorus, "Galoshes and pants! Galoshes and pants!"

Anon has nowhere to hide, nowhere to go. He feels an arm around his neck as someone pulls him down from behind, and then he's lying on his back in the grass while several people pull and tug on his galoshes and pants.

"Iiiiiihhh!!!"

A scream makes everyone stop.

Everyone stands up, everyone stops paying attention to Anon and his clothes, and with small yelps all the girls in the class start running around gathering up their shirts and pants and dresses and putting them back on.

Anon slowly lifts his head. He gets up, and now he sees what happened: Some of the junior high guys came, four guys who are standing there next to the house talking to Henke and grinning and watching with delight as the girls get dressed. And the game is over and Ida and Kristina go over and talk to the junior high guys too. It seems like they know each other. And suddenly it feels like the whole party is over, and everyone seems a little uncertain, and Anon tries to find his shirt. He finds it slung over a currant bush, and he pulls it over his head and thinks: I'm going home now.

"You're not leaving, are you?"

It's Stoffe who comes over, puts his arm around Anon, leaning over him.

"Why shouldn't I?" Anon wonders.

"Because there's going to be dancing, and there's more to eat and drink, we're mixing up a really good punch right now, and there's a video and there's going to be … da-da-da-dum … a surprise. A big show! A performance! A surprise! In just a little bit. And you have to be here for that. So you can't leave yet."

"All right," Anon says, shrugging his shoulders.

Henke seems to have convinced the junior high guys to leave, and Ida is trying to convince Kristina and some of the other girls to stop by their party later. When Ida passes Anon, who has sunk down into one of the soft sofas in the living room, she makes a face and sticks her tongue out at him.

So where is Magdalena? Anon looks around but can't see her anywhere. He gets up and goes out to the kitchen. Some of the guys are standing around the kitchen table. They are busy messing around with some bottles and cans and a big glass bowl.

"Well, if it isn't Anon," Stoffe says, looking up. "Perfect. You can be our guinea pig, heh heh. I mean, you can taste this delicious punch we just made."

"Stop your cruel animal experiments," Fille says, grinning as Stoffe takes a big ladle and fills up a glass for Anon.

"Here you go. It's not dangerous," he says, holding out the

glass. "It's punch. Soda and cider and fruit and juice and ice cubes and lemon."

"And—" Fille starts to say with a little chuckle, but Stoffe silences him by elbowing him in the stomach.

Anon takes the glass, he sniffs the contents, he's still a little suspicious, he cautiously tastes a gulp, mmm, good, sweet and fresh and cold, mmm, really good.

"Really good," Anon says.

Stoffe nods, looks at the guys around the table in satisfaction, and wants to refill Anon's glass right away.

Soon everyone in the class has a glass of the reddish punch, and now the dancing begins. Fille has set the living room up for dancing; he sits in one corner with the music system and a small microphone, the Venetian blinds are drawn, and some red lights on the bookshelf are flashing on and off.

"Dancing!" Fille yells into the microphone. "Come on, everybody!"

Everyone obviously recognizes the first song and they all rush in and form a ring and all start making similar motions, and someone pulls Anon onto the dance floor, and he stands there and tries to imitate the others as best he can, and everyone is happy and Anon is dancing and he's happy too. He feels happy in his head but starts feeling tired in his legs.

For a few more songs, everyone is up and dancing every old which way and this way and that or in a circle, but then some people sit down and some people start dancing in pairs, mostly it's girls dancing with other girls, but Henke and Ida are dancing and Henke is sweaty and his face is beaming.

Anon sinks down into the sofa. He's been sitting there for

only a minute when he feels a pat on his shoulder. It's Stoffe. He smiles nicely and hands Anon a glass of punch. Anon nods and takes the glass: "Thanks, thanks, so nice of you, Stoffe." Mmm, ice-cold punch hits the spot after dancing, mmm, really good.

Anon drinks punch and looks around. The lights are flashing, the music is pounding. Dancers are whirling around. Anon realizes that he's sitting there almost laughing to himself without knowing why. He just feels so giddy and happy. And suddenly Kristina is standing right in front of him, Kristina in her short black dress, and she leans over and says something into Anon's ear, but Anon can't hear. "What?" he yells, scrunching up his forehead, and then Kristina just holds her hand out and pulls him up onto the dance floor and starts dancing in front of him. With him. Kristina is dancing with Anon! And Kristina dances so nicely. So graceful, so vivacious and beautiful, she knows just what to do the whole time, not a moment of hesitation, she dances with her whole body and Anon would rather just stand there and enjoy watching her move to the music, but he has to dance a little too, and he wants to, too, and he tries to imitate Kristina's steps and movements, but it's tough. And the fact that Anon is wearing galoshes on his feet doesn't make it any easier.

But Anon does the best he can, and Kristina doesn't seem concerned. She gets more and more caught up in her own dancing, she doesn't seem to notice Anon at all, doesn't notice anything other than the music and the dancing, her body's supple motions, her heated pulse. And Anon watches her and dances and enjoys everything he's seeing and hearing and doing.

And doesn't notice that all the others have stopped dancing.

And doesn't notice that all the others are standing still, watching him and Kristina.

Anon doesn't notice anything, the music fills him up, he feels happy in his head and his body and his legs … his legs don't seem to want to … work properly … can't quite seem to keep up and … whoops … uh-oh … hello … the whole room is spinning and … uh-oh … Anon is lying flat on his back on the floor and the music stops abruptly.

It's completely quiet. Everyone stands still. The lights are flashing.

But Kristina drops to her knees next to Anon.

"What happened?" she asks. "Are you all right?"

Anon shakes his head and smiles awkwardly. And Fille yells into his DJ's microphone, "Uh-oh, our own Disco King, Anon, seems to have bit the dust on that one, but it doesn't look like he's out for good, I'm sure he'll pick himself back up and start dancing again."

Everyone laughs and the music starts throbbing again.

Anon has a little trouble getting up off the floor, but Stoffe comes over, pulls him up, and helps him out onto the porch.

"Maybe a little fresh air?" he says, parking Anon in the hammock.

Anon nods gratefully. He suddenly feels so dizzy and giddy.

Nice to be outside. Nice to sink down into the soft cushions on the hammock and carefully sway back and forth a bit. And here comes Stoffe with yet another glass of that yummy red punch.

"Here. Have a little more to drink. You need it."

"Mmm," Anon says, taking the glass.

Stoffe disappears, and Anon sits there with the glass in his hand. The throbbing, pulsing dance music forces its way from the living room out into the yard, and the blackbird is still singing from the TV antenna on top of the house across the street. Anon starts feeling a little better right away. But when he raises the glass to take a swig, someone stops him. Someone puts a hand on his arm. Someone says, "Stop! Don't drink any more, it'll just make you sick."

It's Magdalena. Anon didn't hear her coming, but now she's standing there in front of him. Anon stares at his glass and sits there as if he's been turned to stone.

"Don't you get it?" Magdalena asks, seeming almost irritated.

Only then does Anon get it, and he nods at the glass.

"Alcohol, right?"

"Yeah," Magdalena says, nodding. "They spiked it."

"They spiked it?"

"Yeah. They have a bottle in the kitchen. The guys have been talking about it all week."

Anon nods. He gets it. And he sets his glass down on the white plastic table next to the hammock. Magdalena doesn't sit down next to him. She doesn't say anything either, just stands there in silence in front of Anon for a while. And the blackbird sings and sings.

"I want to dance a little more," Magdalena says finally, and she goes back in toward the house.

"Mmm," Anon says, watching her without getting up.

But Anon only sits out there alone for a couple of minutes. Now he's feeling good again, now he wants to go back to the party.

But he's tired. A wave of tiredness has come over him. It takes an enormous effort to stand up.

Now people are making out, slow dancing. Anon notes the slow music as he comes back in from the porch, and he stands in the doorway and looks at all the people dancing. Yes, now almost everyone is dancing, it's crowded in the living room. Kristina is dancing with Henke, they're dancing really close together, one of Henke's hands has found its way in under Kristina's long hair, he holds his hand against the nape of her neck and dances with his cheek resting against her head.

Magdalena is dancing too. She's dancing with a guy named Patrick. Also close, but not as close. Not as tenderly, not as familiarly.

When the song ends some of the couples let go of each other right away, while others stay pressed together in a long embrace.

Fille was dancing too. Now he darts back over to his corner, leans in over the microphone, and says, "Yes, yes, that was the last dance. For now. There'll be more dancing later, but now everyone should take a seat here on the sofas because it's time for tonight's big surprise."

And everyone crowds together onto the sofas and the armchairs again, and everyone is a little giggly and silly now. Some of them have drunk more than one glass of the spiked punch, and when they talk, their voices are unusually loud and shrill.

"Quiet! Quiet!"

Now it's Stoffe talking into the microphone. He's standing in the middle of the floor with Henke and Fille and Ida and Kristina and Frida.

When everyone quiets down, Stoffe continues, "Now our class's very own little theater group is going to act out a few scenes, some highlights from our time in elementary school, and those of us who took drama have been working on this and we did it all ourselves and now we'll get started … So, is everyone here? Is Anon here? Ah, yes, there he is … Hi, Anon … Well, if you're here, I'm sure everyone is here. We'll get started!"

It's funny. Anon laughs as the little theater group acts out scenes with the Janitor and the Evil Cafeteria Lady, and the time the Dead Camels were supposed to play a concert in study hall and all the fuses blew, and when they tricked Miss Larsson and the principal on April Fools' Day, and the time the whole class took turns guarding the school at night to catch some computer thieves and …

It's funny. Anon laughs and everyone laughs.

Then Stoffe says, "Always save the best for last."

His face is red and shiny, and he seems pleased as he looks around the room.

"Do you remember how it all began? It was like this …"

THE FIRST DAY
a short play by the Drama Group

Starring:
Ida as Miss Larsson
Stoffe as Anon
Henke, Fille, Kristina, and Frida as four 4b students

The classroom. Miss Larsson sits at her desk; four students sit quietly and wait. Enter Anon, dressed in hip-wader boots. He stumbles up to Miss Larsson.

ANON: Hi! Oh, am I late?

MISS LARSSON: And who might you be?

ANON: I'm Anon.

MISS LARSSON: That's a strange name.

STUDENT I (*turning to Student II*): He seems like he's a little strange too.

STUDENT II: And he looks strange too.

Anon sits down next to Student II. Miss Larsson passes out books and says a little bit about how much fun they'll have together in fourth, fifth, and sixth grade. Finally she looks around at the students.

MISS LARSSON: So, that's all for today. Does anyone have any questions?

ANON (*stands up and raises his hand and waves it around*): Yes, Miss Larsson, there's one thing I've been wondering about.

MISS LARSSON (*in a friendly voice*): Yes, Anon? What is it?

ANON: Well, what does "orgasm" mean? And what does "penis" mean? And "vagina"? And "cli—"?

The other four students fling themselves at Anon and carry him out while Miss Larsson hides her face in her hands. After a little bit she looks up, smiles at the audience, and says:

THE END

Everyone laughs. Everyone remembers. Stoffe looks pleased again. Anon is laughing too. That was funny. The play is actually over, but Henke stands in the middle of the floor and raises his hands. When everyone is quiet, Henke says, "There's one more scene."

He turns toward Stoffe and grins a little, but Stoffe doesn't know what he's getting at and just shrugs.

Then Henke turns toward the audience and says in a kid's voice, "Um, my name is Stoffe, and I know that orgasms are like tiny, tiny things that are everywhere ..."

Everyone laughs again, even harder. Everyone except Stoffe.

"Shut up," he hisses, staring angrily at Henke.

Stoffe's face is red now, beet red.

When it quiets down again Stoffe says to Ida, "Yeah, Miss Larsson, there's one other thing I've been wondering about."

Now Stoffe is acting again. Now he's pretending to be Anon again and Ida is looking at him, bewildered. They didn't rehearse this.

Finally Ida says, "Yes, what?"

"Well, teacher, I wonder if you could come with me when I pee, and help me hold my weenie, because at home my mother usually does it, and if you don't help me, teacher, I might miss and end up peeing on the outside of the toilet and on the walls and on the doorknob and everywhere ..."

At first there's just silence.

Then someone starts whispering and no one can hear whose voice it is that's whispering: "Piss Anon."

And the words are repeated by several voices and interspersed with words like "Disgusting" and "That's so nasty."

Lots of derisive words and critical voices are heard. Ida stands in the middle of the floor staring down at her hands; she's just remembered something awful she experienced.

And Magdalena's voice drowns out all the noise: "Oh, cut it out! You all know that it wasn't Anon!"

"That's what you say, sure!" Stoffe yells. "That's what hypocritical little Magdalena claims, sure! Because maybe little Magdalena has a little crush on Piss Anon ..."

"You're an idiot!"

There's a commotion and shouting and everyone stands up. There's an uproar in the living room. But what about Anon, what's Anon doing? He just sits where he's sitting, on the armrest of one of the sofas. He thinks: This doesn't have anything to do with me. It wasn't me. I know who it was.

"I know who it was," Anon says.

But no one hears him.

There are three groups in the room now; the class has split into three teams, as if there were another competition. Three teams plus Anon.

Stoffe is in charge of the first team. That team thinks Anon is "disgusting" and that he should be punished in some way or somehow taught a lesson.

The second team, which seems to be almost as big, consists of people who think it's time to get the party going again, especially the dancing. "Cut it out already" is their slogan. Kristina and Henke are on that team.

The third team consists of Magdalena. She's standing right in front of Stoffe and yelling right in his face. She's calling him various names. And she's fuming mad; like an angry hornet she's hopping up and down and waving her slender arms. Now someone grabs hold of Anon, someone pulls him up, and he doesn't resist, he lets himself be guided, shoved, dragged through the house, a swarm of hopping and shouting and noisy classmates crowd around him, until finally someone gives his back a firm shove and he's forced into a bedroom, presumably Henke's parents' bedroom, and Anon stands there in the middle of the floor looking around. Some of his classmates are huddled in the doorway, there's a lot of noise and activity out there, but he's alone in the bedroom until Magdalena hurtles in as if she were flung; she wobbles and almost falls down on her knees in front of Anon but quickly gets up and turns back toward the door. Her small hands are clenched into fists, but she never has a chance to say or do anything because now Stoffe is standing there and screaming, "You can just stay in here! We'll lock you in, then … Then Magdalena can teach Anon what an orgasm is … and … and …"

He slams the door shut.

Magdalena flings herself at the door right away; she tugs at it and struggles to open it, but there are a lot of people holding it shut from the other side, and finally she gives up, takes a few steps back, and stares at the door, seething. There's a lock on the inside of the bedroom door. With a snort Magdalena walks over and locks it.

Then Magdalena turns to look at Anon. He's sitting on the edge of the bed now with his face resting in his hands.

"Anon?"

No response.

Magdalena waits for a little while, standing completely still and looking at Anon, and finally she walks over to him, kneels down on the floor in front of him, and asks, her voice concerned, "Anon, are you sad? Are you crying?"

Anon takes his hands away from his face.

"No," he says, mostly seeming surprised.

They can hear voices outside the door.

Someone moans, someone pretending to have a girl's voice exclaims, "Oh, Anon, it's so big! Oh, Anon, that feels so good, ohhhhh ..."

"What are they doing in there?" someone wonders.

Someone tries turning the doorknob. "Hey, they locked the door! Hey!"

"Ah, we'll leave them alone for now," someone says, and then the voices and the noises disappear.

"No, I'm just tired," Anon says. "And I feel a little sick."

Magdalena studies his face. He doesn't look sad, he hasn't been crying.

"This really pisses me off," she says, casting a glance at the locked door.

"Um," Anon says.

They sit there in silence for a while, Anon on the edge of the bed and Magdalena at his feet. Anon yawns deeply.

"If you're tired, why don't you lie down and rest for a bit," Magdalena says.

Anon nods and looks at her gratefully as if she'd come up with a brilliant idea.

"But if you're going to do that ..."

"Yeah?" Anon wonders.

"... if you're going to do that, you should take off your galoshes. Because surely you don't normally wear your galoshes to bed?"

Anon shakes his head, chuckling as if Magdalena had said something funny. And she starts pulling off his galoshes. It takes a while, but off they come, first the one, then the other.

"Ugh," Magdalena says, staring at Anon's feet.

"What?"

"Your feet really stink. Can't you smell that?"

Anon sniffs. Nope, he can't smell any unusual odors.

"Ugh," Magdalena says, looking around. "Wait a sec."

She stands up and walks over to a little table next to the door, one of those little tables you usually see in old movies, a little table with a big mirror on top, and on the table there's makeup and skin creams and hairbrushes and stuff. Magdalena picks up various bottles and containers, sprays samples out of some of the different spray bottles, and finally comes back over to Anon with a white plastic tube in one hand.

Pleased, she holds it up and reads the label. "Body lotion. Skin care. Apricot. How 'bout that?"

Anon shrugs his shoulders. What is she doing?

Magdalena pulls one of Anon's socks off, holds it from the very edge as she sniffs it and wrinkles up her nose, then tosses it off to the side. She takes hold of Anon's foot, sets it on her knee, sitting there below Anon, squirts a little of the white cream out, and starts rubbing it on his foot. Slowly and carefully, as if she is performing a very important task, Magdalena anoints Anon's foot.

It feels good. Magdalena's hands are soft. And it feels nice to see the top of Magdalena's head and the back of her neck as she kneels in front of him, Anon thinks. He closes his eyes and sighs contentedly. The world is soft and smells good.

"There. And now the other one," Magdalena says, and she pulls Anon's other sock off.

Anon doesn't want Magdalena to finish, he doesn't want her to stop, but she finishes and she stops.

"There," she says and bends over. "Mmm, now your feet smell like two apricots. Can you smell that?"

Anon nods. "Thanks," he says.

Now Anon feels good, mmm, now he doesn't feel sick anymore. But he's still tired. He crawls up toward the head of the bed and stretches out. Mmm.

"Scoot over a little, would you? Then there'll be room for me too."

"Sure," Anon says and scoots over toward the wall.

Anon and Magdalena lie on their backs next to each other in the wide double bed. They lie there quietly. It's not just Anon's feet but the whole bedroom that smells like apricots.

"What funny feet you have," Magdalena suddenly says, giggling.

"What do you mean?" Anon wonders, turning to look at her.

"Well, your index toe is longer than your big toe. A lot longer."

"Index toe?"

"Yeah, or whatever it's called, your second toe, the one next to your big toe."

"Oh, yeah, you mean my long toe," Anon says with a quiet laugh. "My feet are completely normal. Look."

He scoots down on the bed and props both his feet up against the wall, he rests his bare feet on the pale bedroom wallpaper with its delicate floral pattern.

"Look. Completely normal feet!"

"No way," Magdalena says, laughing.

She pulls off her socks, scoots down on the bed next to Anon, and props her feet up on the wall next to his.

"*This* is what normal feet look like," she says. "On normal feet the big toe is the longest."

"There's two kinds of feet," Anon explains. "The kind that you have and the kind that I have. The kind I have are called swamp feet."

"Because they smell so bad," Magdalena says, laughing.

"No, because you can walk in swamps with them. You can do that only if your long toe is longer than your big toe. Your kind of feet are worthless if you have to walk in a swamp. You would just sink. Like a stone."

Magdalena turns to face Anon, looks at him carefully and curiously. Anon studies their four feet on the wall with a serious, contemplative expression, and Magdalena bursts into effervescent laughter: "Swamp feet, ha, ha, ha …"

Anon waits until she's done laughing, and then he says, "Yup, it's true. Actually. My father told me that. He has feet just like mine. But bigger, of course."

It's quiet for a while. Magdalena giggles a little now and then, but then she gets serious and asks, "They're divorced, aren't they?"

"Mmm." Anon nods.

"Mine too," Magdalena says.

"Oh, no!"

Uh-oh—when Anon takes his feet off the wall he discovers that there are two greasy footprints on the wallpaper. Uh-oh.

But that's quite attractive, Anon thinks as he contemplates the footprints for a while. It's like a work of art.

And then Anon thinks it would be an even more attractive work of art if Magdalena's feet participated as well, and Magdalena says "All right then" and giggles as Anon rubs apricot cream on her feet. She giggles because she's ticklish and because she's in a silly mood.

Then Anon and Magdalena make foot art on the bedroom walls.

All of their works of art have titles. One is called "Cold." It's two pairs of feet with their heels facing each other. One work of art is called "Curious." It's a big toe that's sniffing another big toe. One work of art is called "Teased." There are three cruel feet that are teasing a fourth foot.

They create many works of art, "The Attack of the Swamp Feet" and "Big Foot Takes Flight" and "Alone in the Blue Lagoon" and "Not Without My Little Toe" and many more, but finally the wall around the double bed is used up.

"Nice," Anon thinks, letting his eyes wander from one work of foot art to the next.

"Do you think Henke's parents will think so too?" Magdalena wonders.

Anon shrugs his shoulders. "Now I'm tired again," he says.

"Do you want to sleep for a bit? Should I turn out the light?"

"Mmm." Anon yawns.

Anon and Magdalena fall asleep.

Anon and Magdalena sleep.

Anon and Magdalena wake up when someone tugs on the doorknob, when someone knocks on the door, and someone half yells, half whispers through the keyhole, "Psst! Hello in there? Come out now, my parents are coming! Hurry up!"

It's Henke standing out there, and he's trying to make his

voice both loud and soft at the same time because his parents must have already come home and are in the house.

Magdalena turns the bedside lamp on, she shakes Anon carefully, and they sit up on the bed and blink at each other sleepily.

"You snored," Anon says, yawning.

"No way!" Magdalena says, certain.

"Then I dreamed it," Anon says, starting to look for his socks.

He's found one sock and put it on when there's another knock on the bedroom door, a firm, determined knocking now, and they hear a stern male voice on the other side.

"Hello in there? Whoever's in there! Come out of our bedroom right now! Immediately!"

"Henke's dad," Magdalena says, buckling her shoes.

"Presumably," Anon says, pulling on his galoshes.

"What on earth is going on here?"

Henke's dad is so big he fills the whole doorway, just a little glimpse of Henke's mom there behind him. He's irritated and mad. And maybe a little drunk, because he's holding on to the doorframe with both hands and swaying slightly as he stands there.

"What on earth is going on here? What are you up to? Who gave you permission to be in our bedroom? And why did you lock the door?"

"We got so tired," Magdalena says in her nicest voice, taking a step forward. "And Anon wasn't feeling well, he needed some rest and a little peace and quiet, and then we fell asleep."

Henke's dad stares at her and then at Anon, who's standing in the dark behind Magdalena, and it looks like he can't decide whether to be strict or nice.

"But ... but what's that smell?"

"It's just apricot," Anon mumbles.

Out in the hallway someone yells that Magdalena's mom is there, and Magdalena and Anon squeeze past Henke's father, they dart under one of his arms like two speedy mice. At the front door there's a group of classmates heading home, and some parents are there to pick up their kids too, and Magdalena runs right over to her mother as their classmates stare at her and Anon.

"We can give Anon a ride home, can't we, Mom?"

And while Magdalena's mom is saying "Sure," Magdalena hurries her along and almost pushes her out of the house while Anon trots after them.

"What's the rush?" Magdalena's mom wonders as they stand next to the car.

"Just hurry," Magdalena pleads, pulling open the car door.

But Henke has caught up to them, he puts a hand on Anon's shoulder and says goodbye to him, and he gives Magdalena a grateful smile.

"Bye," Anon says, but Magdalena doesn't say anything.

"Come on, get in," she tells Anon instead, practically shoving him into the car.

And after she hops in, she orders her mother: "Go now! Drive away!"

Just as the car pulls out from between two other parked cars, Henke's dad comes running out onto the steps. Magdalena and Anon see through the rear windshield how he's waving his arms and how he's yelling something after them, but they can't hear what. It's something angry, something upset and irate in any case. Probably something involving swear words. Not something nice and friendly, nope.

"He didn't like the feet," Magdalena whispers to Anon.

"Strange," Anon whispers to Magdalena.

And giggles fill the car's back seat.

Magdalena's mom drives around a corner, stops the car, turns off the engine, and turns around.

"What in the world did you two do?" she asks. Her smile is very similar to Magdalena's.

"Nothing much," Magdalena says, giggling and giving Anon a look.

"Nope," he says, vigorously shaking his head. "Nothing in particular."

"Well, you must have gotten into some kind of mischief," Magdalena's mom says, watching them with cheerful, curious eyes. But then she starts the car again and drives on, and outside Anon's house she lets him out. "Bye. Good night."

"Bye. Good night. Thanks for the ride."

"See you tomorrow."

Anon stands there and watches the car drive away. He's filled with joy and not at all tired anymore.

Actually it doesn't matter at all that she doesn't have any breasts, he thinks. She will.

Zarah

"Why are you going to leave?"

"Was it nice in Italy?"

The summer sun beats down on the daycare playground. The kind of sun you have to seek cover from, a sweaty sun that has forced Zarah and Rebecka and Hanna to seek out a shady corner. There they sit on a wooden bench next to a wooden picnic table, Zarah in the middle with one little girl on each side. In front of them there's a melee of activity with tricycles and tire swings and pails and shovels and running and outdoor activities.

"You're wearing such a nice dress," Rebecka says, feeling a little of the cloth on Zarah's short white sundress.

"Hmm," Zarah says, smiling to herself.

Girl talk, she thinks. Girl talk already. Strange. A five-year-old boy would never tell me my dress is nice.

"Why are you going to leave?" Hanna asks again.

"Because it's summer," Zarah says, feeling the summer warmth on her cheeks. "So I can have a summer vacation. I'm going to school actually, even though I'm here with you. And now it's summer vacation, summer vacation starts tomorrow."

"Mmm, I know," Hanna says, nodding knowingly, "because I have a big brother and—"

Rebecka interrupts. "Was it nice in Italy?"

"I've already talked all about Italy," Zarah says with a smile, "a zillion times."

"Not to us," Hanna and Rebecka protest.

Yes, it was nice in Italy.

And again Zarah talks about the beautiful city of Florence with its big, beautiful churches and palaces, and about all the tourists and merchants crowded together on the old stone bridge over the river, and she talks about the arcades in Bologna, yes, that's what you call it when there's a ceiling over the sidewalk, when the buildings go out over the sidewalks, do you know what I mean?

Hanna and Rebecka nod seriously.

And Zarah talks about the mild evenings and nights, about restaurants and cafés with outdoor seating, about young people dancing ballet in the middle of the piazza in the middle of the night. And Zarah talks about Juliet's grave in Verona and about all the people who write letters to Juliet.

"Who was Juliet?" Rebecka wonders.

And then she and Hanna listen with their little mouths hanging open as Zarah tells the story of Romeo and Juliet as best she can.

Afterwards, Zarah is quiet and thinks: Yes, it was nice in Italy.

For four days life was a game and a dance. Never, almost never, have I felt so carefree, have I felt that life is so carefree and easy, Zarah thinks.

Everything was great, everything was nice. Until the last evening, the last night.

"Did you watch Mia play soccer too?" Hanna asks, even though she already knows the answer.

"Mmm." Zarah nods. "I watched Mia and her team play soccer. Twice. One game they won seven-zero."

"Wow!" Hanna exclaims. "Seven-zero, wow!"

"Did Mia score any goals?" Rebecka wants to know.

Zarah shrugs. "You should ask Mia that."

"Mmm, here she comes. Mia! Mia! Come here!" Rebecka shouts, even though Zarah tries to shush her and get her to stop.

"No, not now. I meant … later. Not now."

Zarah has successfully avoided Mia for two days. They haven't exchanged a single glance, a single word. And Mia has let Zarah hide, left her in peace. But last night Mia got only two hours of sleep, she didn't fall asleep until dawn, and it was thoughts of Zarah that kept her awake and wet her pillowcase with tears.

Two days without a glance or a word, and then Mia just comes over and sits down across from Zarah and the two girls, as if everything were normal. She looks normal, too, although maybe there's a glint of paleness underneath her mild sunburn.

"Yes?" she says, smiling at Hanna and Rebecka.

"Did you score any goals?" Rebecka asks. "In Italy?"

"Two," Mia says, nodding. "Although actually I'm a fullback, so the idea isn't for me to score goals. I'm actually supposed to stop the other team from getting any goals."

"Two goals!" Hanna says admiringly, looking as proud as if she'd scored the goals herself.

"Did you hear that?" Rebecka shouts, loud enough to be heard all over the playground. "Mia scored two goals! In Italy! Even though she's a fullback! Two goals!"

And the girls get up and run off to spread the good news: "Two goals, two goals, two goals …"

Zarah and Mia sit there facing each other. A tabletop between them, and an abyss. A Berlin Wall. An Arctic Sea. A mountain range. An infinite distance.

Mia tries anyway. "How long do I have to wait?"

Zarah doesn't look at her, Zarah lets her eyes wander out over the playground as she answers. "You don't have to wait at all. Today's my last day. I brought a marzipan cake to share with everyone and then I'll say goodbye. And then that'll be that. What would you be waiting for?"

Mia shakes her head quietly and swallows. "You're so damn cold. So callous. So …"

Mia quickly gets up and hurries away from the table, but Zarah can hear it, Zarah can hear the tears in Mia's voice, and now she watches Mia run away and bites down on her lip. Hard.

Steady, secure, safe, stable Mia. What's become of her?

Yeah, when they have a coffee break that afternoon Zarah offers everyone a piece of marzipan cake from a gigantic, poison-green, marzipan-covered cake. All the children in the Yellow Group get a piece and all the teachers too, and the director comes in and says that it's been a pleasure having Zarah there and Zarah says something about how she'll miss working there, which is actually true, and Mia stays away.

When Zarah's about to go, when Zarah's going to leave the daycare, she still hasn't seen Mia. She makes the rounds through all the classrooms, she says "Goodbye" and "So long" to everyone, but she doesn't see Mia anywhere.

Not in the little teachers' lounge either. But the teachers' bathroom is occupied. Zarah knocks on the door.

"Hello? Who's in there?"

No response.

Then Zarah starts kicking the door and pounding on it with both fists and she yells, "God damn it, just come out!"

Mia opens the door almost right away. Zarah looks at her and sighs.

"All right already. So we'll talk. When do you get off?"

"I'm done," Mia says, pursing her lips.

"Tag along then," Zarah says as she starts to leave. "Let's sit down somewhere."

Mia follows her like an obedient little child.

Mia follows Zarah across the big grassy field over to the park. Zarah walks slowly, with slow, dawdling steps, and Mia walks just as slowly.

The person who's in love is always at a disadvantage, Zarah thinks. The one who's the most in love. This time it isn't me, Zarah thinks. Usually it's me.

Zarah sits down on an empty bench in the shade under a big weeping willow, and Mia comes up to the bench and after hesitating for a moment she sits down too. She scoots all the way against the armrest, as far away from Zarah as possible.

They sit there in silence for a long time. Zarah stares straight ahead at the air in front of her, and Mia looks at the ground.

Finally Zarah takes a deep breath and turns toward Mia. "I want you to understand."

Mia doesn't say anything, and she doesn't glance up to look Zarah in the eyes either.

"Picture this," Zarah begins. "Picture me sitting alone in a café or something, and a guy comes over and asks if he can join me, and I say sure and we start talking, and maybe he's funny and cute and smart and we talk and laugh and … But one thing is totally clear the whole time …"

Not until Mia looks up and turns to face Zarah with a questioning look does Zarah continue.

"I know that his dick is calling the shots. That little dick, that little earthworm that men have between their legs, that's what's in control. That guy who sits down at my table and starts talking, he's really just trying to get in my pants. His dick is in charge."

Mia smiles a cautious smile and then rests her head on one hand.

"But that doesn't matter," Zarah continues. "I know what he wants, and he knows that I know. There's a kind of tension, a contest, a game; it doesn't bother me, mostly it doesn't bother me."

Zarah stops talking and looks at Mia, who's still sitting there with her head lowered and with one hand in front of her face.

"Mia, for Pete's sake, don't look like that. You make me forget what I was saying when I look at you. Mia, for Pete's …"

Mia obeys and looks up.

"Good. Now listen. I was so happy when I met you, Mia. It felt like I'd found a … friend. I've had more boyfriends than friends for the last few years, lots more, I realized that when I met you. And I remembered how nice it was to have a friend. A real friend. For however much that's worth. And how nice it is not to have to deal with that whole game for a while, that whole mating dance between boys and girls, I mean …"

Mia nods. She's starting to see where Zarah's going with this.

"So suddenly our friendship isn't worth anything anymore?" Mia asks. Her voice is thin, thin as a butterfly's wing.

Zarah looks at her seriously. "I had an amazing time in Italy, I haven't been that happy since ... since I was a little kid. Until that night. But obviously it's worth something. Still. Everything that's happened is worth something. But ..."

Mia has started shaking her head. "Was it such a big deal?" she asks, looking directly into Zarah's eyes for the first time in a long time. "I was happy. I was a little drunk. You were also happy and a little drunk. You make it sound like something terrible happened, as if I'd tried to rape you or something. That's not how it was, right?"

Now it's Zarah who's hesitating. Now it's Zarah who gulps and looks at the ground. When she looks up she smiles sadly and shakes her head.

"God, Mia," she says. "Why don't you get it?"

A very old woman with a walker shuffles past; a friend in a flowered dress limps along next to her.

Zarah doesn't speak again until the women have gone by. Then she says, "I wanted us to be friends. I still want that, but ... I don't know if I'm brave enough. You have this desire that I don't understand, a kind of desire that I can't even understand. That I don't have. And I know ... just a sec ... I know, because I've known a lot of guys, I've been with a lot of guys, I know that desire and friendship are usually an impossible combination. I don't even think it's that easy to combine desire and love; at least I'm starting to doubt it. If I ... just a sec ... if I were to hug you now, because friends hug each other sometimes, don't they, I don't know what that would mean for you. Maybe for you that would mean something completely different ..."

Mia has tried to interrupt Zarah several times, but she stays quiet until Zarah's done talking.

"So you don't think I have any friends?" Mia finally asks, her voice sounding tired and resigned. "Friends that are girls, I mean? You think my desire is so great that I can't control it? You think that I just try to ... seduce every girl I meet?"

"I don't know," Zarah says with a sigh, shrugging her shoulders.

Then Mia gets up off the bench and walks away without a word.

Sit tight, Zarah whispers to herself. Sit still, stay put, don't run after her.

Zarah clenches her teeth and almost has to hold on to the bench while she follows Mia with her eyes until she disappears from view.

Then Zarah exhales. So. That didn't go well, and it was my fault, she thinks, but there's no fixing it now. That was the end. Maybe later, maybe another time, maybe next time.

Shit, Mia. I miss you already, Zarah thinks, standing up.

What if all of my stereotypes are true, Zarah thinks on her way home, smiling sadly at the thought. My worst, most ridiculous, stupidest stereotypes are turning out to be true: Immigrant guys are criminals who hit their girlfriends. Short-haired female soccer players are lesbians.

No, that's not true. I know one guy who's an immigrant, who's my boyfriend, and he hit me and he's a small-time crook, sure. And I know one homosexual girl who plays soccer. But

Victor is just Victor, he's not all immigrant guys. And Mia is just Mia, she's not all girls who play soccer.

But still, Zarah thinks, kicking a rock, which makes some ducks quack in fear and jump out of the way. But still …

Come on, life, surprise me!

Nils

Tienes que enterrarte a tí mismo
Tienes que enterrar a tu proprio Ser
si quieres vivir,
si quieres hacerte hombre.
—from *La Búsqueda*

"Am I crazy?"

"Definitely. Without a doubt!"

Nils and Hannes have been talking for twelve hours straight without stopping. They started yesterday evening at the café, continued during the night, first at a party they wound up at and then at Hannes's house. Now it's Friday morning and they've been sitting at Hansen's Café for half an hour having coffee.

"No, I mean seriously?" Nils asks.

"Seriously: Yes!" Hannes responds. "At any rate, I don't know anyone who's as totally nuts as you. No one. Not a one."

Nils lights a crumpled breakfast cigarette and coughs. He notices the taste of lead in his mouth after a night of smoking and frowns to himself. With the stubble and bloodshot eyes, he looks exhausted, partied out. Hannes, on the other hand, looks almost as smooth-shaven and almost as bright-eyed as ever.

"Listen up now," Hannes says, smiling at his tired friend. "Listen and decide for yourself. You're following around a girl that you don't even know, that you've never spoken to. You followed her to Italy just to watch her. You traveled around in Italy for four days to spy on a girl like you were a twelve-year-old boy. And then, when you get home, you want me to help you out by burying you. Burying you alive, burying you in the ground. You want to know what it's like to be buried, you say. And you spent the night in a coffin. And you slept in the cemetery. Crazy or not crazy? Answer: totally crazy!"

You. You, Nils.

Didn't you used to imagine what it would be like to go crazy? To kind of go a little crazy?

Yes, that's true. I would go a little crazy. Not totally crazy, not someone who sits in a padded cell with mattresses on the walls and smears feces all over himself, not someone who shuts himself off from the outside world. No, I would just be a little crazy.

Why did you want that?

I don't know. So that I would be well looked after, so I wouldn't have to take any responsibility whatsoever for myself. I'd have a bed in a Home or a Nut House and wear a white jumpsuit and be surrounded by gentle people and other slightly crazy people.

But there was something else, wasn't there?

Yes. Yeah. There in the Home I would create ingenious works of crazy art. Write a novel or a collection of poetry. Paint. Create masterpieces on the walls with bits of lead stuck under my fingernails. A Wölfli, a Hill, a Munch, a Hermelin, a Dostoevsky, a ...

Sounds like an adolescent boy's dream, doesn't it?

Yeah, definitely. An adolescent boy's dream.

—

"Seriously," Hannes says, interrupting Nils's daydream memories, "I don't think you're crazy."

"Well, that's fucked up," Nils says with mock disappointment.

"Exactly." Hannes nods. "It's like maybe you want to be crazy. A mad genius, of the old, romantic variety."

"Ach, Doktor Freud," Nils says in a fake German accent, "you are readink my brains as usual, ich bin so impressiert …"

Tired laughter, tired smiles, and more coffee.

"That girl …" Hannes starts.

"Zarah," Nils says, nodding. "Zarah with a Z. I'm going to talk to her tomorrow. After the burial. After the resurrection."

No, sometimes I just don't get him, Hannes thinks. Sometimes I don't get if he's serious about something or if he's just kidding around. Is he obsessed with that girl or is he pretending he's obsessed? Ever since he met her that night at the pub he's been following her, chasing her, trying to catch a glimpse of her, trying to piece together a picture of her instead of …

"You have to keep your dreams alive," Nils says with a somber smile. "You have to live your dreams."

"Amen," Hannes says, clasping his hands together.

"Besides, I talked to her. I told her that I love her."

"You did?" Hannes asks, raising his eyebrows. "And then what did she say?"

"She was the one who spoke first," Nils explains. "I called her. Then she said, 'Hi, this is Zarah. But I can't come to the phone right now (teehee). Leave me a brief message and I'll call you back. If you want.' And then I said, 'I love you.'"

"After the beep?"

"Yes, after the beep. Of course."

Nils stamps out his cigarette, sniffs his fingertips, and scowls with displeasure again.

"But on Saturday," he says, "I'll go to her. Saturday is the first day of summer. And of my new life."

"Saturday is tomorrow," Hannes points out.

"I know," Nils says.

"But first you're going to be buried," Hannes says with a small sigh. "Before your new life starts."

"Precisely." Nils nods. "Exactly."

"Don't you think there'll be a bunch of schoolkids running around in the woods tonight? Celebrating the beginning of summer vacation?"

"Not in the woods," Nils says, shaking his head. "They hang out down by the Strand Café. That's where they try to drink themselves unconscious, the sweet little dears."

"Mmm."

At exactly the same time, an overwhelming sense of exhaustion washes over both of the young men at the café table. Like a club hitting them in the head, the exhaustion strikes, the sleepless night catches up with them and they look at each other, yawn, and grin sleepily.

"Home to bed," Hannes confirms.

"Wish I could too," Nils says yawning. "But I promised Kristina, my sister, I promised I'd go to her elementary school graduation."

Hannes stands up and nods. "Give your little sister a kiss from me."

"Not on your life," Nils says, yawning.

And Hannes shuffles out of the café while Nils remains seated.

"See you tonight!" he calls after Hannes, who waves in response without turning around.

After Hannes has disappeared, Nils gets up too, but just to go to the bathroom. He stands in front of the cracked mirror in there for a while. He leans heavily against the washbasin and looks at his face.

"Tonight you'll be buried, old man," he tells his reflection. "Shit, you look like you've already been buried. Deep down, for a long time. And I don't even have time to go home, have to head straight to the school for Pomp & Circumstance."

He turns the tap on so that cold water is pouring out and he splashes his face again and again. Then he takes some paper towels, dries himself off, and looks at himself in the mirror again. A little better, still not good but a little better.

Nils walks straight to his table, picks up his coffee cup, gets himself a refill, and sits back down again. There's a half hour left until the graduation ceremony.

He pulls a wrinkled piece of paper out of his back pocket. He smoothes it out, tries in vain to flatten it, and lays it on the table in front of him. This is the result of the night's discussions with Hannes. At least, the result of the discussions that had to do with Nils's burial, which will take place tonight with Hannes's help.

There are only a few words on the piece of paper. If you saw it without knowing what it referred to, you'd think it was a shopping list or maybe a list of equipment for someone who was going to go on a little expedition.

The words on the list are:

Raingear
Boots?
Facemask
Snorkel ***SAWED OFF!
Gloves
Shovel
Hat?

Nils sits and stares at the little slip of paper for half an hour, then gets up to go to his little sister's graduation.

Tonight I will be buried, he thinks. But tomorrow I will rise again.

Tomorrow the summer will begin. Tomorrow my new life will begin.

Tomorrow.

Anon

Graduation.

It's a bright sunny day, and a mild summer breeze stretches the Swedish flag out against a completely blue sky. Grouped by class, all the students are standing out on the playground, the teachers are wearing nice clothes and are unusually well groomed, and lots of parents are there.

Graduation, an old-fashioned graduation the way it's always been.

First there's singing. Each class has been working on a song, and now the first graders and the second graders and the third graders and the fourth graders and the fifth graders have all sung, and they sang "Ida's Summer Song" by Astrid Lindgren and a song about nature and one about how short summer is and two songs that Anon has never heard before, and now it's the sixth graders' turn to go up and sing their song. On the way up to the flagpole Anon feels someone take hold of his arm. He turns around.

It's Henke, who whispers, "My dad is super pissed. Thanks for not saying anything. You're all right, man."

Henke pats Anon's arm and then everyone in the class takes their positions, ready to sing. Anon wonders what Henke meant. He doesn't understand. Why is he all right? He doesn't get what he did or didn't do …

"Is everyone ready?" the teacher whispers, looking around at all the students to make sure she has everyone's attention. "Let's sing. Let's do our best! One, two, three …"

And the sixth graders sing. A very difficult song in three-quarter time that has some high notes, a new song that the music teacher has been practicing and practicing with them, and now everyone chimes in: "... songs are delicious, singing tastes so good ..."

But Anon isn't chiming in, he's just moving his lips and looking around. Elementary school is over, he thinks. I've been with these kids for six years. And I went to preschool with most of them too.

There's Ida, she seems like she's sulking today, must be something from the class party yesterday, she looks like a lemon. And Stoffe seemed annoyed too when he came to school this morning; he made a face at Anon *and* a nasty gesture with one finger. But Kristina was perky and happy and a little rosy in the cheeks. She sat close to Henke. Anon thought it almost looked like they were holding hands. And Henke, well, he thought Anon was "all right." Strange.

But where's Magdalena? Anon stretches out his neck, leans forward, looks around, ah, there she is, all the way up in the front, she's standing there singing wholeheartedly. Anon hasn't talked to her today, but she flashed him a cheerful smile as they stood there listening to the other classes sing. Maybe she wants to ...

"Psst, Anon ..."

Anon looks up. The teacher is whispering at him.

"Anon, we're done now ..."

The whole class is walking back toward their seats; only Anon and Miss Larsson are still standing next to the flagpole in the middle of the playground. She looks so pretty today, the teacher does. Her hair is so nice, she's wearing a little wreath of flowers in her hair and a bright, sky-blue dress. She looks happy too, almost a little ecstatic.

Anon nods and follows her, and right as he catches up with the class and is even with the others a laugh comes from the fifth graders. It's because someone whispered to someone else, "Good thing you have galoshes on today, Piss Anon, since the weather's so bad."

Neither the teacher nor Anon, nor anyone in Anon's class, heard the whisper.

After the principal gives a speech all the students head back to their classrooms, and by the time all the parents and students manage to squeeze in it's crowded and chaotic in there. People give the teacher flowers and a present that everyone in class chipped in for, and the teacher opens the package and pulls out a bowl with a wooden lid and everyone can see her eyes are a little misty as she holds the bowl up as if it were a trophy she'd won in some competition.

"Oh, how nice!" she says. "Thank you! I'll keep my home-made rosehip jam in this, and every time I use some jam I'll think of you guys."

"So you don't like rosehip jam that much, right?" Henke says, laughing. "You don't eat it very often, do you?"

All of the parents laugh, finding Henke's quip amusing, and the teacher beams at him and says, "Actually I do, Henrik, I'm very fond of rosehip jam. Very, very, very fond …"

The teacher gives just a short speech, and she says that she'll miss the class, and then everyone has to go up to her desk one by one and say goodbye to her, and some of them have little bouquets of flowers and some have little presents, and the girls hug her and the boys shake her hand, but when it's Anon's turn he just stands there in front of Miss Larsson.

"Goodbye, Anon," Miss Larsson says. "I hope you have a good summer vacation and …"

"Goodbye, Miss Larsson," Anon says, but he doesn't take the hand she's holding out to him.

The room goes quiet, all the fidgeting and chatting and murmuring stops, everyone looks at Anon and the teacher up at the front of the room. But Anon doesn't notice, he keeps looking into Miss Larsson's eyes, he sees how a single tear slowly runs down her cheek, and yet her eyes aren't sad, no, they're something else, something Anon doesn't understand.

He wrinkles his brow and whispers so softly that only Miss Larsson can hear, "Why are you crying?"

But she doesn't respond, just keeps her eyes on Anon without looking away, and shakes her head almost imperceptibly.

"Do I get a hug?" she whispers.

Anon nods and takes a step forward toward his teacher and hugs her for a long time, hugs her tight, and his teacher is soft and smells good and Anon can feel one of her breasts against his arm.

Yes, Anon and the teacher stand there hugging until Henke yells "Yes, yes, yes" and starts making cat calls, and then several people laugh and some start applauding.

And then it's over, then it's time for the sixth graders to leave their classroom for the last time, but then there's a bunch of noise and commotion again, because all the parents want to talk to the teacher and thank her and wish her a pleasant summer, and a lot of the parents want to take a picture of their child with the teacher, so she has to sit for a photo shoot and shake hands and smile and chat politely to people on her right and on her left. And there's a bit of jostling and confusion in the classroom.

But Mother isn't at all interested in taking a picture of Anon with his teacher, so they're the first to leave the classroom and make their way out onto the playground.

"So," Mother says, stopping in front of Anon, "are we ready to go? Are we finished with this school now?"

Anon looks around and reflects for a moment. Mmm, I guess it's over now. Mmm, I guess there's nothing else to do here. Maybe say hi to Magdalena, but ... nah, I guess I don't need to do that.

"Mmm," Anon says. "I'm ready."

But Anon and Mother have taken only a few steps across the playground when someone opens the door of the cloakroom behind them.

"Hello? Hello? Wait a sec!" a deep, firm voice calls.

Mother and Anon stop and turn around. The voice belongs to Henke's father. Now he hurries to catch up to them, almost jogging. His tie flutters in the summer breeze, his beer gut flops back and forth over his belt, and his face is flushed.

"Just a sec!" he says, stopping in front of Mother. "Don't go sneaking off now. There's a couple of things we have to clear up first."

Anon looks at Mother, he sees how she stiffens, how she pulls up her shoulders, how her eyes narrow, and how her stern glare makes Henke's dad take a stumbling step backward.

"Is that so?" Mother says.

Her voice is like ice.

"Um, yes," Henke's dad says. "Something happened at the class party at our house last night and we need to clear it up. Now. Right now."

And then he explains. He describes the ugly, greasy stains on the wallpaper in his and his wife's bedroom, and he uses words like "behavior" and "reprehensible" and "normal" and "responsibility." And he talks about costs and reimbursement.

Mother listens without interrupting or asking any questions, and when Henke's father finishes she stands there looking at him with an icy, scornful expression for a long time.

"Anon and Magdalena?" she says finally.

Henke's father nods. "There's no doubt about it. We caught them in the act, so to speak—"

"Nonsense. Baloney," Mother interrupts.

"Now let's just try to calm down a bit, why don't we?" Henke's father says. "And get to the bottom of this. Together."

Anon squats down. Telling Mother to "calm down a bit" is certainly about one of the dumbest things a fat old man with sweat stains in his armpits could do in his position; it's like pressing the red button, and Anon squats down and waits for the explosion.

But it doesn't happen because Magdalena's mother gets there first. She comes up to them and addresses Mother right away.

"Has he told you what happened?" she asks, nodding toward Henke's father. As if he weren't standing right there next to them.

Mother nods, and soon the women have decided that they have to see how the bedroom looks with their own eyes, and

Magdalena's mother says that Mother and Anon can ride in her car, and they walk to the parking lot together while Henke's father yells after them, "Yes, all right then, we'll see you at our place in ten minutes!"

As if he'd played some part in their decision.

Magdalena is already sitting in the back seat when Anon climbs into the car.

"Hi."

"Hi."

No twinkle in Magdalena's eyes now and her face is paler than usual, but she doesn't seem remorseful or concerned. No, more angry, Anon thinks.

After she takes her seat behind the wheel, Magdalena's mom doesn't start the car. She turns around to face the children in the back seat instead.

"Now," she says. "Let's hear it. Tell us exactly what happened."

Mother turns around too, and Magdalena starts to tell the whole story.

As the words bubble out of Magdalena, Anon starts to understand why Henke thought he was "all right." Because Magdalena isn't all right. She describes everything, she describes the games and the spiked punch and Stoffe and the play, and she's forced to explain about the Pissman, too, which her mother had never heard about, and she explains how she and Anon ended up in the bedroom.

She describes it exactly the way it was, exactly how it happened, although Anon thinks it sounds a little exaggerated. Like he was being picked on. I mean, it wasn't really that big a deal, was it? It wasn't that big a deal at all.

But their mothers think it was. When Magdalena finishes explaining, they look at each other somberly.

"That is just completely fu—" Magdalena's mother says, swallowing the swear word.

"Mmm," Mother agrees.

"Well, let's just drive on over there to that chubby old bastard's house and look at his bedroom wallpaper," Magdalena's mother says, turning the key in the ignition. "And then we'll give him a piece of our minds."

The gravel flies under the wheels as she pulls out of the school parking lot, and two mothers with their cute little well-dressed first graders in tow glare angrily at the car.

"My mom is really mad," Magdalena whispers.

"Mine too," Anon whispers.

"My mom's like a tiger when she's mad," Magdalena whispers.

"Mine's like a lion," Anon whispers. "An angry lion."

Henke's father is pacing back and forth in his house. When the doorbell rings, he opens the door, not realizing that he's letting an enraged tigress and a furious lioness into his house.

Nope, when he lets those two women and their children in he still thinks he's the angry one, the one who's been wronged, that here come two mothers ready to take parental responsibility, ashamed at being forced to acknowledge their children's guilt and ready to apologetically reimburse him for the damage they caused.

"Right, now let's see if we can just clear all this up," he says with a hint of an awkward smile.

Not a word, barely a glance does he receive in response.

Henke's mother is there too. She's standing just behind her husband.

"It's just dreadfully sad, all of this," she says. "When we came home last night we could hardly believe our—"

"Where's the bedroom?" Mother interrupts and Henke's mother stops talking and looks at her husband.

"This way," Henke's father says, leading the way.

Anon looks around. There's no sign of Henke anywhere. And there's no trace of yesterday's party. The house is spick-and-span. As if nothing had happened. Anon thinks of something that makes him shake his head and then follows the others to the bedroom.

When he goes in, the room is full and very quiet. Four grown-up backs and one narrow little-girl back block Anon's view of the footprints on the walls, but he notices something else. He can tell something from Mother's back and also from Magdalena's mother's back: Both mothers are very close to bursting out laughing. Anon can see from their backs how they're struggling to suppress it, and he can see how they're avoiding looking at each other. It's completely silent, and everyone is standing still.

"Sooo," Henke's father says at last, sighing, "here's …"

"Let's see," Magdalena's mother interrupts, turning around. "Was it this?"

She takes a couple of steps over to the little table next to Anon and picks up the bottle of apricot body lotion. When her mother holds it up, Magdalena nods. Magdalena's mother squirts out a little dab and rubs it thoroughly into her hands. When she's done, she smells her right hand and then holds it out to Mother.

"Do you use this stuff?"

Mother sniffs it and makes a face. "It smells like a health-food store," she snorts. "No, I prefer Nivea. What about you?"

"I don't really have trouble with dry skin," Magdalena's mother responds. "But my husband once bought me a bottle at the duty-free store. My ex-husband, that is. It smelled like rancid coconuts. Even worse than this stuff."

Magdalena turns around and gives Anon a look. He nods. Yes, the mothers are putting on a show now. Playing the kind of game ferocious, self-confident predators play. The two women understand each other remarkably well. They just met, they don't know each other, and nonetheless they're putting on quite a show together.

Henke's father, on the other hand, has no idea what's going on. His face is beet red with rage.

"It's time you ladies quit fooling around and listen up," he says, his voice almost sputtering. "We just put this brand-new wallpaper up a few months ago, and—"

"You ladies?" Mother hisses. "Well …"

"Actually you're the ones who should be explaining …" Magdalena's mother begins.

"… just what went on in this house last night," Mother finishes.

But she doesn't explode, and Magdalena's mother doesn't either. No, they speak calmly and patiently, their anger hidden behind a profound seriousness as they take turns repeating what Magdalena told them about the party last night.

Soon Anon stops listening. He forces his way through the crowd to the bed and starts studying the imprints from last night's adventure on the walls. Because it *was* an adventure, a small one, but an adventure nonetheless.

The footprints have darkened; greasy dark brown prints practically cover the walls around the bed. Anon remembers. He remembers every single one. And he remembers what their titles are. When he sees a print where his big toe exactly touches Magdalena's big toe, a little feeling of warmth and pleasure tingles through his body.

Behind him the mothers' voices have grown increasingly heated, and occasional phrases find their way to Anon's ears: "Minors drinking alcohol," "Bullying, if you even know what that word means," "Mob mentality, trapped in the bedroom by your precious son and his buddies …"

Anon feels a soft hand on his shoulder and turns around.

"Maybe we should go wait in the car," Magdalena whispers.

Anon nods and follows her. In the doorway he stops and looks over his shoulder. A lion and a tiger versus an old fat guy and his timid wife—it can end only one way. With the predators going in for the kill. There'll be only a few bones left, with all the flesh gnawed off them.

"I think they looked great," Anon says after he and Magdalena have been sitting next to each other in silence in the back seat for a bit. "I almost think they looked better today. I'd like to have some over my bed too."

Magdalena tries to figure out if he's serious. It seems like he is.

"I mean yours too," Anon continues. "Your feet too. Would you … would you like to?"

"Mmm." Magdalena nods.

"It would work with Nivea too, wouldn't it?" Anon says. "Don't you think?"

Magdalena giggles and nods in assent. A slightly hesitant giggle and a slightly hesitant nod. She seems a little distracted, Magdalena.

Then they sit there in silence. Magdalena looks at Anon; he's staring straight ahead and seems to be lost in some dream. After a while she carefully pokes his arm.

"Hey, you?"

"Hmm," Anon says, turning to look at her.

"I want some too," Magdalena whispers. "Will you come over to my place and help me?"

"Sure. I can bring Mother's Nivea too," Anon says.

Then Magdalena smiles.

Then Magdalena smiles so beautifully that Anon forgets everything else in the world.

Now the mothers come out. The mothers jump into the front seats and slam the doors so that the car sways. The mothers look at each other and burst into roars of laughter.

The mothers laugh for a long time in the front seat. In the back seat Anon and Magdalena watch each other, they shrug their shoulders and let the mothers laugh until they're done. It's Mother who quiets down first. All of a sudden she gets quiet and gets a sad, serious look in her eyes and looks at Anon.

"I didn't know that things were like this ... Why didn't you tell me?"

"Oh, things really haven't been that bad," Anon says. "It wasn't that bad. It was nothing. Just Stoffe carrying on a little bit. Not Henke. Henke's actually ... all right."

Did you learn a new word today, Anon?

Mother looks at Anon questioningly for a long while, but

finally her seriousness gives way to a warm smile. "Footprints on the wall … What were you thinking, the two of you …"

Magdalena's mother turns around too. Her eyes are full of mischief and she's laughing like a schoolgirl. "You should have seen him in there … heeheehee …"

"What did you say?" Magdalena wonders.

The women look at each other and take turns explaining what happened.

"We talked about filing a police report … minors drinking alcohol … the parents' responsibility … that we were going to talk to the school … what's actually been going on in this class … who's to blame … who's responsible … and …"

"And finally we started talking about calling the newspapers," Mother said. "Henrik's poor mother was close to fainting as she pictured the headlines: 12-YEAR-OLDS INVOLVED IN LIQUOR AND SEX ORGY. In her home …"

"Then we left."

"Yup, then we left."

"Are you going to do all that?!" Magdalena asks, shocked. "I mean the stuff about the police and the school and the newspapers?!"

She looks at her mother. Her mother looks at Mother. Mother looks at Anon. Anon shakes his head. Mother turns back toward Magdalena's mother and shakes her head. Magdalena's mother looks at Magdalena and shakes her head.

"Nah."

Anon is astonished. That Magdalena's mother has a Magdalena inside her, he already discovered that in the car last night, but Mother hardly ever gets all girly and giggly like this. Giddy, really. Now she and Magdalena's mother are laughing together for the third time. She's laughing right out loud because she can't help it.

The mothers have turned into happy children. When they're finally done laughing and they've turned back into mothers again, one of them says, "Now let's go have some dessert!"

"Yes, now we'll go have some dessert. And celebrate the start of summer vacation!"

This is how mothers should be. This is how mothers should talk.

So the four of them end up sitting outside at Hansen's Café, they sit there in the shade under an umbrella with a pastry and a cup of coffee or a soda, and the mothers start speaking mother-speak again to each other, and Magdalena turns toward Anon.

"Do you see who's sitting over there?" she says, pointing.

Anon nods. Sure enough, Kristina and her mom and her big brother are sitting over there at another table. Kristina's big brother's face is completely white, it looks like he was up all night partying.

Magdalena stands up and waves, and soon Kristina notices her and comes running over. They step away from the table and start talking excitedly. Kristina is still happy and bubbling over and bursting with things to say, but then Magdalena starts talking and then Kristina settles down and listens, and she turns and looks over at Anon and looks concerned and asks Magdalena concerned questions. The girls stand there talking for a long time, then come back over to the table together.

"Well, hello there, Kristina," Magdalena's mother says. "Are you here too?"

She looks around, spots Kristina's mother, and waves.

"Mmm, but we're going home now, because Oskar, my other big brother, is finishing ninth grade today and we're going to have a little party and …"

And there's a bit of small talk and everyone says "Have a good summer" and then Kristina turns toward Anon and says, "Bye, Anon."

That's what the others hear. "Bye, Anon." But Anon hears more than that. He looks at Kristina and hears her say "I'm sorry." She says it without words, but he hears her loud and clear.

And Anon responds, "You don't have to apologize." He answers without words, and he sees that Kristina hears his response, and he sees that it makes her happy. Relieved. As if she'd been worried.

No one else hears their wordless conversation, no one else hears Anon say anything besides "Bye, Kristina."

And Magdalena and Kristina hug each other and say "See you, see you" and then Kristina runs off.

Why did she apologize? Anon wonders. She didn't do anything to me, did she?

Two mothers who had basically never spoken to each other before are like sisters after this morning's adventure, and now they're saying "We'll have to get together" and "You have our phone number" and "I'm sure we'll find something to do together this summer."

Anon looks at Magdalena. She has powdered sugar on her lips.

"Tomorrow," she says. "I'd like to do something with you tomorrow."

"Sure." Anon nods.

"Not the thing we talked about in the car, though," Magdalena says. "Something else."

"Sure," Anon says. "But …"

"Yeah?"

"There's one other thing I have to do tomorrow too," Anon says, nodding to himself. "I'll do that first. Then I'll do something with you after."

"Is it a secret? The other thing you have to do?" Magdalena wonders.

Anon contemplates it. Telling Magdalena about Sara isn't a good idea, or at least he suspects it isn't. And it would take a long time to explain.

"Yeah, it's a secret," he confirms. "Or … I'll tell you about it later. Another time. Afterward."

"OK." Magdalena nods and doesn't seem concerned about it.

No, Anon hasn't forgotten about Sara, even if several hours have gone by now without his having thought about her. But Sara isn't as real anymore. And maybe Anon has started to understand, maybe he's understood for a long time: the real Sara Enoksson might not be like the Sara Enoksson he sees in his dreams. But she still needs to get her wallet back, of course, and her library card.

Anon will go see Sara tomorrow. First he'll go see Sara and give her her wallet back, and then he'll do something with Magdalena.

Tomorrow.

Zarah

There is a wooded area. East of the city, where no new neighborhoods have sprung up past the old houses, that's where the woods begin.

The woods begin with a sign, a sign with a big map that shows how the blue, white, and yellow trails wind their way through the woods and explains how long each trail is. All the trails start at the sign by the parking lot, and all the trails end up back there again.

The woods are big enough to get lost in—if you really try and if you choose not to stay on the marked trails—but they're hardly big enough for you to stay lost in. If you keep walking, sooner or later you'll find your way out again.

It's late now, almost the middle of the night, and Zarah and Victor are taking a walk in the woods. Even though it's the first night of summer vacation, the woods are quiet and deserted. The kids and teenagers who are celebrating the end of the school year are celebrating down by the waterfront, down by the Strand Café, just like someone mentioned. Some are celebrating by trying to drink themselves unconscious, just like someone mentioned.

Zarah was the one who wanted to go for a walk. Zarah was the one who said that she needed to get out, and Victor said sure, why not, he'd go with her.

They're taking the yellow trail, following the yellow markers posted on trees and rocks, and they've come quite a way into the woods. Victor is talking, he's talking about his plans and ideas, but Zarah only gives him brief responses. She's not really there.

Zarah's thinking about Mia. She's been thinking about Mia almost nonstop since they parted ways on the day Zarah quit working at the daycare center. So many feelings well up inside her when Zarah thinks about Mia, there's sadness and anger and disappointment and guilt and regret, and the feelings fight each other and push and shove each other out of the way and get all mixed up, and Zarah can't find any way to sort out her feelings or to move on. Everything's at a standstill. Everything's at an impasse.

So Victor is talking and Zarah is thinking and trying to respond "Mmm" and "Nah" and "Yeah" in the right places and they're walking side by side until Zarah stops and says, "I have to pee."

"Would you like me to help?" Victor offers, grinning at her.

"No thanks," Zarah says, taking a few steps out into the autumn leaves next to the trail.

She stops there and starts unbuttoning her pants.

"What, are you going to stand there gawking at me?"

"I like to watch you pull down your pants," Victor says, grinning.

Zarah sighs, she pulls her jeans down to her knees, then her underwear.

"Satisfied?"

Victor nods.

"Now turn around so I can pee in peace," Zarah says, and Victor obeys and looks the other way while Zarah squats down.

There's a rustling in the leaves as she pees, and she squats there for a moment contemplating the little rivulet of pee flowing out between her feet, then she gives her rear end a shake, stands up, and pulls her pants up again.

"I had an idea," Victor says when Zarah joins him back on the trail.

When Victor puts his hand on Zarah's hip and pulls her to him, she understands right away what his idea is. She senses it in the weight of his hand and in the small movements his fingers make against her hipbone.

Zarah knows what Victor wants, and she starts searching for her own desire. She rarely, maybe never, has to search. Victor usually lures it out effortlessly; if he just lifts an eyebrow or wiggles his little finger, then Zarah's ready and willing to play love games with him.

But right now Zarah hesitates. Does she want to? She concentrates and discovers to her surprise that she doesn't care one way or the other. But maybe it's a good idea, maybe it'll help her get her mind off Mia for a bit.

Therapeutic outdoor intercourse, sure, why not, Zarah thinks, and smiles at her thought.

"OK," she says, pulling Victor by the hand. "But we can't do it here in the middle of the yellow trail. Come on."

Zarah and Victor wander, hand in hand, through the rustling leaves still on the ground from last fall, between large boulders, up a little knoll. Zarah is slightly in front, she pulls Victor along as if she were showing him the way, as if she knew where they were going. They pass a dense grove of spruce trees and come out into a clearing where a large rock is surrounded by tall, straight pine trees.

"Shhh," Zarah says, stopping abruptly. Victor stops next to her.

"What is it?" he whispers after a minute.

"I thought I heard something," Zarah says. She stands there completely motionless for another minute, listening. "Oh well, I'm sure it was just an animal."

"What, are you afraid the animal is going to watch us?" Victor laughs.

Zarah doesn't respond, just goes over and stands in the middle of the little clearing, stands there as if she were standing on a stage and the full, yellow summer moon is a spotlight shining on her from the ink-black sky.

"Here," she says, doing a pirouette. "Right here."

Victor comes over to her.

Like animals, Zarah thinks. Like the other animals. A hen and a rooster.

She's on all fours, her jeans and her underwear are lying where she flung them in the grass next to her. Victor is on his knees behind her, his hands on her hips, his warm thighs against her naked bottom, and Zarah feels his rhythm as he slowly moves inside her, and the full moon shines down on them, but Zarah isn't really there.

This is the first time, she thinks. The first time with Victor when there wasn't any lust, when the desire didn't come and carry her away. She's never had a better guy, never one so hard and so soft. He's a careful lover. He knows how to play this game and it's never been so delightful to play the game as it has with Victor. And now he's inside her, behind her, he's moving inside her, but Zarah isn't really there. Not now. Not this time. She moves, she follows him, but she isn't there.

Zarah's mind is racing. The thoughts are whirling around in her head at a speed of ten thoughts per second, here and there, every which way. Now Zarah remembers a poem she wrote this one time in ninth grade when they were studying literature and they had a substitute and they were supposed to write a poem about love. And the substitute was young and new and cute and he would get these reddish splotches on his neck and Zarah already knew quite a bit about love, about both kinds of love, and she noticed that her glances and her smile could make the young substitute's neck even redder, and she called him over to her seat and showed him the poem she'd written:

About Love

In out in out
spurt squirt
fun's done

And she smiled seductively at the pale substitute, and he stammered something about there being different kinds of love and turned away from her.

Zarah had to bite her lip to keep herself from starting to giggle at the memory of her love poem. And behind her, in her, Victor's moving a little faster now, he feels her, they feel each other, he knows that he can't bring her along this time, he moves faster, he's almost there.

That's when Zarah sees it.

A little way in front of her, just two yards or so, a short blue plastic tube is sticking up out of the ground.

Zarah is on her hands and knees. Behind her and in her Victor is moving even faster now, and two yards in front of Zarah's nose a bright blue plastic tube is sticking up out of the leaves.

And it looks weird. It looks wrong. What the heck is it? It almost looks like a snorkel, like the one she used when she was in Greece with her dad one hot summer a long time ago, swimming in the warm water where fish sparkled and shimmered like jewels in a dream.

Zarah stares at the plastic tube and tries to keep up with Victor. He's not making much noise, he's a quiet lover, and that's nice, Zarah thinks. She's been with guys who groaned and panted like an old-fashioned locomotive, who thought you were supposed to do that to show that you were enjoying it; boys who had learned how to make love from watching porn on cable TV.

Victor is a quiet, attentive lover. Just a little "mmmm" and then he's finished, still inside her behind her back. But Zarah pulls away from him and slides down to the ground.

"What is it?" Victor whispers, dropping down onto the grass next to her.

Zarah just shakes her head, puts her hand on the nape of Victor's neck, and pulls him toward her.

"Lie here for a minute," she asks. "Lie here with me."

Zarah, naked from the waist down, lying in a clearing in the woods on her back in the tall grass, stroking the back of Victor's head and kissing his forehead. Victor rests there in her embrace and Zarah looks at the moon up above them and hums softly: "How happy you must be, O you moon so bright, to hang in the heavens in the black of night, detached and aloof in your lofty lair …"

It would be like this, Zarah dreams: I would marry some fat, pasty, rich old geezer and live on a lovely estate, and maybe Victor could be my secret lover, my Whistling Gypsy, Black Jack Davy. And we would sneak off and make love in the woods and someday … That's how it would be. In an old folk song. Or on a TV show.

Victor, my highwayman, Zarah thinks, chuckling.

"What's so funny?" Victor whispers, lifting his head.

"Time to get a move on," Zarah says, pushing him away. "My butt's getting cold."

"Hmm, you do seem to have been caught with your pants down," Victor says. "But you know what they say, don't sweat the petty things and don't pet the sweaty things."

He learned that one from Zarah.

They get up and Zarah puts on her pants, and just as they're about to leave the moonlit clearing and go back to the trail, Zarah remembers something and turns around.

"Wait a sec."

The plastic tube. What is it? But wait …

"What is it?" Victor asks when Zarah suddenly freezes.

"Shhhhh," Zarah whispers, training her eyes on the tube. It's moving! The tube is moving. Up and down, a little bit. A little side to side. And it's completely still in the woods, not a breath of wind. That being the case, a blue plastic tube sticking up out of the ground shouldn't be moving.

Now Zarah starts thinking about other TV shows she's seen. The ones about supernatural and extraterrestrial phenomena. But then she swallows and takes Victor's hand.

"Come," she whispers, starting to walk toward the tube.

"Help! Can someone help me? Is there anyone there? Help! Help!"

A voice from somewhere behind Zarah and Victor makes them jump.

"Help! Come help me!"

Victor and Zarah exchange glances, then without a word they start running hand in hand toward the voice.

Nils

El Amor y la Muerte
Cuando te encuentras con el uno,
siempre está el otro muy cerca
Más cerca de lo que te imaginas
El Amor nunca deja a la Muerte
La Muerte nunca deja al Amor
El Amor y la Muerte
Son compañeros eternos.
—from *La Búsqueda*

"Help! Can someone help me? Is there anyone there? Help! Help!"

He yells as he stumbles through the underbrush. The tears are making it hard to see. A few branches whip him in the face and he feels a burning pain from his right cheek, but he doesn't have time to stop, he has to keep going. Away. Away from here.

"Help! Come help me!"

At dusk, in the blue light of twilight, Nils and Hannes had met at the sign at the trailhead by the edge of the woods. Hannes was standing there in the parking lot waiting when Nils came barreling in on his bicycle. He skidded to a stop, tossed his bike in the ditch, and handed Hannes a shovel.

"Here."

Nils was holding a brown paper bag in his hand.

"Come on," he continued, setting out. "We're taking the yellow trail. I know a place."

They walked quite a way down the yellow trail, keeping very quiet as they walked. Hannes walked with the shovel over his shoulder. After a while he started singing: "Hi ho, hi ho, it's home from work we go ..."

But he stopped singing when Nils stopped walking and pointed. "Here. We enter the woods here. Over there. Behind that grove of spruce trees. Over there."

So they left the trail and trudged through the leaves, between the boulders, up a little knoll, past the dense grove of spruce trees, and came out into a clearing. A moonlit clearing surrounded by straight, tall pine trees.

Nils walked over and stood next to a large rock, pointed at the ground, and said, "Here. I want to be buried here. This will be my resting place."

And Hannes nodded and walked over to him.

"As you wish, Master," Hannes said with a sigh, setting the shovel down on the ground. "Lie down so I can measure, so I don't dig it too long. Or too wide."

And Nils lay down on his back on the ground and Hannes marked how long and how wide his grave should be.

"That's good," Hannes said.

Then Hannes started digging. First he sliced out the sod in clumps and set them carefully aside, then he dug down into the loose, sandy soil. After twenty minutes of laboring in silence, he stuck the shovel into the pile of dirt that had grown up next to him.

"Your turn. I think we still need to dig down a little more. It's not that hard. Just a lot of roots."

And Nils got up from where he'd been sitting, leaning comfortably against the rock, watching Hannes. "All right," he said, picking up the shovel and taking over digging.

"If it takes two men forty minutes to dig a grave, how long will it take three men to dig a grave?"

"What?"

Nils stopped digging; he straightened his back, wiped the sweat off his brow, and turned to face Hannes.

"What are you talking about?"

"I'm just sitting here coming up with math problems, that's all. Thought it might energize you," Hannes said, grinning at Nils.

"Twenty-six and two-thirds," Nils said. "In other words, twenty-six minutes and forty seconds. If there were three of us. But now there's only two of us. And I think we're ready. Come and check."

So Hannes got up and walked over to Nils, stood next to him, and stared down into the shallow grave. It was about two feet deep.

"It's your call," Hannes said, shrugging his shoulders. "Maybe you should give it a test run?"

Then Nils decided he might as well change, and he put on the raingear and the boots, fished the facemask out of the bag, and put it on after carefully cleaning the glass lens. He handed Hannes the earplugs and the sawed-off snorkel.

"Leave my head for last."

Hannes nodded, took the earplugs and snorkel, and looked at Nils seriously.

It was the middle of the night. The moon was bright. Two young men were standing out in the woods, one wearing raingear and a facemask. The other one was about to bury him in the ground. Cover him with dirt. Bury him alive.

Maybe I should think this is stupid, Hannes thought. Maybe I should be laughing. We must look ridiculous. But Hannes couldn't laugh, couldn't even smile. Instead he felt ill at ease, and the pale moonlight made him shiver.

Maybe I should refuse, Hannes thought. Maybe I should say, "What the fuck are we doing here?" and just walk away. No, I can't do that. Hannes looked at Nils. The glass in his facemask had started to steam up and he could hardly make out Nils's eyes.

"Quit breathing through your nose, you idiot!" Hannes said, feeling a surge of affection. He put his hand on Nils's shoulder. "Play dead. Simon says: Play dead. Good doggy."

Hannes smiled, but his eyes were serious.

"In you go," he continued. "I'll watch over you. In you go, let's get this over with."

Nils took up almost the entire grave; it didn't take long for Hannes to fill it up with dirt and then lay the blocks of sod back down on top. He covered Nils with dirt and sod all the way up to his chin, then he ran and got an armful of leaves that he spread over the grave, and he looked pleased when he surveyed his work.

"It doesn't show. From up here you can't tell that you're down there. Once we've covered your face too, it won't show at all."

Nils lay there quietly. He stared straight up at the night sky.

Was it the moonlight that made his face so pale and tinged with blue?

"Can you get up?" Hannes asked.

Nils tried. No, there was no way; he couldn't budge his arms or legs even an inch. There was no way he'd be able to get out of the grave on his own. He shook his head.

"Are you ready?" Hannes asked.

A face partially covered by a facemask was all he could see of his friend, and now Nils's lips moved for the first time and he whispered in a dull voice, "Yes. I'm ready."

"I'll wait here the whole time," Hannes said quickly, dropping down onto his knees next to Nils. "After two hours I'll dig you up. If you want me to get you up before then, make a sound through the snorkel. Three times. I'll put the snorkel in your mouth so you can practice."

Carefully he placed the snorkel between Nils's lips.

Nils droned, "Unnnh unnnh unnnh."

His voice sounded like a small, childish ghost voice through the snorkel. He spat it out.

"Bury me now," he said. "Cover me up."

He was a little impatient. Everything had already been said, everything had already been settled. The plan was in place. The only thing left was to do it.

"OK." Hannes poked the earplugs into Nils's ears and put the sawed-off snorkel back between his lips, then he carefully filled the opening around Nils's head with dirt, he filled in the area over his head, above the facemask and around the snorkel, and finally he laid the last two pieces of sod down so that the snorkel stuck up between them by a couple of inches. He sprinkled more leaves on top to hide the seams and then got up and took a few steps back.

—

No one would be able to tell that someone was buried here. True, there was a mound of dirt left, the dirt that belonged in the space Nils was now occupying, but it looked just like a molehill. And the short blue plastic tube that stuck up there between the leaves was impossible to see if you didn't know it was there.

Hannes took a deep breath.

A tingle of little-boy excitement had made him forget his uneasy feeling for a while, but now it came back, and he shivered again.

Two hours. He looked at his watch.

He would sit here for two hours. Nils would lie buried underground for two hours, and then Hannes would dig him up again.

The woods were quiet. Everything was lit by moonlight.

Hannes felt himself trembling. Without letting the blue plastic tube out of his sight he took a few steps backwards. The rustle of the leaves echoed through the clearing. When Hannes felt the big rock behind his back he sank down and sat there leaning against it.

Last night they had sat together laughing and planning.

Last night this had been a Crazy Idea.

Last night this had been One of Nils's Crazy Ideas.

That's the difference with Nils, Hannes thought. There are so many people who talk big, so many who have big plans and wacky ideas. But Nils actually does them. He doesn't just talk about it, he does it.

And the moon shone over a silent clearing in woods, and Hannes sat leaning against a rock and staring at a blue plastic tube that was sticking out of the ground.

And down there in the earth, Nils lay buried.

Since Hannes had just looked at his watch he knew exactly how long he'd sat there before he heard the voices.

He had been leaning against the rock for twenty-five minutes. He'd just thought "Two hours is a long time," he'd thought "I should have brought a book," he'd thought "At least there's no chance I'll fall asleep," when he heard the voices.

Voices in the woods. Voices that were coming closer.

Hannes stayed completely still.

Shit, shit, shit, he thought.

Voices. A girl's voice and a guy's voice. Voices that were coming closer, voices that were heading right for him. And right for Nils. Footsteps in the woods.

Hannes swallowed and looked around.

He whispered to himself: Where should I go? Where should I hide? Can't leave Nils, no, no. But I can't be discovered. Over there maybe, in that dense grove of spruce trees, that way I can keep my eyes on Nils, from up there I'll still be able to hear it if Nils wants to come up …

On his tiptoes, as noiselessly as he possibly could, Hannes snuck in amongst the trees, up a little slope, and he lay down flat on his stomach behind a pile of twigs right where the dense spruce grove started.

The footsteps and the voices approached.

Carefully Hannes peeked out. He had a view of the whole clearing, he saw the short blue plastic tube sticking up out of the ground down there, and he could keep his eye on Nils. But who was coming? Who goes walking in the woods in the middle of the night? Who had left the yellow trail? Who seemed to be heading straight for him?

Hannes had to bite his lip. He wanted to scream, he had to press his right hand over his mouth so that no sound would escape. He whimpered, he swore softly to himself, his eyes wide, as he stared down at the moonlit stage and saw who appeared down there.

It was her.

The girl Nils had been following and pursuing for several weeks, after that meeting at the pub. His angel. His dream. It was her.

Now she was standing there, just a few feet from where Nils was buried. He couldn't see her or hear her. She was standing almost on top of him. Could he feel her steps through the earth, through the ground?

Why was she here?

She wasn't alone. No, now her boyfriend stepped into the scene too, her popular boyfriend, whose name was … No, Hannes couldn't remember, he'd heard the boyfriend's name that night in the pub but had forgotten it.

Now she was walking over to him.

Now she was kissing him.

Now she was unbuttoning her pants.

Through a veil of tears Hannes watched two people make love in the woods in the middle of the night, a young woman on all fours, a young man taking her from behind, it could have been two animals. It could have been a sex club too, Hannes could have been a horny old man, a spectator, but he didn't get excited now, he didn't get hard, a heavy sadness filled his eyes with tears but he couldn't look away, he forced himself to watch, because he had to watch over Nils and protect him, the snorkel was sticking up out of the ground only two yards in front of the girl's nose. Please, don't let her notice it.

God, you're quite the jokester, aren't you, Hannes thought.

Why did she have to come here tonight? Why right here? Why are you letting her have sex on Nils's grave?

God, you want to punish him, right? You want to punish him for playing around with death.

God, you're a bad playwright. And a miserable director.

Lucky for me I don't believe in you, God, Hannes thinks. How could anyone believe in someone who writes such atrocious soap operas?

Through a veil of tears Hannes watched the girl and her boyfriend rest in the grass after their sexual romp.

No, not so much of a romp, Hannes thought. Not that much lust either. More like habit. More … yeah, almost like an exhibition. Almost like a show in a sex club. But without the panting and moaning.

Now they're standing up. Now she's putting her pants on again. Good.

Hannes breathes a sigh of relief. The nightmare is over, now …

Wait! Wait, what's going on now?

She stopped. She's pointing.

She's discovered the snorkel!

She takes a step toward it.

At first, Hannes sits nightmare-still and nightmare-silent just staring. Then he manages to get up onto his feet, and as he takes a couple of stumbling steps away from the clearing he yells, "Help! Can someone help me? Is there anyone there? Help! Help!"

His voice is a crow's dry croak.

He yells again. He runs. Branches whip his face, tear open bleeding sores on his cheeks as he rushes through the dense woods, but he doesn't care, he has only one thought, a single idea in his head: I have to lure them away from the clearing, they can't discover Nils, I have to save him ...

"Help! Come and help!"

Hannes flings himself headlong at the ground. A little bit ahead of him he sees the path and the yellow trail, he rolls around in the leaves, lies there on his back, and yells as loudly as he can, "Help! Help! Help!"

It works. Almost immediately he hears the girl's anxious voice and her boyfriend trying to calm her down. And he hears rapid steps approaching.

"Help! Help!" Hannes yells, making his voice sound tormented.

And they hurry, and now they're there and now they're leaning over him and asking what happened and ...

What was I planning on saying? Hannes wonders. Why am I lying here in the middle of the woods yelling? What was my plan?

But with tears in his eyes and blood on his face it's quite easy for him to convince the girl and her boyfriend that he fell and broke something while he was out jogging. "In the middle of the night?" "Yeah, I have such a hard time sleeping in the summer." And he groans from the pretend pain as they pull him up and he hangs heavily between them with one arm around the girl and the other around Victor. Yes, Victor, that's the boyfriend's name, Hannes remembers when he hears the girl say the name. With one foot dragging on the ground, Hannes hops along the trail between his rescuers.

"What luck that you came along," he pants, smiling idiotically at Victor.

"Uh-huh," Victor mutters.

And they make their way along the yellow trail, slowly and painstakingly, bit by bit toward the parking lot.

In a moonlit clearing in the woods, a clearing surrounded by tall, straight pine trees, there's a sound. A sound that seems like it's coming from down under the earth. It seems to be coming out through a short blue plastic tube.

"Unnnh unnnh unnnh … unnnh unnnh unnnh … unnnh unnnh unnnh …"

A voice from the depths of the earth. A sound that no one hears.

"Soo …"

Victor lets Hannes lean against the sign. Victor straightens up, stretching his back; he has had to struggle to help the injured nighttime jogger get back here. His girlfriend doesn't seem anywhere near as tired.

"Now what?" she asks, looking at Hannes. "We should drive you to the hospital. So that someone can take a look at your foot."

"Um," Hannes says, searching for some clever split-second idea, "um, no, I'm sure that won't be necessary, I'm sure it was just a sprain and …"

"Of course we're driving you to the hospital. Aren't we, Victor?"

"Sure," Victor concedes.

But he doesn't exactly look thrilled.

But the girlfriend's will is stronger than the two young men's, so Hannes is stuffed into Victor's little white car, he gets to sit in the front seat, next to Victor, and he's driven to the hospital's emergency entrance, and there he's helped out of the car, and although he says he can handle it on his own from there, the girl helps him to the doors.

Right there, exactly then, Hannes looks for the first time right into the girl's eyes, and he's dazzled and is almost forced to take a step back. You are beautiful, Hannes thinks, looking at her face. I understand him. You are beautiful in a wonderfully old-fashioned way. So beautiful that it hurts.

"Thanks for all your help," Hannes says, swallowing.

And right then her name floats up to the surface.

"Sara?"

She nods, smiles, and marks her surprise by raising her eyebrows. "How'd you know that? Yes, my name is Zarah. Zarah with a Z. And an H at the end."

"A Z, I see." Hannes nods. "And an H at the end, I see."

A roguish little smile. A glance down at Zarah's rear end. Hannes thinks: An H at the end, yeah, right, an H for "hubba hubba," heh heh.

And Hannes basks in the smile Zarah gives him when she catches his glance and his flirtatious tone.

"Can you handle it on your own now?"

"Mmm. Thanks for all your help," Hannes says again.

Zarah walks back over to Victor, who's waiting in the car, and Hannes waves at them as they drive off.

Wow, it really got cold. And dark.

I understand him, Hannes thinks, feeling a stab of jealousy in his chest, right where his heart is. I understand him all too well. Sigh.

He's already forgotten that he watched Zarah and Victor engage in a real live sexual act right in front of his very eyes in the woods half an hour ago.

Hannes is jealous of Nils. Jealous of a feeling.

At the same time, in the woods.

In an empty clearing a weak sound can be heard.

"Unnnh ... unnh ... unh ... uh ..."

The sound fades away.

The sound seemed to be coming from the earth.

Anon

Mmm, how wonderful to lounge around in bed, half awake and half asleep. Anon is lying in his bed. He stretches and rolls over. Mmm, it's summer vacation now. This is the first morning I get to sleep in and after this morning there'll be a long series of lovely, luxurious mornings of lazing around and taking it easy.

Mmm, summer vacation means sleeping in.

Summer vacation means the alarm clock doesn't go off.

Summer vacation means late nights and long mornings between soft white sheets.

Faintly in the background, in the outskirts of his consciousness, Anon hears the faint murmur of Mother's voice. Now and then he hears a little laugh too. Maybe the phone ringing had woken Anon up, but that was a while ago. Mother must have been talking on the phone for a long time … Anon yawns widely and rolls over to face the wall. Who cares? It's his first morning of summer vacation, his first chance to sleep in, nothing else matters right now. Mmm.

"Up and at 'em, sleepyhead!"

Here comes Mother, like a whirlwind, into Anon's room. Swish, up go the blinds so that the sun blinds Anon when he turns over to see what's going on.

"Up and at 'em, you have a phone call!"

And she flips the soft, warm covers off Anon.

"Up and at 'em, someone really wants to talk to you!"

Anon rubs his eyes but keeps lying there flat on his back while Mother kisses him.

"Up and at 'em, hurry up, someone's waiting on the phone, someone who wants to make some summer plans with you!"

Magdalena, Anon thinks, swinging his legs over the edge of the bed. Magdalena's on the phone.

Magdalena is Anon's first thought. He yawns and stumbles out to the phone in the hall on wobbly legs that haven't had a chance to fully wake up yet.

"Hello! Hi—is that you?"

No, it's not Magdalena, it's not Magdalena's voice that meets Anon's ear when he picks up the receiver.

"Oh, yeah, I just forgot is all, or rather … Yeah, of course … Yes! … No … Of course I want to … Mmm … Good … I don't know, nothing much …"

Now Anon is quiet for a long stretch, he listens attentively to the voice in the receiver, someone is telling him something, occasionally Anon nods, occasionally he smiles a little, occasionally he says "Mmm," otherwise he just listens.

"Do you still have the old one, the red one?" Anon suddenly asks.

It seems as if he interrupts the voice in the receiver, and when he gets an answer he continues eagerly.

"I'd love to learn, is it hard? … Yeah … Sure … Great … No, I'm sure that's plenty. I don't know … Oh, I'm sure she can … Oh, she'll get used to it …"

Anon's face lights up with eager anticipation now, he paces back and forth in the hallway with the receiver pressed against his ear, he laughs, he chats and listens and gets all tangled up in the telephone cord.

"Wait a sec, I just have to untangle myself …"

Now the voice in the receiver is asking some questions. Anon answers, trying to explain:

"The feet, yeah … Mmm … No, that wasn't actually the idea. We were just going to compare our feet and … Magdalena, yes … And then they left prints because we'd put lotion on … With some kind of cream … And then we kept going because they were cool … No … No, exactly … Mmm … Mother talked to him … No, it wasn't anything much, nothing that bad … The whole class, yeah … Mmm, she's in my class … Later today …"

Mother comes in and stands in the hallway outside Anon's room. She leans against the doorframe and smiles at Anon when she hears what he's talking about. And now Anon's done talking. He says, "Bye-bye, I'll see you," and passes the phone to Mother.

"He wants to talk to you again, there was something you were going to arrange."

Mother takes the phone and talks a little about dates and times and locations, then she says goodbye to the phone voice too and the call is over.

After she hangs up the phone she turns to Anon and smiles an expectant morning smile: "Well?"

Anon grins at her. "Father's going to teach me to play electric guitar," he says, doing a little jump for joy so that his pajama bottoms almost slide off.

"That's great," Mother says.

"And I get to borrow his old guitar, the red one, and he has an amp I can borrow too, a twenty-five-watt one."

"That's great," Mother says, nodding.

Mother and Anon sit in the kitchen and eat summer vacation breakfast, the year's first summer vacation breakfast, and the scent of toast mixes with the coffee aroma and Anon has a hot-chocolate-with-whipped-cream mustache.

Mother and Anon don't say much to each other, mostly "Pass the butter" and things like that. Mother and Anon are thinking. Both Mother and Anon seem to be thinking pleasant, cheerful thoughts; their foreheads are smooth and their eyes have a contented, expectant gleam.

"He sure sounded happy," Mother says, no longer lost in thought and back in the real world at the kitchen table and Anon.

He looks at her without responding.

"His voice sounded so happy, don't you think?" Mother persists.

Anon thinks about it. "Yeaaaah ... yeah, I guess he did."

Although actually Anon thinks Father sounded exactly like he usually does. Exactly like normal. Anon thinks that Father sounded like a god. Just like always. A god's voice on the phone.

"I thought we might go for a stroll in town," Mother continues. "And then we could grab a pizza or something later. And then you have to pack and get your things together."

"Mmm, but ..."

"But what?"

"There's a couple of other things I have to do today. I told ... Magdalena I would show her something ... and ..."

"We could meet in town anyway," Mother suggests. "We'll invite Magdalena to have pizza with us too."

"Yes, but ... there's another thing I have to do today too. This thing that I have to ... to do today ..."

"You're a busy young man," Mother says, smiling. "Then I guess I'll have to scrap my pizza plans. Nonetheless we *can* establish that you'll be home by six o'clock. You have to pack. It's an early day tomorrow. So you'll be home by six o'clock?"

"Sure," Anon says, nodding and getting up from the table.

Anon goes into his room, gets dressed quickly, and unlocks the right desk drawer.

You. You, Anon.

Yes?

You're going to return Sara's wallet now, right?

Yes.

Are you brave enough to do it?

Of course I'm brave enough. I've been brave enough the whole time. I just haven't wanted to before now. Because ... because I wanted to hang on to it.

You wanted to hang on to the dream? The dream of Sara?

Mmm.

But now you don't need it anymore?

Nah.

Zarah

Something's wrong. Zarah senses it right when she wakes up.

Something isn't right. Something's off. Something happened, something is going to happen.

She hears Victor snuffling and snoring there in the bed next to her. He's lying on his back with his mouth open, and she nudges him so that he rolls over onto his side without waking up. But the snoring stops.

She sees all the boxes stacked along the wall of her bedroom and thinks: Shit. He promised. I don't want to sleep in a warehouse, in a thieves' den.

She tastes lead and ash on her tongue. Time to quit smoking now. Only failures, miserable idiots, and little girls smoke.

She smells how the scents of dust, leftover food, dirty linen, mold, filth, full ashtrays, sour wine remnants, and sewage fill the apartment, and she wrinkles her nose in a disgusted grimace.

She feels a dank, shut-in coldness against her skin when she gets up out of bed and stands naked in the middle of the living room. She shivers.

All of Zarah's five senses say the same thing: Something is wrong.

And the sixth one says: Watch out. Be on your guard. Something is going to happen.

The sun finds its way in through the dirty windowpanes, the

sun highlights every single splotch on the glass, every single little bug splatter glows like punctuation in some invisible writing, the window is filled with periods and commas and semicolons and big, milky splotches.

Zarah opens all the windows, fills her lungs with the morning air, and stands naked in the sunlight.

It's not helping. Something is still wrong.

Zarah takes a hot shower. Zarah puts on clean, white clothes. Zarah flings the trash bag down the garbage chute. Zarah does the dishes. Zarah tidies up. Zarah dries the dishes. Zarah plays soft music on the stereo; beautiful guitar music bubbles out of the speakers. Zarah makes coffee. Zarah combs out her pretty, long hair in front of the mirror.

She doesn't know she's doing it for the last time. She doesn't know that this is the last time in her life that she'll comb her long hair. She only knows that something is wrong.

Even so, a little smile lights up Zarah's face as she goes back into the kitchen. A thought has popped into her head and an image, an image of that guy, the one who hurt his foot in the woods last night. He never said what his name was, did he? Who was he? What was he really doing in the woods? He probably saw me and Victor, Zarah thinks. He was probably spying on us.

But that doesn't matter. He had such pretty eyes. Happy and sad. Real Jesus eyes. I'm going to see him again, Zarah thinks.

And that little thought makes her smile even though everything is wrong.

While Zarah drinks coffee and eats a piece of toast, she looks at her pictures from Italy. At first Zarah had thought about chucking the two rolls of film without even developing them, then she changed her mind and dropped them off at the photo shop down on the corner, then she changed her mind again and decided not to pick up her pictures, but yesterday she did it anyway, yesterday she picked up seventy-two color photos from her brief trip to northern Italy with Mia and her soccer team.

Now Zarah's drinking her morning coffee and remembering Italy. She remembers how playfully simple and easy life was for some of the days, she remembers all the laughter, she remembers how friendship felt, she remembers all the scents, the long, mild nights, the melodically beautiful language, the colors, the food ... All until that last night. Then something shattered. Then something fell apart, something ran out, and the trip home turned into a long, painful silence, an ice-cold game of hide-and-seek.

Zarah sighs, looking up from the pictures. What really happened? Zarah shuts her eyes and remembers. It was in Bologna, it was the very last night, and they had eaten a good dinner at a restaurant, a three-course meal where each course was beautiful, like a painting on the plate, and the wine was good and easy to drink. After the meal, they wandered through the city, silly and giggly and full of laughter, and they wound up in a little bar with outdoor seating just off the Piazza Maggiore. Sixteen happy young Swedish women. And they flirted and tried to make themselves understood in various ways to all the handsome, attentive, young Italian men who were flocking around them, it was just an innocent, harmless game, and they were offered wine and drinks, what was that yummy stuff with the coffee beans in it called again? No, Zarah can't remember, but she remembers what happened later when they finally got back to the hotel, when she and Mia finally made it back to their room.

No, Mia didn't try to seduce her. Not at all.

No, Mia had only revealed her desire and her longing, she couldn't hold it in anymore, and ...

Now Zarah's eyes gleam, she sighs and remembers, and bitter tears blur her vision.

Without motives, without expectations or anticipation, Mia had explained, but Zarah had run away full of dire disappointment and finally fell asleep later on a sofa in the corridor. The trip home had been silent and chilly, not a single word between Mia and Zarah until that last day at the daycare center.

Damn it, Mia.

Now salty tears are dripping down onto the pictures.

Damn it, Mia. I was unfair to you. I miss you, Mia. Forgive me. I was stupid, forgive me. I was so disappointed, but I still should have been more understanding. Sweet Mia. Come back. I want us to be friends again. I need you, Mia.

Zarah quickly gets up from the kitchen table, dries her teary eyes on her sweater sleeve, and walks with quick, determined steps over to the phone. Her heart is pounding as she picks up the receiver and dials Mia's number. Answer. Please answer!

Zarah waits with the receiver pressed against her ear for a long time, but no one answers. Where are you, Mia? Zarah thinks about it. Today is Saturday, it's the first day of summer vacation, it's morning. Maybe Mia's at soccer practice. Maybe she's in town. Because I'm sure she's not on vacation yet, she hasn't left town, she did say she was going to be working until Midsummer, didn't she? Zarah concentrates, trying to remember.

No more tears fall as Zarah hangs the phone back up. She's made up her mind.

Right then Zarah remembers her answering machine. It's been on since the Italy trip. What if Mia called, what if Mia left a message?

Zarah hears Victor open the bedroom door behind her, he's awake, he got up, but she doesn't care right now, she wants to hear Mia's voice on her answering machine and she hits "play" and … yes, there is a message on there, yes, someone called.

But that isn't Mia's voice. It's someone else, it's a voice Zarah doesn't recognize. It's a guy's voice that says "I love you."

That's it. The tape ends with a click.

"Who was that?"

Zarah turns toward Victor, he's still standing in the bedroom doorway, in just his underwear, and the voice from the answering machine startled him.

"Who was that?"

"I don't know," Zarah answers. "No idea. I don't know who that was, I don't recognize the voice. Some idiot probably."

Suspicion in Victor's eyes as he stares at Zarah. To have to wake up and hear some other man say "I love you" on her answering machine … there are better ways for a day to begin. Much better. He sighs, staring at Zarah. Is she lying? Is she telling the truth?

"Why have you been crying?" he asks, his eyes narrowing.

"Sit down and have some coffee," Zarah offers. "I'll tell you. I'll explain. I'm just going to go to the bathroom first. Have a seat for a sec. But I don't know who called and left the message, I promise. Sit down, I'll be right back."

As she disappears into the bathroom she hears Victor pull out a chair and sit down at the kitchen table.

—

Zarah stands in front of the bathroom mirror for a long time, she rinses her face with ice-cold water over and over again, and she looks at her wet face and thinks about Mia.

Mia, Mia, Mia. I have to get hold of you. I have to talk to you. You have to forgive me.

Zarah has already forgotten that someone said "I love you" on her answering machine.

The fact that Victor's sitting at the kitchen table sulking for just that reason doesn't bother her for an instant. She's not even concerned when she hears a sharp "Damn it" from out in the kitchen right as she opens the bathroom door. That's how preoccupied with thoughts of Mia she is.

But when she enters the kitchen, she senses right away that something else has happened, something even more wrong. A menacing chill streams out of Victor, an icy hatred, he's sitting there staring at two of Zarah's Italy pictures, and without raising his eyes he orders, "Sit!"

Zarah slides down into the chair facing him. What happened?

"Now listen," she starts, "I'll explain. It—"

Zarah doesn't get any further into her explanation than that, because Victor interrupts her. "Who did you go to Italy with?"

He doesn't look up from the pictures.

Zarah hesitates. What's he getting at? He's playing a cat-and-mouse game with her now. What does he know, what does he think he knows?

"You know who I went to Italy with," she says. "I went with Mia and her soccer team. Mia who works at the daycare center. Just girls. Not a single guy went, if that's what you're afraid of."

"Not a single guy?" Victor asks without looking at her.

"Nope."

Then Victor pushes two pictures over to Zarah, the two Italy pictures come sliding across the kitchen table like two playing cards, and Zarah looks at them, more curious than worried. What's happened? What has Victor seen?

One of the pictures is from Florence, it was taken outside a big art museum, and there's Mia and some of her friends and everyone's laughing and someone is holding two fingers up behind Mia's head. The second picture is from Verona, one of the girls from the soccer team took the picture, it shows Zarah standing with her arm around Mia, it was near Juliet's grave, a group of tourists is in the background being led by a little old man holding an umbrella high up in the air.

Two pictures from Italy. One picture from Florence and one from Verona.

"I don't get it," Zarah says, looking at Victor. "What's your point?"

In a flash Victor is standing. Before Zarah has time to react he's standing behind her and holding her neck with his hand. Firmly. Not tight, but firmly.

"You don't get it," he says. "Well, look here then."

And Victor bends over forward and points. Without relaxing his grip on Zarah he points first to one picture and then to the other.

"Now do you get it?"

Now Zarah sees. In the background in both pictures she sees a young man. The same young man, dressed in the same striped sweater, in Florence and in Verona. Zarah sees, but she doesn't get it.

"I don't know who he is," she says.

For an instant Zarah feels how Victor's grip on her neck tightens, for an instant she thinks that he's going to push her face down against the kitchen table and she tenses all her muscles to resist, but then Victor relaxes his grip, he lets Zarah go and takes a few steps away from her.

"You don't know who he is?"

"No," Zarah says.

That's true. She doesn't recognize that guy. Strange that he's in both a picture from Verona and one from Florence, but Zarah doesn't recognize him.

"You're lying!"

Zarah doesn't recognize Victor's voice either. It's different. The change in Victor's voice probably should have caused Zarah to be on her guard, but at the moment she's too preoccupied, too full of her own conjectures and her own sadness to really pay attention.

"Whores lie. You're a whore. You're lying."

Zarah's startled, she turns around in her chair and stares at Victor. "What did you say?"

"That you're a whore. And that you're lying," Victor says, spitting on the floor between them.

Doesn't Zarah hear that Victor's voice is piercing and cold like a knife? It doesn't seem like it. She's angry, but still not scared, when she scowls at Victor and taunts him.

"Poor immigrant boy, your language skills really aren't that good, are they? You don't even know what the word 'whore' means, do you?" Zarah says in a pretend foreign accent and then continues in her own voice: "So let me explain it to you. A whore is a woman who gets paid to fuck. And who does it with everyone who's willing to pay. I'm not a whore. Do you get it? And now it would appear that you have a little mess on the floor to clean up; you know where the paper towels are."

Zarah's words don't make it through to Victor. Maybe he doesn't hear what she says at all. His eyes are narrow and his voice is sharp, like a knife, sharp like the kitchen knife lying there in the dish drainer just a few feet away from him.

"You are a whore and you're lying. You were with that guy in Italy. That's the guy you were making out with at the pub a few weeks ago. I recognize him. You're lying, you whore. And that's his voice on the answering machine."

Zarah stops.

Bewildered, she turns and picks the pictures up off the table. Is Victor right? She studies the guy in the pictures, he's standing in the background and his face isn't in focus in any of the pictures. She tries to remember the guy from the pub. What did he look like? No, she can't remember, he was just someone she used to get back at Victor. But how could it be that guy? No, that's impossible. And the guy who said "I love you" on the answering machine. Same guy? No.

"Victor, I promise …"

No, Victor doesn't want to listen. "Quiet! No more lies now. Quiet!"

His voice is sharp and cold like the kitchen knife in the dish drainer.

The kitchen knife that's lying there just a couple of inches from his right hand.

"I've been fighting, you know," Victor continues. "For us. For you and me, you know. I believed in you."

"Fighting," Zarah scoffs. "You've filled the whole goddamn

bedroom full of boxes, as if it were—"

"Quiet!"

Victor's voice is sharp like a knife jab, the kitchen knife is no longer visible in the dish drainer, it's probably behind his back, and Zarah still hasn't noticed the knife and she is still more angry than afraid. Yes, she's angry, and she gets up from the chair with a jerk, marches into the bedroom, takes the first box she sees, a flat cardboard box, very heavy, schleps it out into the living room and over to the window that's still wide open. She lets the box balance on the windowsill for a second before she gives it a push so that it falls out the window.

Zarah doesn't follow the VCR's path toward the ground. Her eyes are on Victor, who's still standing in the kitchen staring at her.

"Fighting, huh?" Zarah snarls, taking a few steps toward him. "That's what it's worth to me, do you get it?"

There's a crash behind her as the VCR lands. A crash but no scream.

What's Victor doing? He's bending down, Zarah tries to see what he's doing, but it's not until Victor's standing in the doorway that she understands.

"What the hell are you doing? Put Simson down!"

Victor's face is stony as he stands there with Simson in his arms, and the fat yellow-white cat is twisting and arching and purring.

Victor heads toward the window.

"What the fuck are you doing? Are you crazy?" Zarah screams, putting herself between him and the window. "Put Simson down!"

Zarah can't stop Victor. They're not in the same league. It's as if a little peewee player were trying to tackle someone on the varsity team, or an NFL pro. Even Zarah's anger isn't enough. Victor takes a swipe at her with his right arm as if she were an annoying little bug and she tumbles over backwards, falling on the coffee table.

Zarah lies there. All she can do is watch as Victor throws Simson out the window.

As if it were nothing. His face expressionless. As if he were tossing a garbage bag down the trash chute.

Zarah gapes and stares. A scream is stuck in her throat.

"That's what a whore is worth to me," Victor says. "Do you get it?"

He looks at his arm where a few drops of blood glisten. "Shit."

From down on the street the sound of cars can be heard. Nothing else. No desperate shouts. No voices. No human noises and no cat noises. Nothing besides car noises.

Zarah gapes and stares.

And starts to feel scared.

Only now does Zarah start to feel scared.

You. You, Zarah.

Run! Get out of here! Hurry!

Huh? No, I can't. I can't do anything. And I don't get it, what's happening?

Go, Zarah, go! Leave him! Now!

What's going on? I don't get it. No, I can't move. Scared? No, not scared. Empty. Just empty. I don't understand anything.

Zarah!

Huh? Wait a sec …

Zarah!

Nils

Estar vivo es:
desayunar con la que amas,
caminar al sol,
ver crecer a los niños.
Estar muerto es:
nada.
Ninguna amante, ningún sol, ningún niño.
Nada. Y nada que temer.
—from *La Búsqueda*

Hannes ran.

Hannes ran through the city, through the night, toward the woods. Toward a clearing in the woods where his friend Nils was buried alive. He looked at his watch as he ran. An hour and fifteen minutes. Nothing to worry about. He would be there in twenty minutes or in half an hour maybe, at any rate in plenty of time before two hours was up and it was time to dig Nils up.

Hannes ran. The image of two smiling eyes, the image of a Zarah "with a *Z* and an *H* at the end" pushed its way to the forefront and blocked out his thoughts about his friend Nils out there in the woods. But he was on his way there, as fast as he could. Just as fast as he could.

Hannes ran, and now he came to the edge of the woods, he pulled up Nils's bike that was lying there in the ditch where Nils had flung it and hesitated for a bit. Which would be faster: to bike or to keep running? After considering it briefly, he flung the bike down and ran into the woods.

Hannes got there.

His heart was pounding and he was breathing hard with his mouth wide open. He finally got there. And there was the snorkel sticking up out of the ground and nothing had happened and two hours wasn't up yet.

And he had saved Nils from … a catastrophe!

As Hannes plopped down onto the ground and sat, leaning his back against the rock, the image of Zarah popped into his head again.

"Uh … uh … uh … uh …"

Hannes gave a start, frozen in fear, and it took a few seconds that felt like forever before his brain figured out where the faint sputtering noise was coming from: It was Nils crying out from underground. Nils wanted to come up!

The shovel! Where had he flung the shovel? Oh, you don't need a shovel, just pick up the blocks of sod with your hands! Hannes dropped down on his knees next to the snorkel and started clearing away the leaves. Then it was easy to pick up the blocks of sod, one by one. From under the very first one a facemask gleamed, and Hannes brushed the gravel and dirt off the glass and smiled at Nils.

"Hello there! Welcome to the light."

Nils's eyes weren't smiling. Nils's eyes were big and round inside the facemask and there wasn't a trace of a smile in them.

Hannes took off two more chunks of sod, and then he could carefully lift the snorkel out of Nils's mouth and pluck the earplugs out of his ears.

"Hello down there! Is everything all right?"

Big, round eyes stared at Hannes, and a thin, deadpan voice whispered, "Dig me up."

Was it the moonlight that made Nils's face so scarily pale and bloodless? Hannes avoided looking at Nils while he pulled up clump after clump of sod. As soon as the blanket of dirt was off Nils's grave-bed, he extricated himself, arduously rolling himself up onto the ground next to the shallow grave. But he didn't stand up. He just lay there carefully stretching his arms, wiggling his feet, moving his fingers one by one and bending his legs.

Silence. Not a word. The eyes in the facemask were empty.

"How was it? How was it?" Hannes asked, carefully squatting down next to Nils.

No answer. Empty eyes staring at the night sky. Two hands clenching into fists and opening, again and again.

Hannes waited.

Nils lay quietly, his face as white as the full moon. With enormous difficulty he managed to lift one of his arms so he could scratch his head. He scratched his scalp harder and harder, violently, while his face tightened into a tormented scowl. "Shit ..."

Hannes sat quietly and waited. "Does it itch?" he finally asked.

Then Nils closed his eyes and laughed flatly, motionlessly, for a long time with his mouth open. Then suddenly, without warning, he screamed straight out into the night, straight up at the sky: "*Shit!*"

Brief pause.

"*Shit, shit!!*"

Slightly longer pause.

"*Shit, shit, shit!!!*"

Like a wolf howling at the moon.

Out of desperation. Out of anger. Out of grief. Out of wrath.

With great difficulty, Nils succeeded in turning over onto his side and pulling himself up so that his upper body was elevated, leaning on one elbow. He stared at Hannes with cold, vacant eyes.

"Where … were … you …?"

"I—" Hannes started, but Nils interrupted him.

"Where the … hell … were you?"

"I—"

"I was lying here moan … moaning into that goddamn plastic tube for several hours. You were supposed to … you were supposed to come when …"

Tears in Nils's eyes now, tears of anger, tears of pain, tears of grief.

"Someone—" Hannes attempted, but Nils didn't let him explain.

"I couldn't breathe. I had a cramp. I couldn't move. And I was calling you. But you didn't come."

"Someone …"

"And small animals were crawling in my hair. *Do you get it? Small, disgusting animals and worms and shit were crawling around in my hair! They were eating their way into my head. Do you get it?*"

"Someone came," Hannes said. Did he have tears in his eyes too? There was something glistening there in the corner of his eye, at any rate.

"Why the hell didn't you come?"

Hannes wasn't prepared. So when Nils tore off the facemask and threw it, Hannes didn't have time to duck. And even though it was a feeble throw, his shoulder and cheek burned with the pain. "Ouch, damn it …"

"Why didn't you come?" Nils's voice was a tormented whisper now.

"But listen, would you?" Hannes said. He had decided to explain. "Someone came. Someone was about to discover you. I was forced to lure them away. I ran all the way back here from the hospital, for Pete's …"

Did he expect gratitude?

Did he expect "Oh, I'm sorry, I didn't know that"?

Did he expect friendship and love?

He didn't get any of those.

He got nothing.

Just a contemptuous stare from Nils before he started struggling to get up. He almost fell down right away, but reached out to the rock for support, stood there with his back to Hannes for a while, and then started undoing his raingear. After a few minutes of groaning and exertion the raincoat and rain pants and boots were lying on the ground next to him and without a word he stumbled off. Away from the clearing and Hannes, off toward the yellow trail.

Hannes watched him go.

"Shit," he mumbled to himself. The most frequently used swear word of the night scored yet another point.

It took Nils two hours to get home from the woods; the sun had already started to glow in the east as he stood in front of his building. He crawled and dragged himself up the stairs, all the energy had run out of him, and when he entered the apartment he flung himself flat on the floor of the hallway.

The apartment was empty. Mom and Göran and Oskar and Kristina were off on a three-day trip to Denmark to celebrate the start of summer vacation and Oskar's graduation from ninth grade.

I'm still alive, Nils thought, lying with his cheek against the rough hall carpet. But barely. Oh, my head. My hair.

He struggled to wriggle out of his clothes, crawled into the shower stall, and took a long shower in scalding hot water. He shampooed his hair five times. He used dandruff shampoo, sports shampoo, shampoo for greasy hair, shampoo that prevents split ends, and shampoo with balsam, and it still itched as if a thousand little red ants were crawling around on his scalp.

I'm going crazy, Nils thought.

Wrapped in a large, moist bath towel he collapsed, half asleep, onto his bed and slept a brief and fitful sleep filled with murky dreams.

I've been buried.

Nils leans over the sink and looks at his face in the bathroom mirror. It's Saturday morning, it's the first day of summer vacation. Some of the energy has returned to his body, but he's still weak like after a long sickness, and his face still shimmers with a bluish pallor.

You. You, Nils.

Yes?

There aren't that many people who've been buried. Who've been buried alive in the earth.

No.

Maybe you're the only one, the only one who's come back to life.

Yes.

How was it?

Dark. Lonely. Cold. I felt the Chill of Death.

Did you also feel the Fear of Death?

Wait a sec. I can't think. My hair! It feels like millions of tiny bugs are still eating their way into my skull. What should I do? It's driving me crazy.

Nils stares at his reflection. Then he opens the medicine cabinet and shrugs. He has no choice. He takes out the razor and puts in a new blade. There's really no other option. Shave or go crazy? Answer: Shave.

But first the clippers, the trusty old clippers. Nils takes them out and puts them on the shortest possible setting.

He studies his reflection again before he starts.

"Good day, sir," he says to the face in the mirror. "And how would you like your hair?"

"Gone," the reflection answers. "Gone. Cut it all off. Telly Savalas. Bald. Same haircut as when I was born, thank you."

"As you wish, sir."

It takes only half an hour.

Nils stares at his reflection with his mouth hanging open. He strains, trying to feel … No, no, the itching's gone, it doesn't itch at all anymore, and he lets out a sigh of relief, a liberated sigh, and then bursts out laughing.

"Hi, Egghead!" he says to his reflection and then laughs until he's practically choking.

Oh, how wonderful, the itching stopped, oh …

Nils runs his hand carefully over the skin on his head. It feels weird. Cold. A cold that comes from up above. And strange. The skin up there is so soft, he doesn't recognize himself. He gets blood on his fingers when he lets his hand slide down along the back of his neck, the razor must have nicked some small zits. A little blood is a small price to pay in exchange for this relief …

"Hi there, Baldy!"

Slowly returning to life, slowly waking up.

That's what it feels like now. Only now does Nils feel like he's starting to come back from the events of last night.

And he's hungry! Empty!

And naked! Cold! Clothes! Food!

Black clothes today, black jeans and a black sweater that will make his corpse-white skin glow.

Food, now!

Then she'll be the first one to see me, Nils thinks.

After my resurrection. Without hair.

I will go to her.

Anon & Zarah

"Come in!"

Anon rang the doorbell three times. After the third ring a hesitant voice could be heard from inside the apartment. A girl's voice.

Anon opens the door and steps in.

It's quiet and empty in there. And it smells ... different. Not like home. Anon walks slowly down a dark hallway. On the left is an empty kitchen. A few pictures are spread out on the kitchen table.

"Hello? Who is it?" a girl's voice calls from the large, light living room. Anon heads in that direction, but stops in the doorway and stands there.

It feels as if he's walked out onto the stage in a theater, right into the middle of a play. The girl is sitting on the sofa. She's wearing white pants and a white T-shirt, her long hair is freshly washed and still damp, and she's so beautiful that it's almost uncanny, Anon thinks. She looks like someone you'd see in a movie or on TV, like a model, like a celebrity, like the woman the hero falls in love with, like someone who doesn't belong in the everyday world.

A guy is standing by the open window. Anon recognizes him. His picture was in the wallet, the wallet that Anon is holding in his left hand, but Anon threw the picture away. That guy looked like a gangster in the picture, and he looks like a gangster in real life, Anon thinks. Even more so.

The guy by the window and the girl on the sofa are silent and motionless; everything on the stage has been frozen to ice. Anon's ringing the doorbell interrupted the scene.

"What the fuck are you staring at?" the gangster guy finally says. "And what the fuck do you want?"

Anon turns toward the girl. "Your name is Zarah, isn't it? Zarah with a Z?"

She nods.

"Enoksson?"

Zarah Enoksson nods.

"Is there a Sara with an S too?" Anon asks.

Zarah doesn't seem to understand the question at first. She seems preoccupied with something else, and she doesn't really seem to care about Anon, who's standing there in the doorway, but eventually she answers, in a weak voice, "I'm sure there is. But not here."

"In that case," Anon says, walking over to her, "then I think this must be yours. Even though it says Sara with an S on the library card."

He holds the wallet out to her. Zarah takes it, takes a peek inside and confirms that the money is gone, and then tosses it on the coffee table. "Mmm."

As if nothing had happened.

Well, that's that, Anon thinks.

For several weeks he's been fantasizing about this meeting, about when he would give the wallet back to her. But he'd been dreaming of a different Sara then, a twelve-year-old Sara with an S, a Sara with bangs and bright eyes. The Zarah who's sitting there on the sofa seems almost paralyzed, she's not really present and her eyes aren't focused on Anon, her eyes are focused on something far away, something that only she and no one else can see.

The guy by the window suddenly says, "I'm not going to touch you. Do you get it?"

The scene that was under way starts up again after the intermission that took place when Anon entered the apartment. Act Two is beginning now. Anon understands that he's not in this scene, he's just the audience, and he follows the guy's eyes over to Zarah on the sofa. She doesn't react, doesn't move, sits there quietly.

"I don't want to touch someone like you. Do you get it?" the guy continues. "Never again. Do you get it?"

Then it's as if Zarah wakes up from a dream, from a spell, and she turns toward Anon.

"Did you see a cat? Down there? When you came in?" she asks.

"A yellowish, fat one?" Anon asks.

"Yes. That's the one. Did you see it?"

"Mmm," Anon says.

Zarah leans toward Anon.

"Well?! Tell me! Did it live?"

"Not at first," Anon says calmly. "Right when I came it was lying there in the bushes and it was dead. But I resurrected it."

Zarah stares at him. "So where is it now?" she asks.

"It wanted to go into the courtyard. So I let it in there," Anon says.

Zarah stares at him in disbelief. "For real?"

"Of course for real," Anon says. "I never lie."

Zarah gets up with a start, rushes past Anon, and disappears out through the front door without closing it behind her. Her footsteps echo in the stairwell as she runs down.

Anon and the cross guy by the window stay there in the apartment. Anon doesn't know that his name is Victor. Anon only knows that he's bad and he says mean things to Zarah.

And now Victor turns toward Anon and hisses, "Get out of here!"

"Nope," Anon says.

He's not scared. And he's not planning on leaving, not now, he wants to see if Zarah finds her cat first.

Victor spits out the window, he takes a couple of steps back and forth as if he can't decide where he's going, or if he's going. He casts an irritated glance at Anon and then stands there, leaning against the windowsill.

Now they can hear footsteps in the stairwell again, slower footsteps, heavy footsteps on their way up the stairs. Now they can hear Zarah in the hallway, now she comes in and stands next to Anon, and now he can see what made her steps so heavy: a fat cat in her arms.

Carefully she sets it down on the floor and right away the cat lifts its tail straight up in the air and starts nudging and rubbing itself against Anon's galoshes and pant legs.

"He's alive," Zarah says, sounding surprised.

"That's what I said," Anon says.

Zarah stands there for a while, watching the cat swish back and forth around Anon's legs, then she lifts her eyes and turns toward Victor.

"Get out of here," she says.

Victor nods. "I was planning to. And I'm not coming back."

"Good," Zarah says.

"But I'm going to kill that asshole," Victor says.

"Yeah, do that," Zarah says.

Anon lets his eyes wander back and forth between Zarah and Victor. This is a serious play he wound up in. A drama. Terse, icy lines fly through the air, and the room resonates with a cold hatred.

When Victor starts walking, Zarah and Anon both move aside to let him past.

"I'll come up and fetch ..." Victor says, nodding toward the bedroom.

"Mmm," Zarah says. "Do it soon."

Victor disappears without a word. He slams the door behind him so that the hall mirror rattles. Bang!

There goes Victor. Curtain. Exit Victor.

Ten seconds later, the air goes out of Zarah.

She sinks down into the sofa, deflated and spent. She sits there with her hands in front of her face while Anon stands on the other side of the coffee table, watching her. She sits there for a long time. He stands there for a long time.

Is she crying? It doesn't seem like it, she's not making any noise and no tears are trickling out between her fingers either.

Anon sinks down onto his knees right across from Zarah. What should he do? Should he say something? What does a boy do when a beautiful girl is sad? He tries to comfort her, of course. But how?

No, Zarah hasn't been crying, Anon can tell when she finally takes her hands away from her face and looks at him. But her eyes are red and full of pain.

What does a boy do when a beautiful girl is suffering?

"Life sucks," Zarah says, looking straight through Anon.

He doesn't say anything.

"Listen," Zarah asks. "My best friend is mad because I did something stupid. I was unfair to her. She probably hates me. She should hate me. And Victor is gone. He was a jerk today, but that's because he was jealous. Actually ... actually things were going well between us. It felt like I'd made up my mind ... about him ... We could have done well together. In some ways we're alike, Victor and me ... but he's too proud to come back now, and I'm too proud too. I don't want to be treated like ... Yeah."

Anon listens. What does Anon know about friendship and love and jealousy and pride? Not much. But he listens to Zarah.

"And some perverse idiot," she continues, "has been following me and spying on me. It's his fault things turned out like this. Everything is his fault. I could kill that asshole."

Anon is startled. "Someone's been ... been spying ... on ... on you?" he stammers.

"Come," Zarah says. She gets up and pulls Anon into the kitchen.

The pictures from Italy are still lying on the kitchen table and Zarah shows Anon and explains.

"I recognize him," Anon says, almost right away.

"What?" Zarah exclaims.

Anon thinks about it. "Yeah, I know who he is. That's Kristina's big brother. Kristina who's in my class. *Was* in my class. And I've—"

I've seen him here by the front door to your building, Anon is about to say, but stops himself. If Anon says that, it would incriminate him too, and Zarah doesn't like spies. So even though Anon had been spying on a different Sara, he bites his lip.

"I have his address," Anon says instead. "And his phone number. In the school directory. I can get it for you."

"Good," Zarah says. "You'll do that today, right? I'm going to kill him."

Anon nods. "Sure."

"Why are you wearing galoshes?" Zarah's been leaning against the sink for a while, looking at Anon.

"I always wear galoshes," he responds, shrugging his shoulders.

"That's not an answer," Zarah says. "I asked why."

Anon swallows and looks at her, his eyes serious. "Radiation and waves," he whispers. "There's so much radiation and so many waves."

"What? Radiation and waves? Huh?"

And then Anon tells Zarah what no one else knows, what he's never told Mother or the school nurse or the counselor, even though they nagged. Even Father doesn't know. Not even Father. But for Zarah, because she's so beautiful and sad, Anon explains:

"There's so much radiation and so many waves these days. Everywhere. Haven't you ever thought about it? There's radio waves from zillions of radio stations and TV radiation and tons of electrical devices all over the place and high tension wires and nuclear power plants and radioactive waste. And computers and screens. And telephones. The air is full of radiation and waves. Millions of rays and waves pass right through your body. The whole time. All the time. Haven't you ever thought about it?"

Zarah stares at him. "But if you wear galoshes you're protected?" she asks.

"Mmm," Anon says, nodding. "Then I'm insulated. I always wear galoshes."

Zarah is still staring at him. "Take off your galoshes!" she orders.

It would be hard to prove that Zarah was threatening Anon as she stood there leaning against the sink and pointing at him with the big kitchen knife. I was only pointing, Zarah would be able to say. I asked him to take off his galoshes and he did, she would be able to say. It would be hard to prove otherwise.

True. And once Anon has pulled off his galoshes, Zarah says, "Put them on the table."

Anon obeys.

Then Zarah walks over to the kitchen table and slowly and methodically cuts the two blue galoshes to bits with the kitchen knife. She shreds the sides. She perforates the soles. She bores big holes into the heels. Anon sinks down onto a chair. He sits there and watches it happen without trying to interfere.

When Zarah is finished, she takes two steps back and looks at her work. The galoshes sit there on the kitchen table like two slouching, exotic jungle creatures.

"There." She turns to Anon. "Now, how do you feel? Are you still alive?"

Anon nods without taking his eyes off the shredded galoshes.

"Do you feel listless? Sick to your stomach?"

Anon shakes his head.

"Well, all right then," Zarah says contentedly. "Doctor Zarah has cured you. One quick and simple treatment. And it's free. But damn—your galoshes stink!"

She pinches her nose as she walks over to the table, picking up the remains of the galoshes with her right hand. With her arm held straight out in front of her she carries them to the window in the living room, holds them out the window for a second, and then lets go.

"There."

Then she goes back to the kitchen, pulls out a chair, and sits down across from Anon. She tilts her head to the side and contemplates him for a minute.

"Are you mad?" she asks.

"I hardly ever get mad," Anon says, shaking his head. "Hardly ever."

"Are you sad, then?"

Anon keeps shaking his head. "I hardly ever get sad either. I never cry."

"Never?"

"Hardly ever."

Zarah contemplates Anon in silence for another minute, then reaches out with her right hand and lays it on top of Anon's left hand, which is resting on the table. She takes hold of his hand plays a little with his fingers.

"I'm sorry," she says. "I'm just so tired of people who … who get ideas stuck in their heads. Who imagine stuff. There are plenty of real problems out there, if you ask me. But I'm sorry."

Anon looks at his hand, which is resting in Zarah's soft, warm grip, like a baby bird safe and sound in a nest.

"Mmm," he says, nodding.

He could forgive anything right now.

Anything at all. But what will he tell Mother?

"What's your name?" Zarah asks. She's still holding Anon's hand in hers.

"Anon," Anon answers.

"Anon? Like Shannon without the *SH*?"

"Nah. Like 'Frère Jacques' without the *C*," Anon replies.

"Huh?"

"Shannon without the *SH* is Annon," Anon explains. "But 'Frère Jacques' is a canon. You get it? And canon without the *C* is Anon. And that's my name. You know what a canon is, right? One of those songs that—"

"Yeah, yeah, yeah," Zarah says, cutting him off. "I know what a canon is. I sang in the school choir. Soprano."

"Look at me," Zarah says a little while later.

She's still sitting across from Anon at the kitchen table. She's still holding Anon's hand in hers.

Sure, Anon would be happy to.

"Am I beautiful? Pretty? Cute? Attractive? Sexy?"

"Mmm." Anon nods. All of those. And plenty more.

Zarah nods too. "*That's* what my problem is," she says. "That's why it all happens. That's why it all happened. All of it."

She keeps nodding to herself.

"I'm going to become ugly," she says intently. "Then I'll be spared all these problems. Will you help me?"

Anon shrugs. Sure, he wants to help her. But how will they do it?

"Good," Zarah says, getting up.

With determined steps, she walks over to the far side of the kitchen, pulls out drawer after drawer looking for something, and then disappears into the bathroom. Anon hears her rifling around in there and then she comes back with her arms full of odds and ends that she sets on the counter.

"There." She hands Anon a large pair of kitchen shears. "Here. Take this. Cut my hair off."

"What?"

"You heard what I said. Cut my hair. As short as possible. Then you're going to shave my head. I'm going to be bald. No more bad hair days. I'm going to be ugly. I think this is a great idea. It's the only thing I can do."

"But …" Anon says, staring at the large pair of shears.

"Come, come. Don't be silly," Zarah says. "Stand over here behind me and start cutting. Think about how I destroyed your galoshes. Now you have a chance to get even with me."

Anon doesn't want to get even, not at all. But he does want to help Zarah, of course. So he gets up and goes and stands behind her. But after he picks up a lock of her long hair and holds the scissors up, ready to cut, he stops, uncertain. The soft, shiny hair. The sharp scissors. This isn't right, Anon thinks.

"This isn't right," he says.

"Don't be silly," Zarah says. "Chop, chop. And cut it as short as you can. And put the hair on the table. I'm not going to throw it away. You can sell it to wig makers or donate it to Locks of Love, at least that's what I've heard."

Anon gulps and starts cutting.

—

Slowly and carefully Anon cuts Zarah's hair.

When he's finished there's a big pile of long hair on the kitchen table, and about half an inch of uneven stubble remains on Zarah's head.

Anon sets the scissors down, walks around to the other side of the table, looks at Zarah from the front, and sighs.

"Ugly?" Zarah asks expectantly.

"Uglier than before," Anon says with a sigh. "Do you want to see yourself in the mirror?"

"Not yet. Not until you're done. Now you're going to shave me. Have you ever shaved anyone?"

"Nope," Anon says.

"That won't be a problem," Zarah says as she starts rinsing her head in the kitchen sink with hot water.

Then Anon gets to massage shaving cream into Zarah's short hair, and then she pulls her chair over and sits down next to the sink.

She shivers and says, "Brrr, my head smells like Victor," handing Anon the razor. "Now shave me. And rinse the razor in hot water."

"What if I cut you?"

"Then I'll scream."

Anon carefully pulls the razor through the white foam. It leaves a narrow little trail across the top of Zarah's head, as if a snowplow had gone through and plowed a road that had been snowed in.

"Did that hurt?" Anon asks, rinsing the razor.

"Not at all," Zarah says contentedly. "Keep going. Just like that."

Slowly and carefully Anon shaves Zarah.

"OK, go ahead and rinse," he says finally.

Zarah sticks her whole head under the tap again and rinses off the remaining shaving cream.

"Am I done?"

"Wait a sec," Anon says.

His fingertips make their way over Zarah's smooth scalp. In several places he finds strands of hair that he missed and shaves them off. Then he dries her head with the dishcloth and lets one of his hands caress Zarah's clean-shaven scalp.

It feels weird. Strangely soft.

"Brrr, your hand is cold," Zarah says, shivering.

Anon swallows and stands in front of Zarah.

"OK. I think you're done now. Let me see."

Zarah looks at Anon expectantly. She's scanning his eyes for some kind of reaction. What does he see? What will she see?

"Am I ugly?" she asks.

"Different. You look stylish. You look like an alien. Your ears … they're kind of … they're more visible."

Now, finally, Zarah wants to see how she looks without hair, and she rushes out to the hallway to look in the mirror. Anon waits in the kitchen. He has to wait a long time before Zarah comes back.

"Were you crying?" he asks, a little afraid.

Then Zarah squats down next to Anon, takes his hand and puts it against her damp cheek, and smiles at him.

"I was just surprised," she says, smiling wistfully. "I wasn't prepared. But it's good. I'm ugly. Thanks for helping me. Now I'll be spared all those problems. And I'll get to find out what life is like for ugly people."

Your eyes are the same, Anon thinks. And your lips. You'll never be ugly, he thinks, still holding his hand against Zarah's cheek. But he doesn't say anything, just chuckles quietly to himself.

Not ugly, just different, he thinks.

Zarah's going to make a phone call; then there'll be food, she promises. She's "as hungry as a bald horse."

Anon tries to hear what Zarah's saying on the phone. He hears the name "Mia," he hears the word "sorry," and "tonight," but he doesn't hear much else of the conversation out in the living room.

Zarah's cheeks are a little flushed when she comes back to Anon and her eyes are a little glazed. But she doesn't seem sad. No, quite the contrary. And she walks right up to Anon and holds his head firmly between her hands and she gives him a tender kiss on the forehead.

"Anon, you bring me good luck," she says, laughing merrily. "Since you came, everything's been going so much better. Can't I keep you?"

Anon considers it. He really wouldn't be opposed to having Zarah keep him.

"My mother would probably get worried," he says.

Yes, Zarah thinks so too, and she lets go of Anon and starts hunting around in the fridge and pantry.

"Hot dogs and mashed potatoes," she calls happily. "That's a classic. I'll boil some hot dogs and whip up some instant mashed potatoes. And mustard and ketchup. And some kind of vegetable so we don't get scurvy. That sounds good, doesn't it?"

"No," Anon says.

"Huh?" Zarah says in surprise, stopping dead in her tracks. "What? Maybe you don't eat hot dogs. Are you a vegetarian?"

"Just the opposite," Anon responds.

And then he has to explain how he never eats potatoes, or anything that grows underground. Not carrots. Not onions. Not beets or parsnips or other root vegetables.

"Why not?"

And Anon explains that the earth is made up of poop, decayed leaves, the rotten remains of animals and people. And slimy worms, grubs, rats and mice and other icky things crawl around underground. It's disgusting to eat things that grow in the ground, Anon says. He will never do it.

He'd never told anyone that before either.

And Anon explains how they tried to force him at school, but that he flushed his potatoes and vegetables down the toilet.

"You're a little nuts," Zarah says when Anon finishes explaining. "But I like you. And you bring me good luck. So I won't force you to eat the mashed potatoes or vegetables."

"Thanks," Anon says.

While Zarah makes the food, Anon puts her hair in a box she brought in from the bedroom. It's a really big box that obviously used to contain a computer monitor, and Zarah's cut hair nearly fills it up.

"I feel so light," Zarah says, touching her scalp. "I feel liberated."

"Me too," Anon says.

"Mmm," Zarah says, nodding. "That's because you're rid of those disgusting galoshes. Let me keep you for a week and I'll teach you to eat mashed potatoes too."

"I don't think so," Anon says calmly.

Zarah and Anon talk during the whole meal; in other words, Zarah asks a lot of prying questions and Anon answers them.

About his school and his classmates and everything that had happened in the last few weeks.

"So who was the Pissman?" Zarah asks. "Did they ever find out who it was?"

"Nope," Anon responds. "But I know who it is."

"What?" Zarah says, so surprised that she drops her fork.

"It was someone in my class," Anon says. "A guy in my class."

"Why didn't you tell anyone?" Zarah asks. "I mean, you got blamed for it. Why didn't you say it was him?"

"I didn't think it was necessary," Anon says.

After Anon explains about Magdalena, Zarah asks, "Do you have a crush on her?"

Anon thinks about it. "I don't know."

Then Zarah tells Anon to think about Magdalena, and Anon thinks as hard as he can, and then Zarah asks, "Do you feel hot and cold? Like your earlobes are on fire? Like ants are crawling around on your skin? Butterflies in your stomach? Achy legs?"

Anon concentrates. Yeah, he has some of those symptoms. But it doesn't feel life-threatening.

"Anyway, you probably have a crush on her," Zarah says. "That's good." She laughs enthusiastically.

"Why is it good to have a crush?" he wonders.

"Because then you feel like you're alive," Zarah says.

—

Then Anon and Zarah talk about their parents.

Zarah says she has a dad she loves and a mom she doesn't love. "Do you have to love your parents? Both of them? Equally?"

"I don't know," Anon says.

"It always turns into some stupid fight between my mom and me. Like it's some kind of competition," Zarah says. "But maybe that will change."

Yes, Anon thinks, maybe that will change.

"What about you?" Zarah asks.

Anon shrugs. Then he says, "My father is a god. My mother is an ordinary woman, but my father is a god."

At first Zarah thinks that Anon means his father is dead.

"No, no." Anon laughs. "He lives in Gothenburg."

"Your father is a god, who lives in Gothenburg?"

Anon nods. Of course.

And then Anon explains about his father. He explains everything that he was going to tell Sara, the other Sara who he's already forgotten. She doesn't exist, but Zarah with a Z, Bald Zarah, is sitting right across from him and Anon tells her all the things he's never told anyone else before. And Zarah listens.

"You're nuts," she says when Anon finishes. "You're nuts but I like you."

Anon shrugs.

Then Zarah says, "I'd like to meet your father."

"Come with me," Anon says. "Come with me and you can meet him."

But that won't work. Zarah can't go to Gothenburg with

him tomorrow. No, she has to get her life in order first. But another time.

"Sure," Anon says.

It's gotten so late that Anon suddenly has to hurry so that he's on time to meet Magdalena in the park. That's where they're meeting, by the ponds in ten minutes.

Zarah doesn't want to let Anon leave, but of course she understands that he has to get going.

"Can we meet later?" Zarah asks. "If I come to the park, to the ponds? I could bring some coffee and snacks. Because tomorrow you're going to your dad's ... to your father's."

"Sure," Anon says.

He stops by the front door.

"But what do I wear on my feet?"

"Go barefoot," Zarah says, shrugging. "It's summer. Or, hang on, you can borrow a pair of flip-flops from me. Wait a sec."

She finds a pair of puke-green plastic flip-flops for him in the closet. Anon tries them on.

"Will that work?"

"Sure," he says, pleased.

"And you ..." A shadow falls over Zarah's face. "I want to get that phone number from you. For that guy."

"Sure," Anon says. "You'll get it."

He looks at Zarah. He's already gotten used to it.

Hasn't she always been bald?

Zarah & Nils

Ugly.

Ugly and free.

Zarah sticks her tongue out at her reflection. Oh man, are you ugly!

Liberated and ugly. Zarah's reflection grins at her, but the grin disappears in a flash and the face in the mirror becomes serious and thoughtful.

Something is happening. Life is turning a corner.

In just a few hours, her whole life has done an about-face. That's what happened, Zarah thinks. There are turning points in life. There are times when everything heads in a new direction.

You grow a little. You learn something. You get a little wiser. And you decide for yourself, you make a choice. That's what's important, Zarah thinks. I hate being a pawn in someone else's game, a cog in someone else's wheel. Hate it. And hate that guy in the pictures from Italy. I hope Victor beats the crap out of him.

Victor.

Victor was a jerk today. But Victor is a jerk I understand, Zarah thinks. He doesn't trick me. He doesn't keep any secrets from me. And he didn't mean to throw Simson out the window. He just wanted to scare me. He was blinded by jealousy. He was just going to hold Simson out the window to scare me, but Simson panicked and started clawing him and then Victor dropped him.

That's what happened.

Her reflection smiles at Zarah. "What do you think Victor's going to think about a bald Zarah?" the reflection whispers.

"We'll have to wait and see," Zarah whispers back, smiling. Someday, Zarah thinks. There's no rush. Que sera, sera.

I'm free, Zarah thinks, skipping down the hallway almost as if the feeling of freedom made her weightless, buoyant.

And Mia said yes. Mia said, "Yes, we can meet. Yes, we can talk."

Mia, Mia, Mia.

And Anon, my little good luck charm, Zarah thinks. What luck that you came right when you did, and what a strange, clever little guy you are. I'm going to buy you a present. I'll buy something nice and—

Right then, right when thoughts of Anon have Zarah and her reflection on the verge of laughter, the doorbell rings.

Not Victor, Zarah thinks. I recognize his ring.

Not Mia. Not now.

Maybe Anon. Maybe Dad.

Maybe the police. Maybe today's the day. Maybe I'll finally be rid of all this stolen property. And maybe I'll have to spend the rest of the day being interrogated by dreary, boring policemen, Zarah thinks.

She shrugs. "Well, let's find out," she tells her reflection. "Life is full of surprises."

And she walks over to open the door.

Nils didn't hesitate.

After breakfast he felt full of energy, full of life. He put a Band-Aid on his neck and set out.

Liberated.

With long, bouncy strides he made his way along the sidewalk. People stepped aside and let him by. People turned and stared at him as he walked by. People made comments about his silly grin as he walked by. "Probably on drugs," "Mmm, high as a kite."

Liberated.

He stopped in front of a store window, studied his reflection in the glass there, and shook his head to himself.

"What was I thinking? Why did I want to play dead? Instead of living … Why do I pretend? Why am I such a coward? Why do I stand on the sidelines watching instead of participating? What was I afraid of?"

His reflection in the storefront didn't answer a single one of his questions, but an elderly couple on their way downtown to do a little Saturday shopping stopped and stared at him.

Nils turned to face the couple and smiled broadly. "Good morning! It sure is a lovely day today!"

The old man nodded politely to Nils, but his wife was nervous and tried to pull him along.

"Don't be scared," Nils said, laughing. "There's nothing to be afraid of. First we live. Then we die. There's nothing to be afraid of."

The old woman pulled and tugged on her husband's arm. "Come on," she whispered, her voice anxious. Finally he went along with her.

Nils stood there. He watched the old couple, laughing to himself and shaking his head.

Next Nils encountered a young woman with a baby carriage.

"Good morning!" he said, smiling, and did a couple of dance steps.

She smiled and nodded at him but didn't stop.

"There's nothing to be afraid of!" Nils called out after the woman. She kept walking nonchalantly and Nils turned back to the store window again.

"I've turned into a preacher," he says, laughing at his bald reflection. "I'm standing here on the street like one of those goddamned sanctimonious soapbox preachers."

And he turned toward the street, stretched both arms out to the sky, and shouted, "*I lived in darkness, but now I have seen the light! I've seen the light! He visto la luz! J'ai vu la Lumière!*"

And then mumbled to himself as he lowered his arms, "La luz? El luz? Hmmm …"

Nils didn't hesitate.

He walked to Östra Storgatan, he entered the front door of number 14, he trotted up to the third floor. It said Z. ENOKSSON by the mail slot. He rang the doorbell. He heard some footsteps in there; someone grabbed the doorknob on the inside of the door, turned it, and opened the door.

Now the door is open.

There's Zarah. There's Nils.

Now Zarah and Nils meet.

Both freeze. Both are struck dumb.

Nils sees a bald young woman dressed in white standing there in front of him. It takes a minute before he recognizes her, but then he realizes: It's her. It's her, but without hair.

Zarah sees a bald young man dressed in black standing there in front of her. She doesn't recognize him, but she knows who he is: My mirror image, she thinks. You finally came. So you were a twin brother, not a sister. No problem. That's good.

Zarah and Nils stand there facing each other in silence.

One in white and one in black. About the same height.

Neither of them can explain what happens next. Of course both of them probably took drama in school at some point, but

no one decides, no one leads, and yet
a mirror game takes place there in the doorway
a mirror game
and white is reflected in black and black in white
and when white slowly raises her right hand and her arm
black raises his left hand and arm
at exactly the same time
and when black blinks with his right eye
white blinks with her left
and neither of them makes a sound
and they're two perfect mirror images of each other
every movement and every expression is mirrored
and no one leads and no one decides
and even their voices mirror each other when,
at exactly the same time, they say
"Hhii, Eegggghheeaadd"
and two bright smiles reflect each other
and they look deep into their mirrored eyes
black and white
and time stands still
like in a dream

no, like in a reality, a denser and more profound
reality
until

Until Zarah furrows her brow and says, "It's you!"

Then the mirror breaks, and Zarah stomps around on its shards.

"I hate you!" she says.

Her eyes are different now. She is staring angrily at Nils. He can't defend himself from her look, but ...

He doesn't back down. He stands his ground.

"It's you," Zarah continues. "You're the one who followed me. You even followed me to Italy. You've been spying on me. You've been sneaking around. You ... you left a message on my answering machine! It was you, wasn't it?"

Nils nods.

Zarah's voice is full of unmitigated hatred as she continues. "Who do you think you are? What gives you the right to mess around with my life? I don't want any part of it, of your childish games. Do you get it? Do you even know what you've done? Do you even see what a mess you've made for me?"

She puts her hand on the doorknob and is about to pull the door shut.

"Now you even went and shaved your head just because I did. You must be fucking crazy! Cut it out. And get lost. I never want to see you again. Do you get it?"

But like an old door-to-door vacuum cleaner salesman, Nils sticks his foot out so Zarah can't shut the door.

"Wait a minute!" he pleads. "I had no idea you shaved your head. How could I know that?"

Zarah stops being angry for a second to contemplate that. No, how could he have known that? She wrinkles her forehead.

"Do you know Anon?" she asks, suspicious.

Nils shakes his head.

"Well then, you explain it to me!" Zarah orders. "Explain why you shaved your head right now. And then you can go to hell!"

"Stop pulling on the door, then," Nils asks. "It's hurting my foot."

And Zarah stops pulling, but her hand stays on the doorknob while Nils explains.

"I was forced to shave my hair off. Because I got all these bugs in it. When I was buried. It hurt and itched so much that I was going crazy. I shaved it this morning."

"Buried?"

Nils explains.

And Zarah listens. She shakes her head several times and her eyes get big and round and her mouth hangs open, but she listens quietly until she cries out, "What?! A snorkel? A blue snorkel?"

She puts her hand over her mouth, as if the shock had made her speechless. Or as if to suppress a laugh.

Nils nods.

Then he thinks: How could she know that? That it was blue.

Zarah looks pensive. Her thoughts are whirling around in her head. Now and then she is close to bursting out laughing, but she stops herself and presses her fingers against her lips. No, there's no way he could know, even if he had spied on her there's no way he could know that she and Victor would end up at that exact spot, in that clearing, and …

"Did you have a periscope too?" Zarah asks, looking at Nils with suspicion. "Could you see anything? When you were buried in the woods, I mean."

Nils shakes his head. "No, I didn't see anything. I didn't hear anything. It was black and cold and lonely down there in the earth. The only thing I could feel was how a zillion disgusting little bugs were crawling around in my hair." He shivers. The memory still hurts.

Zarah still seems pensive, and Nils waits patiently.

"You have a friend, right?" Zarah says suddenly, laughing. "A guy with short black hair and … and pretty, cheerful eyes. You have a friend who was with you in the woods, right?"

What do you mean, pretty eyes? Nils thinks, stiffening. His voice bitter, he says, "He's not my friend anymore."

"Oh yes he is," Zarah says, nodding her head.

Zarah is pensive.

And while she's thinking, a feeling of joy starts bubbling deep down in her stomach, a crazy, giggly joy. This is just insane. This guy, the one standing here in front of her, the one who followed her, he was buried in the ground last night, in the woods, in the exact same clearing where she and Victor … And he doesn't know about that. And he didn't know that she had shaved her head. He was just standing there being her mirror brother by chance. No, that can't be true. But yes, it is true and what a crazy day this is. And what a crazy world this is that we live in.

Now Zarah laughs. She laughs right out loud, a liberated laugh that echoes through the stairwell.

But she stops suddenly. Then it's deathly silent, a silence that echoes through the stairwell.

"I still hate you," she says.

Nils looks at her. His face is calm and his gaze is steady. "Actually," he says, "you're the one who started it. You're the one who came up to me that night in the pub. All of this is your fault."

"Well, there was certainly no way I could know you were crazy," Zarah says.

Nils doesn't comment on that. Instead he asks, "Well, why'd you shave your head, then?"

"I wanted to be ugly."

"It didn't work," Nils says, smiling.

Right away Zarah hisses, "Cut it out! None of that talk! Do you get it?"

Nils nods.

Zarah alternates between laughter and rage.

Nils remains calm.

One in black and one in white, in a doorway. Two bald young people.

"What do you want?" Zarah sighs.

Nils thinks about it, he hadn't gotten any further than this in his head, any further than the doorway, any further than meeting her.

"To get to know you," he says after a moment of consideration.

Zarah hesitates. Thinks about it for a long time. Weighs her various feelings. For a second she wrinkles her forehead and thinks about slamming the door shut in Nils's face, but finally she says, "You can come with me on an outing."

Nils nods, pleased.

"But I have two conditions," Zarah says quickly.

"Sure," Nils says, shrugging.

"One," Zarah says. "You're not allowed to touch me. Not ever. And two: You're not allowed to talk about you and me as if there were some kind of 'us.' Because there isn't. And there won't be. Not ever. Do you understand?"

"But—" Nils starts.

Zarah holds up her finger and gives him a stern look. And Nils gives up right away. He holds his hands up in front of his chest to show that he accepts her terms.

For now, Nils thinks.

"Do you have any money?" Zarah asks.

Nils nods.

"Good," Zarah says. "We're going to go to the bakery to buy some pastries. We'll bring a thermos of coffee with us. We're going to go meet Anon in the park."

"Anon?"

"He's in the same class as your sister," Zarah explains.

Nils considers this. "Anon? Is he the one with the galoshes?"

"He's finished with the galoshes," Zarah says.

Anon & Zarah & Nils

Here come Zarah and Nils.

Here come Zarah White and Nils Black out through the front door of number 14 Östra Storgatan. Nils is carrying a cloth tote bag in his hand; Zarah isn't carrying anything.

Here come bald Zarah and bald Nils.

When Nils stops on the stairs and seems like he wants to just stand there blinking and squinting at the sun, Zarah says "Come on" and pulls Nils along.

Whoops. There are two police officers in the planting bed on their left, in among the short, dense bushes, just a few yards away from them. One policeman and one policewoman. The woman is holding up what's left of a pair of tattered blue child-sized galoshes. The man is using his foot to poke at a brown box containing a smashed VCR and peering up at an open window on the fifth floor.

Zarah pulls Nils along, past the two police officers in the planting bed.

"Hello there, boys!" the policewoman says.

Zarah and Nils freeze in their tracks with their backs to the police officers.

"Stand behind me," Nils whispers out of the corner of his mouth.

"Why?" Zarah whispers.

"Because you have breasts," Nils whispers.

And when they turn around, Zarah stays behind Nils.

"Listen, boys," the policewoman says, "do you know a girl named ..." She takes a little slip of paper out of her pocket. "... named Zarah Enoksson, who lives up there?" She points up at the open window.

Nils shakes his head. "No, we don't live here. We just stopped by to say hi to a friend."

Now the policeman has also turned to face them, and for a few long seconds both officers stare at Nils and Zarah. Then the woman says, "Well, then."

And when Nils and Zarah turn around and keep walking, no one shouts anything after them and no one tries to stop them.

That may mean that they caught Victor, Zarah thinks. Most likely. Probably. Maybe. Sooner or later that means the police are going to visit my apartment. That means that I'll finally be rid of the boxes in the bedroom. That means interrogation and questioning. Possibly a trial. It may also mean that the kids at the daycare center will get their new computers back.

"They thought you were a guy," Nils whispers with a little chuckle. "What? What is it? Don't stop now. Come on ..."

He tries to pull Zarah along with him, but she's dragging her feet. She has discovered something on the other side of the street, something that Nils hasn't noticed since he's looking straight ahead as he walks.

What does Zarah see?

A police car.

Who's sitting in the police car?

A policeman.

Yes, but in the back seat?

Victor. It's Victor. And he's noticed Zarah and he recognized her even though he couldn't believe his own eyes at first and ...

Victor's laughing. He's laughing, an angry, out-of-control laugh, there behind the car window. Zarah can't hear it, but she sees his silent laughter.

Reluctantly, slowly, with her eyes fixed on Victor, Zarah keeps walking while Nils tries to get her to move faster. Then she sees how Victor stops laughing, all of a sudden. Zarah sees his expression. She sees a sadness in his face.

"I'll come," she whispers without making a sound. "I'll come later."

And as she turns away from him and follows Nils she thinks: He won't rat me out. He'll never rat me out. Then she thinks: But I'll get caught anyway.

And Zarah shrugs and walks on.

Nils and Zarah are standing outside Hansen's Café.

"What did the police want?" Nils asks.

Zarah shrugs again.

"It's Victor," she says after a moment's hesitation. "Victor, my boyfrie— My friend. He's done … some stupid stuff."

"Are you involved?" Nils wonders.

"My apartment is involved," Zarah says. "But let's drop it for now. No more police today. The sun is out. And we're going to buy some yummy pastries. Come on!"

Zarah and Nils in the café, at the bakery counter.

Now Zarah and Nils are standing at the bakery counter and in the tote bag Nils is carrying there's a thermos of coffee and a small bottle of strawberry juice.

Two bald people, one in white and one in black, up at the counter. And people are staring and both Nils and Zarah are a little exhilarated and inspired by it, and are suddenly in the mood for a little theatricality, a little play. Without anything being said between them, Zarah and Nils decide to practice their twin-speak. Slowly and precisely, simultaneously and without knowing who's leading and making the decisions, they say:

"Wwee'dd lliikkee tthhrreeee aallmmoonndd ttaarrttss."

They let their eyes wander over all the baked goods behind the glass.

"Aanndd tthhrreeee Ddaanniisshheess, pplleeaassee."

Nils starts fishing for his wallet in his back pocket, but Zarah nudges him with her elbow and they continue:

"Aanndd tthhrreeee cchhooccoollaattee bbiissccuuiittss, aanndd …"

"Stop!" Nils cries.

Zarah turns to face him and smiles knowingly. But she doesn't say anything, just lets Nils pay and then they leave the bakery. And everyone is staring. And Zarah giggles a little and Nils looks up at the blue sky.

Zarah and Nils walk through the park.

Nils swings the tote bag. He looks around at everything as if he were a tourist visiting the city, as if he were walking around in a world that's new to him. Zarah dances along next to Nils, skipping and doing little dance steps and small leaps, and then she stretches her arms out and twirls around and around in a wild pirouette until she gets dizzy.

Nils stops and waits until she gets her balance back. Their eyes meet, their smiles almost meet, but then Zarah puts her hands on her hips and shoots Nils a look.

"Don't go getting any ideas," she says.

And Nils shakes his head, tilts his head back, and laughs at the sky.

Zarah and Nils walk across the green grass.

And Zarah takes off her shoes and lets Nils carry them too while she runs around him like a puppy. And it's the first day of summer and the sky is blue and the sun is shining and there are already a lot of people in the park. Old people are sitting on the benches mumbling to themselves, single men and young women with their friends are lying stretched out in the grass to tan their pale legs and stomachs and backs. A few families are having picnics with bread and beer and Frisbees. A few boys are playing soccer. A little one-year-old in a sunhat is toddling around; she's just learned how to walk. She plops down on her butt and her mother rushes over to help her up again.

Zarah stops on the hill overlooking the ponds. She sits down on the slope and says, "Here."

And Nils sets the bag and her shoes down next to her, and flops down on his back on the grass, looking up at the sky.

The sky is clear and blue; just a few small, fluffy summer clouds sail tranquilly by. But the earth is cold and heavy. Nils feels the cold ground under his back, shivers, and remembers. His eyes fill up with tears, and choking back a sob he sits up, makes a fist with his right hand, and starts hitting the grass.

"I don't want to, I don't want to, I don't want to." Like a little kid he pounds his hand against the grass and tears flow down his cheeks and Zarah looks at him with a concerned crease between her eyes.

"What is it?"

She gets only a sob in response. "Here ..." Zarah says,

stretching out her legs and patting her stomach. "Put your head here. But don't get any ideas."

Nils stops sobbing and stretches out with his head in Zarah's lap, and she carefully smoothes the tears off his cheeks and gently sings, "Hush, little baby, don't say a word, Mama's going to buy you a mockingbird, and if …"

After she finishes singing all the verses, Nils sits up.

"First we live," he says, giving Zarah a faint smile.

She nods.

"There's nothing to be afraid of," he says.

Zarah shakes her head.

"Can I kiss you?" Nils asks. "Just on the cheek …"

"Nope," Zarah says decisively. "Absolutely not."

Zarah and Nils are drinking coffee when they hear happy shouts and laughter from down by the ponds, and Zarah cranes her neck to see and, sure enough, she heard right. She did recognize one of the voices. Anon comes trotting up the slope. He's not alone, there's a girl next to him. Both of them are barefoot and they're laughing and talking excitedly.

And Zarah, who'd been about to call out to Anon, stops herself. But he notices her anyway and waves happily with both arms. And she waves back and Anon says something to the girl and she says something to him and they laugh again and then she scampers off. And Anon runs up to Zarah and Nils.

"Was that Magdalena?" Zarah asks, nodding toward the girl who's disappearing behind the hill.

Anon nods, staring at Nils.

"Did you shave him?" Anon asks, and Zarah shakes her head.

"Are you going to kill him?" Anon asks.

"I haven't decided yet," Zarah answers.

"What's his name?" Anon asks. His eyes are focused on Nils, but it's Zarah he's talking to. She thinks about it.

"I don't know," she says. "Why don't you ask him?"

"I'm Nils," Nils says before Anon even has time to ask the question.

"His name is Nils," Anon tells Zarah.

"Oh, I see," Zarah says.

"And you must be Anon," Nils says.

Anon nods.

"Hi, Anon," Nils says.

"Hi, Nils," Anon says.

Anon and Zarah and Nils drink coffee and juice and eat the yummy things from the café and the sun warms Zarah's cold scalp and Nils's.

"My little sister's in your class," Nils says.

"I know," Anon says.

And the sun shines and the chocolate on the chocolate biscuits melts and gets sticky.

"Yum," Nils says, licking his fingers.

"Mmm," Zarah says, licking her fingers.

Anon licks his fingers too.

"Where are my flip-flops?" Zarah asks, glancing down at Anon's bare feet.

"Where are my galoshes?" Anon fires back with a mischievous glint in his eyes.

Zarah bites her lip and laughs.

"Seriously, though," Anon says, "something happened to

your flip-flops. They're gone. They, um, sank."

"And what were you guys up to?" Zarah wonders, pointing at Anon's feet, which are covered with mud and clay and gravel up to his ankles.

Anon chews his biscuit slowly and carefully before he answers. "Walking on water."

He chuckles to himself.

"Or walking on mud," he continues. "In the marsh by the pond. Down there. I wanted to show Magdalena that swamp feet are better for walking on marshy ground. I was right, of course. She sank right away. Just like your flip-flops. Not me, though."

"Swamp feet?"

And Anon explains what swamp feet are and holds his feet up in the air, demonstrating what a pair of first-rate swamp feet look like, and Zarah holds her feet up and Anon says that her feet are worthless on marshy terrain, and Nils pulls off his socks and holds up his feet and Anon thinks that Nils has "fairly good swamp feet" but that his "pointer toes are slightly too short."

"Compare them to mine," he says. "They should look like this."

Now Anon and Zarah and Nils are lying on their backs holding their feet up against the blue sky and the cottony clouds.

"When I die," Zarah says, "I'm going to be an angel and live on a cloud like that one."

"I'm not going to die," Anon says.

And Nils remembers something and tells them the following story:

"I walked on clouds once. It was when I was a kid and went with Göran, my dad, to Umeå. We met some of his friends there and it was a sunny winter day and we went for a walk on the lake below their house. It was completely frozen over and the ice was as smooth as glass, just like a mirror. Yes. And when you walked on the lake, the clouds were reflected in the ice and … it felt like you were walking on the clouds. Like being in heaven. It felt like flying."

He falls silent, stretching his bare feet toward the clouds.

And Zarah remembers too. A little bell goes off way down in her subconscious. That memory. That sensation. Exactly like that. The smooth ice, the clouds under her feet. Maybe she was there too? As a little girl, a long time ago? A memory that she'd forgotten.

Then Anon and Zarah and Nils lie on their backs and study the clouds for a long time. Zarah and Nils are lying next to each other, their heads closer together than their feet. That's just how they all ended up.

Anon is lying crosswise, by their feet. Periodically he tickles the soles of Zarah's feet with a blade of grass and then she tries to reach him so she can pinch him with her toes.

Nils raises his head and studies the three stretched-out bodies for a while. Then he laughs. "You could almost say that the square root of my height is equal to the sum of the square roots of your heights," Nils says.

Zarah cocks her head to the side and gives him an apprehensive look.

"Because," Nils continues, "we basically form a right triangle, where I'm the hypotenuse and you two are the two catheti or right-angle sides. And therefore, of course, we can apply the Pythagorean theorem, which—"

Zarah interrupts him by yawning. "Enough already, Professor," she says, yawning again. "You're disturbing the peace."

"The hypotenuse?" Anon says, looking at Nils with curiosity.

"Yes, the hypotenuse is the—"

"Enough already!" Zarah commands. "I hate math. And besides, it's summer vacation now."

You and you and you. You, Anon. You, Zarah. You, Nils.
Now you're lying here in the grass. Together.
And now the adventure is almost over.
No, no, no. Here's where our adventure begins.
Most of it is yet to come.
The best is yet to come.
The adventure will never end.

"I have to go now," Anon says. "Home to Mother. Because I'm going to Father's place. To stay with him."

"But you're coming back, right?" Zarah asks, sitting up.

"I always come back," Anon promises.

He stands up and brushes the grass off his pants.

"You'll come by and see me when you get back in town, right?" Zarah asks.

"Certainly," Anon says.

"I need you," Zarah says.

And she almost doesn't want to let Anon go. She wants to thank him for this and that and the other thing, and she wants to give him a hug and tousle his hair and finally he has to wriggle away from her.

"Bye," he says, taking a few quick steps backwards to get away.

Bye and bye and Anon leaves.

Exit Anon.

Nils reclines, watching him as he trots down toward the ponds. It's probably a trick of the sunlight, some sort of reflection in the water perhaps, or maybe he dozed off for a minute and it was actually a dream, or maybe there's some other explanation, but Nils sees Anon walk on the water.

Anon is walking on the water.

Anon walks right across the bottom pond, on the surface of the water as if it were a floor, and he gets over to the other side and continues walking as if nothing had happened.

Nils thinks he sees Anon walking on water. But of course there must be some logical explanation.

"Did you see that?" Nils asks, turning to Zarah.

"What?" Zarah says.

No, Zarah didn't see anything. She's thinking:

Imagine that someone like Anon exists. Someone who has so much to offer. If you saw him and didn't know him, he would just look like any old person. Just a little dumber, a little slower, a little clumsier.

And imagine that someone like Nils here exists. Who buried himself.

And imagine that someone like Victor exists. And someone like Mia. And someone like me.

Aren't there any normal people out there? Zarah thinks. Seriously: Are there any normal people? People who are only interested in their appearance and their clothes and earning money and getting drunk on the weekends. And sex. People who are just as simple and normal on the inside as they appear on the outside. Are there any people like that?

That's what Zarah's thinking.

Nils has also been thinking. He says:

"Do you think there are turning points in life? Do you think you can look back and say *that's* exactly when my life changed, exactly when that happened? Or when I met that person my life started moving in a different direction? Or do you think that people are actually marching straight ahead, like stupid mechanical puppets, even though they think they are growing and changing and learning things?"

Zarah doesn't answer. She just wrinkles her forehead.

"I think people can change," Nils continues. "That you can turn into someone else. Or become yourself maybe. Become more who you really are. Find yourself. That's how I feel now, I feel like—"

"Words, words, words," Zarah says, flopping down on her back again. "Talk, talk, talk. You talk too much."

Nils is sitting on the grass. Zarah is lying on her back. Nils looks at Zarah and smiles. Zarah closes her eyes.

"And you know something else weird?" Nils asks.

Zarah lies there silently with her eyes closed.

"One time when I was a kid," Nils says, "I dreamed that I had a twin. I dreamed about everything we did together; it was one of those warm, fuzzy dreams. And when I woke up from it, I missed my twin. Life was so lonely and cold after that dream and I haven't forgotten that feeling. And when I met—"

Zarah is up in a flash. She topples Nils over so that he's on his back and starts pounding on his chest with the palms of her hands.

"I hate it," she screams. "Hate it, hate it, hate it!"

"Cut it out! Quit it! What are you doing?" Nils yells, trying to wriggle away from her.

But Zarah straddles him, grabs hold of his wrists, and he gives in right away and lets himself be overpowered.

"I hate it," Zarah says, glaring angrily at him. "I hate it when you steal my thoughts and my dreams and my ideas. And my memories! Let me have them in peace. You're devouring me piece by piece …"

"I don't know anything about your thoughts," Nils says, chuckling at Zarah's anger. "But if we have the same memories and the same thoughts, I suppose that just means that we're twins. And that we belong together."

"Ugh," Zarah grunts, letting go of him.

"Hey, what's your friend's name anyway?" Zarah asks with a sly smile. "The one with the nice eyes."

Nils's eyes narrow. "His name is Piss Hannes, Shit Hannes, and Stupid Idiot Hannes, and his eyes are the same color as doodoo."

"Hannes is your friend," Zarah says.

"No!" Nils says fervently. "Not anymore. Not after last night."

"Yes," Zarah persists. "I know something you don't know. Someday I'll tell you. But I know that he's your friend. And his eyes don't look anything like doodoo. He has pretty eyes. He looks nice."

"He's cruel. He rapes little girls. He does painful animal experiments on little puppies. He …"

Zarah gets up.

"What is it? What are you going to do?" Nils asked nervously.

Zarah looks at him. "I have to go," she says.

"But … what … why?" Nils asks, scrambling onto his feet as well.

"First of all," Zarah says, "I have to go and see Victor at the police station. If he's still there. And see how he's doing, and—"

"But," Nils interrupts, "what if they arrest you when—"

"Nonsense," Zarah says, brushing aside his objections. "Second of all, I'm meeting Mia tonight. And third of all, you promised that you wouldn't talk about you and me, that you wouldn't talk about some hypothetical 'we.' Remember? And now here you are going on and on about twins and shit."

"But …"

"You promised. Remember?"

Nils sighs and nods, resigned.

Well, this fairy tale certainly didn't have a happy ending, Nils thinks.

Nils the Knight liberates Princess Zarah from the evil Victor. But the princess falls in love with the knight's assistant Hannes instead. And she still doesn't want to leave that villain she lives with. What a terrible ending for the story. Fairy tales are supposed to have happy endings. The hero gets the princess. And half the kingdom.

"Well, I suppose I might still get half the kingdom," Nils says to Zarah, who's still standing there, looking at him.

And when he looks into her eyes, he understands that the fairy tale didn't have an unhappy ending. Not at all.

You are my twin sister, he thinks, nodding to himself. And that's the best, because a sister never disappears. She's always there. You get to keep a sister for life.

He looks happy, Zarah thinks as she stands there in front of Nils. Almost idiotically happy. Obviously he's her twin brother. She knew that the second she saw him standing outside her door a few hours ago. But he needs to chill out a little. Twin brother and nothing more.

"There's one thing I want to do before you go," Nils says. "Please?"

"What is it?"

"I want … I want to hold your earlobes. I know what I promised, but … Please?"

"OK," Zarah says without much hesitation at all.

And Nils reaches out and takes hold of Zarah's earlobes carefully between his thumb and his forefinger and he laughs gently to himself and nods.

Yes, that's exactly how soft they were. Exactly the way he remembered.

"Thank you," he says, letting Zarah go.

Zarah leaves.

Nils stands there and Zarah leaves.

"Might I be permitted to call?" he yells after her.

She waves without turning around. Her wave means: Yes, but don't leave any messages on the answering machine.

"Might I be permitted to be happy?" Nils yells.

She waves. Yes, that would be fine.

Now Zarah disappears.

Exit Zarah.

Nils is left alone.

And the grass is green and the sky is blue and the clouds sailing around up there are fluffy and it's the first day of summer and children are playing and a woman is sitting alone on a bench reading a book.

"Is it possible?" Nils mumbles to himself. "Is it possible to be happy? In this world, at this time? With all the evil that exists, all the danger and all the injustice? With all the things that are worth fighting for? Is it possible to be happy?"

Nils, you think too much.

You can't know all the answers.

I know, I know.

Now Nils leaves.

Barefoot, through the grass, with his shoes in one hand, Nils goes straight down toward the ponds. And when he gets there he carefully puts his right foot on the surface of the water.

I'm alive, he thinks.

And he takes a step and for a brief second he feels like the water will hold him, but just for a brief second, then he sinks down into the mud and loses his balance and winds up on all fours at the edge of the water.

And he laughs out loud and scrambles to his feet while the mud and water run out of his pant legs and he turns around and sees that the woman on the bench has set down her book and is looking at him with a worried expression.

"I'm alive!" he yells to her and waves.

"Good," she yells. And she sits back down again, picks up her book, and continues reading.

Translator's Note

In the original Swedish version of *You & You & You* some passages were in English, the most widely studied second language in Sweden. To preserve the author's contrast between the main language used in the book and the second language used for these passages, I have translated the passages into Spanish, the most widely studied second language in the United States. I did this in order to convey the same effect that the author intended in the original. Here are the passages in English for readers who don't read Spanish:

p. 24: To know Life you must know Death, / to know Life you must die. / —*The Quest*

p. 44: To be a man / you must remember death / Every living day / you must remember death. / —*The Quest*

p. 70: The old sage from China said: / The hard and the strong / are the comrades of death, / the supple and the weak / are the comrades of life. / I say: Yes! / —*The Quest*

p. 100: Are you looking for someone / to change your life? / A guru, a teacher, an angel? / Maybe you are looking for a holy scripture, / or a sacred place to visit. / Do not fool yourself. / It is all within you. / —*The Quest*

p. 122: To know Love you must know Death, / to know Love you must die. / —*The Quest*

p. 147: But if you find your angel, / follow her. / Don't let her disappear, / don't let her fly away. / —*The Quest*

p. 152: A bible for the beat generation. / Cristóbal Carbón / *El Universal*

   After reading *The Quest* I found myself looking upon the world with the eyes of a child; the same astonishment, the same warmth and the same curiosity. This book changed my entire outlook. / Isabel Metralla de Astilla / *La Opinión*

p. 153: Funny and clever. / Nestor Furbank / *El Nuevo Día*

   Lorenzo Montero was born in Salinas, California, on February 13, 1934. He spent his whole life there, living with his mother and his little sister. On May 20, 1963, he walked out of the house and never came back. The day before he had sent the manuscript of *The Quest* to a publisher. Nobody has seen him since.

   The photograph below shows the author between Jack Kerouac and Neal Cassady outside the Montero home in June 1959.

   You must live your dreams, at least one of your dreams. Pick your deepest desire, and make it come true. If not, you will live forever like a small child, caught in self-pity. Be a man, face the world, stop crying. Make one dream come true.

p. 154: But if you find your angel, follow her. Don't let her disappear, don't let her fly away.

p. 190: You must bury yourself / You must bury your Self / if you want to live, / if you want to become a man. / —*The Quest*

p. 220: Love and Death / When you meet the one, / the other is always close / Closer than you think / Love never leaves Death / Death never leaves Love / Love and Death / are eternal companions. / —*The Quest*

p. 249: To be alive is: / to have breakfast with / the one you love, / to walk in the sun, / to watch the children grow up. / To be dead is: / nothing. / No lover, no sun, no children. / Nothing. And nothing to fear. / —*The Quest*